PROLOGUE

Season's Streaming

Your favorite holiday streaming channel is back with the cheeriest of line-ups for you and yours.

This season's streaming programming includes old favorites like holiday movies, baking shows, shopping tips and tricks, news about the best light displays across the country, children's shows, and MORE!

New Addition!

This year, we're adding in a fun competition show called Once Upon a Christmas House.

We'll follow ten couples from around the country as they compete for viewer votes over eight weeks. Each couple will live in their own home as our team records their daily goings-on and completion of challenges. Viewers will vote each week and the couple with the lowest scores and votes will be removed from the show. At the end of the competition, we'll be left with our final two couples. The winners of *Once Upon a Christmas House* will share $500,000 *and* get their home remodeled. And YOU, the viewers, decide who wins! Who will be your favorite couple? STAY TUNED FOR UPDATES AS THE SHOW DRAWS CLOSER!

If you'd like to be considered as one of our competing couples, head to the Season's Streaming website and submit an application. We'll pick our ten couples in late October and begin recording in early November.

Rules and regulations apply and can be found on the application.

*Nothing says **Season's Greetings** like a little bit of competition and teamwork, a dash of romance, and a splash of holiday magic with the **Season's Streaming** channel.*

CHAPTER 1

IVYRSON "IVY" LANE GREGORY

"YOU'RE ONE HUNDRED PERCENT SURE YOU WANT to do this?" I asked.

My best friend, Trevor, nodded. "Sure. I agreed to it when we first applied and I'm not changing my mind now. Accept the invitation."

With my finger hovering over my phone screen, anticipation, dread, anxiety, and hope filling me, I thought about what accepting the invitation to be on *Once Upon a Christmas House* would mean.

The chance at $500,000 and getting the old house I'd recently purchased in my little hometown remodeled.

Distracting myself from all the holiday spirit and Christmas cheer I knew would be popping up around town, while simultaneously throwing myself right smack dab in the middle of said holiday spirit and Christmas cheer.

But I'd be with my best friend the whole time.

As in *the whole time*.

If Trevor and I opted to do the show, we'd live together for eight weeks.

The pros of *Once Upon a Christmas House* included the fact contestants would live in their own homes, still be able to go to work, and only be recorded for challenges, interviews, and *some* day-to-day stuff.

The cons of the show included it centered around the holidays and focused on *couples*.

Which meant I would be forced to acknowledge Christmas—the worst holiday of the whole damn year —*and* Trevor and I would have to pull off a fake relationship.

Don't get me wrong, my best friend was a catch, but we definitely weren't into each other that way. Trevor was straight and I—well, *I* mostly shrugged off any thoughts I'd ever had about other guys and had only ever slept with women. Sure, I found guys attractive, but I couldn't see Trevor and I ever hitting it off romantically. The show called for contestants to be a couple, so that portion of our participation would have to be fudged a bit.

Why would I want to compete on a show where I had to fake a relationship with my best friend while being surrounded by a holiday I hated?

Did I mention $500,000 and a remodeled home?

As the local auto mechanic in Peppermint Hollow—no, I'm not kidding, that's the real name of the small Midwestern town I call home—I needed my share of the $500,000 to expand my shop and be able to pay for the big old house I'd just purchased.

Old being the operative word.

Growing up, I'd been fascinated by the old home.

It was magical, mystical, creepy, and heartwarming all rolled into a nice package.

Before life went to shit, I'd called it *The Christmas House* and swore one day I'd live there.

But that was before I hated Christmas.

One night, after drinks with Trevor and a hook-up with some girl I barely remembered—yeah, that's my usual M.O., I don't *do* relationships. Why should I? They don't work, everybody ends up leaving in one way or another in the long run. Anyway, I saw *The Christmas House*, recalled how much I used to love the place, and clearly lost my mind because I called the number on the For Sale sign the next day.

Voila. I was now the owner of *The Christmas House*.

And the old girl was in desperate need of remodeling.

Actually, she was in desperate need of *repair*.

Now, some of that, I could handle myself—I was handy in the auto shop, and I wasn't too shabby with other fixes —but money was the issue.

If I could win *Once Upon a Christmas House*, money and free labor would be my prize.

Which was the *why* behind our application and the reason I wasn't too concerned about faking a loving relationship with my best friend.

I tapped my phone screen, accepted the invite to be on the show, and breathed a sigh of relief.

"I still can't believe you guys applied *and* got accepted," Emory, my best friend's little brother, said as he took a seat next to Trevor.

Trevor and I had gone to eat at the little café where Emory worked. We'd waited to meet up until the lunch rush was over and having Emory join us after clocking out was expected.

Trevor and Emory were close.

Pretty much as close as Trevor and me, despite their age difference.

I'd met my best friend in elementary school—before all the bad shit started—and Emory had been a presence ever since.

With a seven-year gap between us, Emory had never really been someone I considered a *friend*—well, until recently, when he'd graduated college and come back home—since he'd been so much younger. Now though, his twenty-three to our thirty-years-old still seemed damned young, but I could see he was a full-grown adult.

Trevor insisted Emory was intimidated by me. I did kinda have the dark, broody, tattooed bad-boy thing going on, but Emory didn't seem the type to stereotype by appearances. I wasn't sure *why* he felt intimidated by me —I thought we were friendly enough and, in reality, his family was more *my* family than my actual blood-family.

Emory was *smart*. Had that nerdy, preppy look going on. Caramel brown hair, chocolate brown eyes, and a sweet smile.

He idolized Trevor—and my best friend pretty much thought the world of Emory, had ever since the kid was born.

Ever since Emory's graduation from college and return to Peppermint Hollow, the brothers had been pretty much inseparable. I didn't mind sharing my best friend— especially not with his little brother—we all three got along just fine.

"Tell me again how you think you're going to convince

people you're a couple," Emory said, his eyes sparkling behind his glasses. I'd noticed he opted for glasses *most* of the time and I wondered idly if his contacts weren't as comfortable.

"Easy," Trevor said with a shrug. "We've known each other for years. All we have to do is add in a bit of PDA and *boom* you've got a couple."

Emory cocked a brow. "And you're both okay with PDA? For a camera? With a guy? Have either of you ever even touched another guy?"

He had a good point.

Emory was gay—we'd all known it since he was just a kid and no one had a problem with it—but I'd never touched or kissed a man, outside of a few brief fantasies here and there, and I was about ninety-nine percent sure Trevor hadn't either.

But we *could*.

I didn't have a problem with same-sex couples.

Hell, I could name some dudes I'd say were totally hot, completely fuckable if I let my head go there.

Didn't mean I wanted to fuck my best friend, but that wasn't the point.

For $500,000 I could pretend to be a couple with Trevor.

Easy.

I loved my best friend—he was pretty much the only family I had left now that my little sister, Iris, had taken off for bigger and better...her words, not mine, I liked Peppermint Hollow just fine.

Trevor was my family.

His parents and brother were my family.

I maybe wasn't super close to Todd and Lisa Bell, but

they'd been nothing but welcoming of me in their son's life since I was just a kid. It wasn't their fault I didn't get overly attached to people these days.

The fact Trevor and I had stayed friends even after the shit-storm blew up in my life probably had to do with us having a bond long before the negative started. Ever since my family had imploded, I'd made it a point to keep people at a distance.

So, yeah, for $500,000 and a free home remodel I could totally kiss my best friend.

"You know the audience is going to *have* to buy you as a couple if you want to get votes. If they think you're faking, you'll be out in the first week." Emory popped a fry from Trevor's plate into his mouth. "Viewers on shows like this are relentless. They tune in if the basis of the show catches their attention and you better believe they're going to expect what's advertised. Which means a *real* couple."

"Yes, baby brother, we know," Trevor said with a chuckle. "I've seen him naked, known him forever, we'll add in hand holding and a bit of kissing, we'll be golden."

"You can't fake chemistry," Emory insisted.

"Do you not want us on this show?" Trevor asked with a bit of irritation.

"It's not that," Emory said, stealing another fry. "I just want you to have a real chance since you both have plans for the money. I've watched enough shows and read enough romance novels to know the audience expects some drama and real romance—I've known the two of you my whole life, you really don't put off the *in-love* vibe."

Emory knew my plans for the money included expanding my auto repair shop—hell, he'd been the one to offer suggestions on how I could make it better when I first started thinking about growing my business—*and* of my recent purchase of a home in need of some tender loving care.

He also knew his brother, who excelled at anything and everything he put his mind to, planned to invest his half of the winnings and likely quadruple the money over time. My best friend had decided he wanted to be an engineer of some sort way back when we were kids. He now had a large savings, no debt, and a stable job he loved in addition to several investments he enjoyed watching grow.

Trevor didn't *need* the money the way I did.

But I appreciated the hell out of my friend for being willing to play the game so I could at least have a chance at the prizes.

If I didn't win, it wouldn't be the end of the world.

The shop would just expand more slowly. I already had a strong base of customers, I just wouldn't be able to bring on more mechanics or grow the business as soon as I'd hoped. *Ivy's Auto* was my baby and I could be patient.

And the house would eventually get finished, it would just be a longer project than I'd hoped. I could hire out some of the repairs to be taken care of first, then when I saved up a bit more money, I'd slowly do remodels on my own here and there.

But damn, winning sure would make things easier—I'd take that holiday miracle, even if it meant my jaded heart had to admit not everything went to shit and Christmas wasn't cursed.

"We'll do some practice kisses before the cameras start rolling, it'll be fine," Trevor said.

Emory glanced between us and shook his head. "I hope so. I'm just saying, I love you two as friends, but if you're going to get votes from people who are expecting a couple, you're going to have to step it up and get some chemistry brewing."

He had a point and I'd be lying if I said I wasn't somewhat nervous about our ability to pull off the fake relationship. Hell, I'd never been able—or wanted—to have an actual relationship, let alone a fake one.

But Trevor and I had been friends for years, there was no one I'd rather try to fake a relationship with than him.

It was actually the perfect setup.

Someone I'd known forever and trusted with my life.

A man I could be around for eight weeks straight without wanting to kill him—mostly.

And a person who knew my extreme dislike and anxiety over the holiday season.

Who else would I rather pull off a fake relationship with than Trevor Bell?

Absolutely no one.

It was a risk, but I knew I was safe with Trevor.

And I was beyond grateful my best friend was willing to go along with my scheme.

CHAPTER 2

EMORY SHAE BELL

MY PHONE VIBRATED IN MY POCKET AS I balanced a tray of food for table fourteen at the Peppermint Café where I worked as a server. I couldn't exactly answer calls in the middle of my shift if I wanted to keep my job.

And I did.

Want to keep my job.

Mostly.

In high school, I'd found myself filled with apprehension over making decisions about my future at such a young age. Everyone else was applying to schools for degrees that would help them land their dream jobs and I was stuck in a perpetual cycle of worry.

What if I made the wrong choice?

What if I opted for a degree and no one wanted to hire me?

What if I decided on a career and ended up hating it?

What if...

What if…

What if…

The anxiety over my future was real way back then.

And I couldn't say it had changed much if I was being honest.

I ended up graduating from college with a degree in general studies. The plan was to then use the four years of classes to help me decide on a career and either move into it or continue my studies to get a degree for said career.

Instead, I'd graduated after four years of college—it was a fairly neutral time in my life, nothing *bad* but also not *amazing*—and moved back to Peppermint Hollow with absolutely no idea what I wanted to do with my future.

Hence my desire to keep my serving job.

I knew the type of job I wanted for my future—something where I could use my organizational skills, my love of numbers, my desire to make sure things ran smoothly, my ability to lead a team, and my skills with schedules and computers—I just wasn't sure what job that would be.

I wasn't even sure I wanted a life-long *career*. Honestly, just having a job I liked, I was good at, and paid the bills sounded perfect. I wasn't sure I was the type who wanted to dedicate my whole life to a career.

If I could help people in some way—and I wasn't sure I meant the traditional way of helping like in medicine or charity or whatever—and keep a roof over my head, I'd be happy.

Speaking of people, my people-ing skills weren't terrible, but I did best when we were speaking for an actual purpose rather than just idle small talk.

Unlike my older brother, Trevor, who could charm a corpse and had known exactly what he wanted to do from the time he was old enough to even think about a career in engineering.

Throw in his penchant for smart investments and the guy had been set for life from the age of twenty-five.

Then there was me.

A useless degree.

Working as a server in Peppermint Hollow.

A gay man with very few prospects—mostly because I'd shut myself off from dating back in high school when two relationships took major negative turns, and now had very little clue how to get back into the dating scene. The few forays I'd taken into attempting to date in college had been major letdowns. Probably because my anxiety over guys cheating or hurting me forced me to go *safe* routes when it came to choosing dates and *safe* for me usually meant guys I liked but had no romantic or sexual interest in.

So, that was Emory Shae Bell in a nutshell.

Single, lonely, desperate to find love, facing my absolute favorite holiday alone in Peppermint Hollow serving café food to people I didn't want to talk to while wishing for more.

So much more.

I had absolutely no idea what I wanted to do with my life—

Okay, that wasn't true.

I wanted to meet the man of my dreams—someone I could trust with my heart, someone I'd never see coming, someone who would make it hard to breathe and form sentences—find a job I felt good about, and settle down with a happy life in Peppermint Hollow.

I just needed the job.

And the guy.

Maybe I'd get a Christmas miracle this year.

Despite the nagging loneliness and perpetual fear I'd never live up to Trevor's charm and success, I couldn't help but be excited about Christmas.

Peppermint Hollow always went all out during the holidays and turned into a regular little Hallmark-esque town. The sidewalks bustled with joyful folks, homes, storefronts, and light poles rolled out their finest holiday décor, and a general feeling of holiday cheer filled the air every season.

I loved the little town.

Plus, I had my family.

He might have outshone me in every single aspect of life, but Trevor was my brother and I loved him beyond reason.

And my parents?

They were the best ever.

My family had likely known I was gay long before I did, but they took it in stride, never batted an eye, offered to take me to my first Pride parade in middle school, and supported me ferociously.

So, yeah, maybe I was lonely and longing for the love of a lifetime, but I wasn't *alone*. I had my family, our town, and the quickly-approaching holidays to keep me company.

I just needed to be patient.

Wasn't there some saying about finding what you're

looking for when you least expect it? Or in the least likely of places?

Maybe that was what I needed to do.

Just go about my life as usual, stop worrying about finding love and a future, and just let it find me.

What was meant to be would be and all that jazz.

Yeah, I'd keep telling myself that.

After delivering my tray of food and heading back toward the kitchen, grateful my shift was ending, my phone buzzed again. Ready to block the telemarketer, I yanked my phone from my pocket and started to decline the call, but I noticed it was Ivy.

My brother's best friend.

Ivy had starred in the majority of my sexual fantasies from the first time I realized I found guys attractive.

"Hey," I answered, willing my voice not to get all breathy and desperate. "What's up?"

"Emory, hey." Ivy cleared his throat. "Are you driving?"

"Huh? No, I'm at work. Why?"

"Trevor's been in an accident—"

My vision grayed and I leaned against the kitchen counter.

Trevor.

Accident.

I had a vague impression of Ivy speaking, but the roar in my head was too loud.

"Emory? Em? Come on, man, I need you with me." Ivy's words were loud and firm, a life preserver on the other end of the line as the wave of panic washed over me. "Em, he's alive. He's hurt pretty bad, but he's alive and going to be okay. Emory, damn it, answer me."

"I'm here." Dashing away tears, I took a deep, shuddery breath and pushed myself away from the counter. "I'm here. Sorry. I'm sorry. I—"

"It's okay. Piss poor way to let you know, but I'm heading to the hospital and figured you'd want to be there, too."

"Yeah, of course. I'll leave now. Can you text me which door and floor?"

"Yeah," Ivy clipped out. "They said he'd likely be in surgery by the time we got there, so don't rush. Last thing we need is another Bell getting hurt. Be careful, I'll see you there."

I'd been considered an adult and responsible for myself for five years.

In reality, despite not being able to commit to a career or find someone to love me, I'd been taking care of myself for even longer—not that my parents weren't great, I was just a fairly independent person. But having Ivy's firm words, his calm, confident voice coming through the speaker, telling me what to do had been the grounding I needed most at that moment.

Wiping the tears with my shirt sleeve and taking another deep breath, I clocked out ten minutes early.

"You okay?" Shelly, my boss, asked when she entered the employee break room.

"Gotta head out a little early. My brother was in an accident and I need to get to the hospital." Maybe I should have *asked* rather than just told her what I was doing, but Trevor was worth more than a job, and I'd risk my position if needed.

Shelly's eyes went wide. "Trevor? Oh, God. Of course,

go. Go. Please keep us updated. I'll start the prayer chains at the local churches if they haven't already been alerted."

That was Peppermint Hollow for you. A town of less than a thousand—hell, less than seven-fifty if we're getting exact—but four churches spread along the landscape.

Smack dab in the center of town on two opposing corners was the Christian church and Methodist church. A bit further down, off a little side road was the Baptist church. And on the outskirts of town sat the Catholic church.

Now, each and every one of these churches were full of wonderful people—people who would give you the shirt off their own back, fix you a meal, and help you find a job all with a smile on their face and love in their hearts.

And each and every one of those churches had some folks who needed a lesson in the reality of *what would Jesus do?* Judgmental, hateful, selfish, and downright mean, all in the name of the god they served.

The churches were a big part of Peppermint Hollow. I knew they'd send up prayers for Trevor and I appreciated it. Even though I sometimes wondered how to reconcile differing outcomes when prayers *worked* for some and not for others—did one deserve healing and the other didn't? Were the prayers for one somehow better than prayers for the other? Or was there really no correlation between prayers and healing? Would the good church-going, god-fearing people of Peppermint Hollow pray just as hard for the gay boy as they would for his golden boy brother?

Whatever the answer, and whatever my beliefs, I wasn't against the town praying for Trevor's healing—I'd take thoughts, prayers, good vibes, whatever folks wanted to send his way.

"Thanks, I'll let you know," I said with a quick wave to Shelly as I grabbed my jacket and headed out the back door of The Peppermint Café.

Sliding into my little red Mazda Miata, I cranked the heat up, unsure if my hands were icy from the cold outside or fear. Taking a deep breath in hopes of centering myself—Ivy was right, if I got in an accident I'd be no help to an already injured Trevor—I replayed Ivy's words.

Trevor was going to be okay.

He was hurt.

He needed surgery.

But he was alive and was going to be okay.

My chest rattled—worry and relief at war—but I clung to Ivy's reassurance that Trevor would be okay.

What had happened?

An accident.

That was all Ivy had said.

For a brief moment, my heart clenched. Why had the hospital called Ivy and not me? Just because I was his little brother didn't mean I wasn't responsible enough to take important calls.

Or my parents for that matter.

Shit.

My parents.

Should I call them?

No.

Best to focus on driving and get to the hospital in one piece.

If Trevor had to have surgery, Ivy could fill my parents and me in while we waited.

My parents would be a nervous wreck.

I didn't know how any parents wouldn't be, but mine would be a mess.

They'd been our biggest supporters our entire lives.

Despite the fact Trevor was absolutely perfect and had been the golden boy since birth, I'd never felt favoritism for him from either of my parents.

They'd supported me the same as they'd supported Trevor.

True, they thought I had more of a career plan than I actually had, but they supported me no matter what.

It was *me* who floundered in Trevor's perfection as I struggled with just what I wanted to do with my future.

Peppermint Hollow didn't have a hospital, but the county hospital wasn't too far out of town. Forcing myself to obey the speed limit and count my breaths so I didn't hyperventilate, I made the final turn into the hospital parking lot just as my phone buzzed.

Parking in the first spot I found closest to the door, I grabbed my phone and shoved my wallet in my jacket pocket as I headed toward the entrance.

Ivy: Main entrance. Surgery waiting room. They say he'll probably be on the 4th floor for a while. I'm here now.

Me: Heading in.

The October wind bit at my cheeks—colder than an average fall day with Halloween just around the corner—

and pushed me toward the door. The older woman at the front desk smiled kindly and I did my best not to demand directions to the surgery waiting room.

"Of course, dear," she answered. "You're going to follow this hallway quite a ways down. When you reach a T, take a right. There will be signs for surgery. You can get some coffee in the waiting room if you'd like. I wish you all the best."

Thanking her, I all but sprinted down the hallway and careened around the corner into the surgery waiting room only moments later.

And there he was.

Ivyrson Gregory.

Ivy.

My infatuation.

My brother's best friend.

My rock in that moment.

Pushing aside my usual feelings of...intimidation? Shyness? Self-consciousness? Deep concern over drooling in his presence? Whatever it was I often felt around Ivy, I ignored it and made a beeline for the man as he stood from the chair he'd been slouched in and tucked his ever-present key chain into his pocket. Taking in his carelessly tousled hair, black from head to toe—Chucks, jeans, t-shirt, leather jacket—the ink peeking under his sleeves and collar, and the five o'clock shadow, I caught his dark brown eyes right before launching myself into his arms.

Ivy wasn't a hugger.

Thanks to some shitty dating experiences in high school and pretty much shutting myself off from dating until late in college—and finding dating much harder than I'd been prepared for—I hadn't done a lot of hugging lately, at least not outside of my family. Not because I didn't want the contact, just because it wasn't something I was accustomed to—but I needed the grounding effect of being in Ivy's arms.

He held me tight and the fear he'd been holding onto seeped from his body.

"What happened? Do my parents know?" *And why did they call you?*

"When you went to college, Trevor listed me as his emergency contact since you were away and he didn't want your parents to get life-changing calls from strangers," Ivy said in answer to my unasked question. "Just hasn't switched it to you. I'd rather I get those calls anyway—you shouldn't have to hear something from a random person on the line."

All I could do was nod. His words made sense, but my brain could only comprehend fear and worry about Trevor combined with the absolute perfection of being tucked under Ivy's chin. At five-eight, I fit just right against his six-two frame and I never wanted to leave his warm, safe embrace.

But all good things come to an end and Ivy released me, gesturing toward a little couch at the far end of the waiting room.

On shaky legs, I made my way to the brown, orange, and green checkered sofa—the functional-but-oh-so-uncomfortable type—and sat on one end, turning toward Ivy as he lowered himself to the stiff cushion on the other end. Tucking my leg under me, I met those deep brown eyes again. "He's in surgery? What happened?"

Ivy produced his keychain—a black and silver key organizer of sorts with a variety of keys and tools all neatly folded and attached to a small metal carabiner clip —and began his usual flick of the wrist keychain flipping. It was something I'd noticed he did a lot—when he was nervous, stressed, bored, angry. I hadn't spent *as* much time with the man as Trevor had, but I'd been around him enough my entire life to know he flipped his keys almost as often as he breathed, and I wondered if he even recognized the habit.

"I missed a call at the shop while I was elbow deep in an engine." Ivy's brows furrowed and I recognized guilt and regret. "When my phone immediately rang again, I wiped off enough to check the caller ID and see Wintergreen County Hospital. They said Trevor had been in a car accident and asked me to come in. All I could get from them over the phone was he was seriously injured and would need surgery, but he was alive." The keys clicked faster in Ivy's hand. "Called you, called your parents, got here and finally got a nurse to talk to me. Her understanding was he'd hit some sort of large construction vehicle. The paramedics who brought him in said he was able to tell them he swerved to miss a dog that ran out of nowhere."

I pinched the bridge of my nose. "I bet he was right over there by his office on Winterberry. They're doing that construction project. He wouldn't have been going very fast on that stretch, but swerving to miss a dog sounds just like him."

Ivy nodded. "That's what I was thinking. And slamming into a big piece of equipment, even going at a low speed, would still do quite a bit of damage."

Wincing at the thought of how badly my brother might be injured, I cleared my throat. "What did he hurt?"

"Face is banged up—the air bag went off, kept him from smashing his face through the windshield, but beat him up pretty good—broke his collar bone. Surgery is to put pins in his thumb and wrist, and to pin his leg. They said his upper leg is pretty messed up, whatever that big bone is."

"Femur," I muttered. "Damn. What's recovery like?"

"Good thing he's not a marathon runner because they said he likely won't ever be able to run, but with physical therapy he should be walking with a walker in about eight weeks, should be able to walk pretty much on his own in about twelve weeks. They said he should recover completely, may have some residual aches and pains in the leg with weather and overuse. Said he'd be in the hospital about a week, then they'll move him to the rehab place. How long he's there will depend on how well he sticks to the exercises and commits to going home."

Ivy's eyes met mine and we both chuckled. We knew Trevor. The man would make it his personal mission to beat every goal and milestone and be home in the shortest time the rehab place had ever seen.

"They said a doctor would come talk to us when the surgery is done—let us know if any of their prognoses change. Said he's young and healthy, no reason to think he won't fully recover—just gonna be a bitch of a time getting to that point." Ivy continued to flip his keys. "I'm guessing he slammed on the brake, tensed his arm and leg, that's probably why the bones on his right side broke."

I winced. "You called my parents?"

"Yeah, they're on their way. They were shopping and at lunch with friends when I called—hated to worry them, but knew they needed to know—they should be here soon."

The hug from Ivy had opened a flood gate and I wanted to scoot closer to him and cuddle into his warm strength. Which was a new enough desire for me—I'd kinda closed myself off from physical touch way back in high school.

The first guy I'd ever dated as a freshman in high school strung me along for a year all while cheating on me. As a sophomore, I bounced right into the arms of a senior who pushed and pushed for more until one night it all came to a scary conclusion.

I didn't like thinking about the party, the loud music, the dark room, and Joe getting meaner and more persistent as the night went on. I'd avoided his advances all night with others around, but when he got me alone, I knew without a doubt he was going to keep at it until he got what he wanted.

I was young and scared.

It wasn't that I didn't want some of the same things Joe was pushing for, but I realized with sudden clarity I didn't want them with him.

And I most definitely didn't want my first time to be rough and mean.

I'd told Joe I didn't feel good and was about to puke.

He cussed me out, pushed me toward the bathroom, and told me to hurry up because he expected me back and on my knees in five minutes.

I'd called Trevor, told him I was at a party and freaking out because there was alcohol, asked him to come get me. Knowing Joe was waiting for me in the bedroom across the hall, I fled down the stairs and out the front door.

By the time Trevor and Ivy had shown up and found

me out by the mailbox—I wasn't sure they bought my reason for needing picked up, but they never pushed it— I'd calmed myself down and swore off guys until it felt right and I found someone who wouldn't force me into a sexual situation I wasn't ready for.

Which was how I ended up hanging out with friends only for the rest of high school—all while lusting after the one guy I'd ever truly felt safe around outside of my family. And also, how I ended up getting through almost four years of college doing the exact same thing.

It wasn't until my last year in college that I decided I wanted to give dating a chance. By then, only willing to date *safe* guys, and feeling as if I'd missed out on several years of honing my relationship skills, my experiences with dating had fallen pretty flat.

So, I'd resigned myself to just letting things happen. If the universe wanted to send me the love of my life—a man who would light up my world, set me on fire, and fill every little crook and cranny of my lonely, love-starved heart, I was ready and willing.

Instead, I found myself pointlessly lusting over my brother's best friend. Why did the only guy I'd ever considered safe *and* hot-as-hell, sex-on-legs, a walking wet dream, have to be Ivy?

Not only was I sure he considered me nothing more than a pesky little brother—sure, I was an adult now, but he'd grown up with me as the snot-nosed tag-along—but as far as I knew, Ivy was straight.

Or, if he was bi-curious or bi-leaning, he'd never let on —at least to me. Ivy didn't date, but he did sleep his way through any and every girl he could get his hands on. Never at his place, never sleeping over, never any repeats

—all facts I'd gathered on the sly over the years since I turned eighteen and the guys considered me enough of a grown-up to talk about their sex lives around me. From what I could tell, Trevor dated, wined and dined, and looked for someone special to build a life with—although, no one had yet to strike his fancy.

Ivy, on the other hand, pretty much just found like-minded and willing women to scratch an itch from time-to-time. And more often than not, he rubbed one out and went to bed instead of getting tangled up in the mess of random hook-ups. Truly, just keeping your ears open when your brother and his best friend were shooting the shit was a great way to gather information.

So, there I was, worried sick about my brother and longing for his best friend. Why did all the other *safe* guys in my life feel like kissing my brother, but the thought of kissing Ivy set my blood on fire? Probably because he was off-limits. Straight, older, and Trevor's best friend.

But none of that made me want to kiss him any less.

Everything about Ivy intimidated me—not in a scary way, nothing about the man had ever scared me. He turned me on, made me aware, sent shivers through me, made me feel seen like no one else ever had.

So, maybe intimidated was the wrong word.

Confused.

Energized.

Challenged.

Did I mention confused?

Pushing the thoughts away—it was what I'd done my whole life, ever since realizing I had a *thing* for Ivy—I stood and rushed to my parents when they walked into the waiting room.

I listened again as Ivy filled my parents in and then we sat in the tension-filled little waiting room for what felt like days. Dad finally paced his way to the little coffee station and busied himself making a new pot. Twenty minutes later, the tiny corner of the room was washed, wiped, straightened, and stocked. Dad delivered steaming cups of coffee to us, all doctored just the way he knew we liked them, and we resumed the waiting game.

Finally, a doctor appeared and explained what he'd done during surgery. For the most part, everything Ivy had been told about the procedure and recovery remained the same. Trevor would go to post-op and then be moved to a room on the fourth floor.

"You're all four welcome to go up and see him. The new sedation we use wears off pretty quickly, so he shouldn't be *too* out of it. The pain medicine should help keep the majority of pain tolerable, but he might be a bit groggy depending on how he reacts to the medication. The goal will be to get him to the rehab facility sooner rather than later. Once he's able to move to outpatient there, he'll need a one-story living area—unless there's an elevator—absolutely no stairs."

We thanked the doctor and pretended to drink our coffee until a nurse arrived and directed us to Trevor's room on the fourth floor. By the time our little quad peeked our heads around the door to my brother's room, I was nearly crawling out of my skin to see him and assure myself he was going to be okay.

"Come on in," a cheery nurse said as she clicked away on a keyboard. "I'm just getting our patient all set up here on the computer and then I'll be out of your way. My name's Mindy and I'll be with Mr. Bell until shift change this evening. Let me know if you have any questions."

All of her words floated distantly on the air as the four of us beelined for Trevor's bedside. His face was discolored and swollen, butterfly bandages on three small cuts, but my brother cracked open a puffy eye and did his best to smile.

"You see," he croaked, "there was this dog..."

We all chuckled, Mom taking his good hand, Dad touching Trevor's shoulder. Ivy and I stood at the foot of his bed.

Over the next hour, Trevor told us of the wreck and dozed in and out while the nurse went over his vitals and their plan for getting him ready for rehab.

Dad checked his watch. "Well, Leese, we better get on out of here and take care of the car and dogs." Trevor had asked them to look into getting his car situation started with insurance and taking his two dogs to their house for the time being. "We'll be back tomorrow to check on you. Text if you need anything."

Mom hovered a bit, making sure Trevor had water and could reach the call button. "We'll have your old room all ready, you just focus on getting yourself rested and healed up."

It had easily been decided Trevor would report to Mom and Dad's place once he was released from in-patient rehab since they had a ranch-style home with only one story. His apartment was on the second floor, and he was out of luck with stairs for a while.

"And no working at least until you're out of here and settled at rehab—the doctor said you needed to rest for at least a week," Mom warned. "I'll call your boss myself if you push me on this."

Trevor smiled weakly. "No worries. I've got plenty of sick time built up. Luckily, I'm between big projects right now so nothing pressing at me. I'll rest here—but once I'm up and around a bit more, no promises. You know I'll be itching to work, even if it'll have to be remotely for a while. Gonna suck not being able to drive."

Dad patted Trevor's good leg. "Wouldn't even be able to get that big ol' cast tucked into the driver's side—looks like you're stuck with Mom and Dad Uber for a while."

Our parents left with love yous and hugs and promises to return.

Ivy finally slumped on the little sofa Dad had pulled up next to Trevor's bed and smacked his good arm. "You damn idiot," he grumbled. "Next time, please hit the dog. Don't wanna get another call like that ever again."

Trevor rolled his head on the pillow and patted Ivy's hand. "You know me and dogs. I'd be devastated if I lost Sassy and Stella," he said, his words a bit groggy as he spoke of his two American Staffordshire Terriers. "I wouldn't be able to live with myself if I knew I'd killed someone else's dog. He was a beauty, too. Big ol' boy, looked scared to death running across that street."

"Yeah, well, *we* were scared to death, too," I added, flopping down next to Ivy on the small couch.

"I'm sorry, I hated that part too," Trevor said. "Oh shit…"

"What? Something hurt?" Ivy asked.

"Man, I'm so damn sorry. I fucked it all up," Trevor said, true regret filling his bruised, swollen face.

"Fucked what up? The car? If it's fixable, I'll work on it, no worries."

Trevor dropped his head back on the pillow with a defeated sigh just as dawning washed over me.

The show.

"The damn show, I messed it up so bad." My brother's words were slurring as his most recent dose of pain medication kicked in.

"Fuck that," Ivy huffed out. "Hadn't even thought of it. None of that's important. What matters is you getting back on your feet."

"Noooo," Trevor groaned. "We were gonna win and get you that money for your shop and house. And now it's all fucked up. Shit."

Without a single drop of my usual anxiety or over-thinking, words poured from my mouth before I had a moment to examine them. "I'll do it."

Ivy nearly gave himself whiplash looking my way.

Trevor's brows shot up—as much as they could with the swelling and his doped-up state.

I shrugged. "What? You signed up as Bell and Ivy, right? That was kinda your nickname for the show. We'd still be Bell and Ivy. I can keep working, do the show with you, and hopefully we can win that money for you." Freezing, a terrible thought overtaking me, I eyed Ivy. "Unless you'd rather not have to live with me and do the whole fake couple thing."

Holy shit.

I'd been so focused on bailing Trevor out and giving Ivy a chance at the win that I hadn't even given much thought to the logistics.

I'd have to live with Ivy.

Pretend to be a couple.

All the shit I'd said about chemistry and the audience expecting the real deal between them would still apply.

Fuck.

I liked Ivy. I'd have no issues living with him. And the chemistry was there on my side of things. But faking a relationship with your straight best friend was very different than pretending to be boyfriends with your best friend's gay little brother—maybe Ivy wouldn't want to get involved with me like that.

Maybe even just pretending to be my boyfriend would be too much...

"Fuck, little Bell, let's do it," Ivy answered with a smirk.

I shot him a sidelong glare. "As long as you never call me that again."

Ivy winked, sending sparks of heat through me. "We'll see."

"Wait," Trevor mumbled. "Emory, no. We can't ask you to do that."

Ivy looked torn between feeling bad for accepting and frustrated with Trevor for shooting down the idea.

"Good thing no one asked me then," I said. "Seriously, it's the only real answer. We'd have to get it cleared by the producers—they may not be on board—but it's kinda perfect."

Ivy huffed. "Shit, yeah, they probably won't be too happy with a switch—they'll know right away we were faking it—either that Trevor and I were faking, you and I are faking, or both."

I shifted on the couch. "We'll just have to see what they say."

Trevor shook his head, his eyes getting heavier by the second. "I don't know if it's a good idea."

"Why? You can't do it, I'm available, it's a no brainer. Buys me more time to figure out what the hell I'm doing *and* I get to be on a holiday-themed show. Plus, if we win, that money would be nice."

Ivy grunted and tensed beside me, the keychain going a mile a minute. "Um, you know how much I hate Christmas."

I patted his knee. "I do. And you know how much I love the holidays. For five hundred grand, I'm pretty sure we can find a happy middle ground."

"But you'll have to kiss him." Trevor's words were definitely slurred. "Like you said, *real* kisses."

"You were going to kiss him," I countered.

"Yeah, but like Emory and Ivy," he mumbled. "Kissing. Like *kissing* kissing."

"And?"

"It was different when it was us," Trevor said.

"Why? Because you're straight and I'm not? Are you afraid I'll turn your friend gay?" I kept my words as light as possible, but a stab of irritation ran through me.

"Not that," Trevor said and I could tell he was having a hard time gathering thoughts and putting them into words thanks to the medication and exhaustion. "It's just..."

I stood. "Promise, I won't taint him." Softening, because I knew Trevor was drugged up and had never once shown anything but love and support for me, I squeezed his hand. "Can't promise I won't get him to love Christmas though."

Trevor chuckled. "Now that would be a damn miracle."

"Not happening," Ivy growled as he stood beside me. "Producer probably won't even let us on now. But definitely not going to ever like Christmas."

I knew Ivy had a history of shitty things happening around the holidays and he'd adamantly hated anything and everything to do with Christmas for almost as long as I'd known him.

"Text us, let us know how things are going. We'll figure out what's going on with the show and let you know," I said.

We said our goodbyes and left Trevor to rest.

On the way to the elevator, Ivy cleared his throat. "You know you don't *have* to do the show with me. I'm not in dire straits—I'd survive without the money. There's a good chance we'd get knocked out in the first round anyway—even if they let us do the show with you instead of Trevor."

"I know I don't have to, but I'm willing to help if we can make it work."

"I really do hate Christmas," Ivy said, an edge to his voice. "So, like, best not to expect anything super holiday-ish from me."

I smirked, my next words making Ivy scowl. "No expectations, but I can't promise you won't love it by the end of our time together."

If we even got to do the show.

If we lasted past the first week.

We exited the elevator and made our way to the parking lot.

"You know I'm not worried about you turning me gay, right?" Ivy said, a serious look on his gorgeous face. "I'm not against shit like that. Gay, straight, bi, pan, demi, ace, all of it, none of it, that shit doesn't matter to me, you know that, right? Labels aren't my thing, but I'm cool with people needing them. I figure, you're attracted to who you're attracted to. You love who you love." His cheeks pinked. "If you're into love and shit. It's not for me, but I'm down with people loving their person, no matter the label or whatever." He ran a hand through his hair. "Fuck, I think the day is catching up with me. Imma shut up now."

Ivy being flustered and vulnerable was something I'd never really had the pleasure of seeing. Not going to lie, it was adorable.

"So, what do we do? Call the producer?" I moved the conversation away from potential awkwardness.

He took hold of the subject change. "Yeah, I've got the guy's number. I'll reach out, explain the situation. Are you free to meet with him within the next day or so if he doesn't automatically boot us out?"

"I'll text you my shifts." We reached my little red Miata and I noticed Ivy's car—a gorgeous black 1970 Plymouth Cuda he'd rebuilt last year and was constantly tinkering with—was just a couple spaces from mine. "You sure you want to do this? I don't want to put you in an uncomfortable position having to fake something with me."

"I'm down if you are," Ivy said, flipping the keychain. "You sure you wanna give me eight weeks?"

I chuckled. "Time is something I have plenty of, unfortunately."

Ivy studied me like he wanted to ask something, but just gave a quick nod. "I'll let you know what the show guy says."

"And if we get the go ahead, maybe we have a conversation about logistics and whatnot. If we're going to pull this off, we need to be prepared."

"I like the sound of that. Trevor was all about just wingin' it, but I like the way you think, little Bell." He winked at my glower. "We need a plan if we're going to make this happen."

CHAPTER 3

IVY

"How mad is he?" Emory asked the next day when he walked into Ivy's Auto a few minutes before the producer was set to arrive.

"Pissed, but he seemed resigned to making it happen. Figure he wouldn't have come here if he was going to say we were out. Guessing he's going to hand us our asses and then do his part to make the show go on." I'd cleared space in my office at the shop for the meeting and pointed to the chair I meant for Emory to sit in.

Next to me.

A real couple would sit together, right? Present a united front?

Obviously, the producer was going to know we weren't a real couple, but I figured it wouldn't hurt to show him we could pull it off.

"I think honesty is our best policy when talking to him," Emory said as he took the seat behind my desk and next to my chair. "There's no reason to try to make him think we're together, but if he thinks we can pull it off, he may be willing to let us through."

"Once again, little Bell, I like the way you think," I said, ruffling his hair and chuckling when Emory squawked.

Part of me felt bad for letting Emory step in and take Trevor's place, but I also couldn't help being excited about the chance to win. Doing the game with Trevor had been a no-brainer. His little brother maybe wasn't my best friend, but I was closer to Emory than I was to my own family for the most part—Iris and I weren't estranged, we just didn't have a lot in common; we'd both dealt with our father's infidelity and mom's subsequent disconnectedness in different ways.

If Emory was willing to play the game, I wasn't going to stop him.

Had anyone else offered to step in, I would have balked immediately. But I had no problem living with Emory for eight weeks—hell, I could only hope we made it through all eight weeks—and the thought of faking it with him was only slightly more anxiety-inducing than pretending to be boyfriends with Trevor.

Why?

There were a lot of thoughts and feelings involved in an attempted answer to that question—most of which I had no desire to examine at that moment, so I pushed it all aside.

I could kiss a guy. Kissing was no big deal. I didn't hate it, but it also wasn't something I loved—never really saw the point in kissing if I'm being honest. When I hooked up with a girl, I was there for something quick and easy.

Kissing took up too much time and often seemed more intimate than the actual sex.

Emory and I could totally pretend to be a couple. Sure, maybe I didn't *do* relationships and emotions and all that, but Emory and I were friends. That was already kinda couple-ish. Add in some PDA and well-planned couple-y things and we'd be golden.

This show didn't get *super* up close and personal, so it wasn't like they'd be filming us beneath the sheets.

I mean, I knew we'd have to share a bed, but it wasn't like the cameras would be *in* the bed. This game was more about completing the challenges and winning votes. We just had to compete well and get the viewers to like us more than the other couples.

Maybe I wasn't super likable, but Emory was a doll.

We could do this.

I watched a car pull into the drive on the small security camera and a well-dressed man about my age climb out of an expensive car.

"Here goes," I mumbled to Emory as I moved toward the front of the shop to greet Silas Corwin. "Hi, thanks for coming," I said with my hand outstretched.

Silas sniffed and rolled his eyes. "Let's get this mess settled."

Okay, then.

Silas looked as if he wanted to put a handkerchief on the chair before he sat down—which was offensive because my shop was spotless—but he took his seat. Crossing his legs at the knee and his arms over his chest, the man studied us for a tense moment before speaking.

"Tell me again what's going on," Silas said in a bored and annoyed voice.

I cleared my throat. "Myself and Trevor Bell applied to be on the show and were accepted. He was recently injured in a car accident and won't be able to participate. His brother," I gestured to Emory who smiled and gave a little wave, "Emory Bell, offered to step in and compete on the show with me."

"And you feel no one would notice this switch?" Silas asked with a cocked brow.

"It's not that," Emory said. "The show hasn't started. From what we know of the application process, only that one picture was submitted. So, as far as *who* would know, the number is pretty small. We know *you're* aware, obviously. And probably some of your staff. We understand if you have to go with another couple, but I wanted to help my brother. I'm available and willing."

A suggestive glint filled Silas's eyes as he devoured Emory from head to toe. "Available and willing, indeed."

I cleared my throat, not liking the way Silas leered.

Not liking the weird stab of...what even was that?

Protectiveness. That was all it was.

"So, what are your thoughts?" I asked, drawing the man's attention away from Emory.

Silas steepled his fingers under his chin. "We're going to pretend that you and the original Bell brother didn't get on the show by duping us into thinking you were an actual couple. And we're going to pretend that you and the new Bell brother *are* a couple. Aside from the three of us—and the incapacitated Bell—no one knows *who* you were when you applied—except for my last assistant, but I fired her and sent her on her way with a nondisclosure, so we should be good." He tapped his chin with his fingers. "I truly hope the other producers are having just as much *fun* as I am with these last-minute snafus." Cocking his head, Silas pursed his lips, deep in thought. "The official images for the show haven't been shot yet—we'll get a few today and then you'll do the professional ones before we start filming. God knows you two can't look any less *in love* than the first version of Ivy and Bell."

The man seemed to be talking more to himself than to us, almost as if running it through his head to see if it would all work.

I wasn't sure whether to be offended he thought the picture of Trevor and me as a *couple* had sucked, or excited because he thought Emory and I would maybe be better.

"Yes, I think we can make it work." Silas nodded as if he'd officially decided. "This show needs to go well for my future career, so I'm dedicated to making it work. That means we start with ten couples in a couple days and I'm not interested in finding your replacements." He glanced between Emory and me. "I couldn't care less if the viewers believe you're a couple—whether or not you stick around isn't my concern, that's on you two. So, if you think you can fake a relationship well enough to win the viewers' hearts, more power to you. Keep in mind, you're up against some actual real couples so you better bring your A game. But in the long run, my only concern is ramping up viewership, making money, and moving on to bigger and better."

I quickly realized *Once Upon a Christmas House* was simply a stepping-stone for Silas. It wasn't a passion project—he wasn't concerned with anything but moving on up. Which actually worked perfectly for Emory and me. Silas wasn't going to worry about the integrity of the show and that meant Emory and I had a chance.

Or at least a *start*.

Silas pulled his phone from his pocket and moved to the edge of his seat.

"Let's get a few shots now, then I'll leave you two to strategize and prepare for your eight weeks of bliss—assuming you make it that long." He gestured between us. "Here's your first challenge, look couple-y. Be cute. Show us the love and good holiday cheer."

Shit.

Okay, we could do this.

Before I could give it any more thought, Emory took my hand, stilling the flipping of my key chain, and leaned close. The press of his lips against my cheek wasn't uncomfortable, just surprising, but I went with it as Silas snapped a couple pictures.

"Look at each other," Silas instructed.

I turned to look at Emory. He was all up in my space, but it was an easy closeness and we shared a slightly uncomfortable chuckle as we tried to decide what to do.

"Do the whole foreheads together thing, people like that shit," Silas grumped.

Shifting slightly, I pressed my forehead against Emory's.

He smelled of coffee, citrus, and mint along with the subtle undertone of *just Emory*. Was it shampoo? Product? Deodorant? Whatever the mixture of scents, I definitely couldn't complain.

In our little bubble, for a fraction of a second, my body relaxed for the first time since finding out my best friend had been injured. Closing my eyes, I just enjoyed the soft, easy quiet of the moment.

"Well, hot damn," Silas muttered as he stuffed his

phone back in his pocket and stood. "You know, part of the selection process was pure chance. Part of it was having a great story—the type that would capture the audience and really pull them in. Part of it was having the look—attractive people are easy to root for. I remember thinking when you and the original Bell were chosen that, one, you made it through on pure luck, and two, you at least had the right look—both hot." He paused with his hand on the door, Emory and I following him from the office to the front. "Don't get me wrong, I still think *this*," he gestured between us, "is going to be a hard sell, but you've got a thousand percent better chance than the original fake relationship had."

Silas gave a nod, still having nothing to do with shaking hands, and pushed open the door into the sunny fall day.

"We'll see you soon. Best wishes on your completion of the game." He gave a smile as fake as Emory's and my coupledom. "And remember, nothing says Season's Greetings like a little bit of competition and teamwork, a dash of romance, and a splash of holiday magic with the Season's Streaming channel," he said in a way that made me think he died a little inside with each word.

We watched the producer drive away for a few moments before Emory turned my way with an excited smile.

"I guess we're in," he said, reminding me so much of Trevor's contagious jovial nature, but adding in Emory's unique twist—innocence? Vulnerability? Whatever it was, just under the surface, I couldn't exactly put my finger on it.

But I liked it.

I wanted to keep Emory smiling.

Wanted him to know he meant something to me just like Trevor—but in his own way.

"We're in." I clapped him on the back.

"Should we meet after my shift to make plans?" Emory had come to meet Silas before his mid-morning shift and I had appointments out the wazoo for the rest of the day.

"Yeah, since we start the show day after tomorrow, why don't you bring your belongings over after work. Probably best to get our little scheme set up sooner rather than later," I said.

"Shoot," Emory said, a cute little scowl pinching between his brows. "Hadn't even thought of the fact most of the town is going to know right away we aren't a couple. Or they'll decide I rubbed off on you and made you gay. I don't want to cause a problem for you around town."

"Em," I said, the nickname Trevor had used for his brother our entire lives rolling off my tongue as easily as breathing. "Look at me. I'm the dark and broody, inked, holiday-hating auto mechanic. First, I don't think that many people care. Second, they won't say much. Third, fuck 'em if they do. I say we approach it as if we're trying to fool the whole damn town. That way, we don't risk someone blabbing their suspicions."

Then a thought struck me.

"Wait," I said.

Emory bit his lip and glanced my way. "Yeah?"

"Do you think people will give *you* shit?"

He shrugged. "It's not terrible. Peppermint Hollow as a whole is pretty tame. I doubt too many people will say anything. I think the worst of it will be from people who might be pissed you pop up as *taken*—you've got quite the fan club of droolers around town," he teased.

I huffed and waved him off. "This town knows I don't do relationships."

Emory cocked a brow.

"Until now," I amended. "We'll play it off that I'd never been into relationships *until* I realized I was into you. No one else except your parents knew Trevor and I were going to do the show, so we can say what we've got is new, the show was a whim, and falling for you had me re-evaluating my stand on relationships."

Emory nodded, biting his lip. "Yeah, sounds good."

"You sure?"

"Yeah."

"No, something's bothering you."

Emory took a deep breath. "I've only ever had two shitty relationships and a couple attempts that failed massively because there was just no spark between us." He crossed his arms around his middle, curling in on himself. "It's just kinda sad the closest thing I'm going to get to a *real* relationship is a fake boyfriend with my brother's best friend."

His words drew me up short.

Shit.

Weird flitty feelings in my chest made me want to ask Emory about these shitty relationships, make things better, make it *good* for him, but it didn't feel like the right time.

Smiling in a way I hoped seemed easy and fun, I said, "Well, you'll be the first relationship—real or fake—I've ever had. Maybe we can learn something together for later on down the line when we get to the real deal."

Something flashed in Emory's eyes—sadness? Doubt? A challenge? I couldn't tell, but he smiled and nodded. "Yeah, that sounds like a plan. I'll be over after work. I don't plan on bringing a ton of things, just clothes, books, laptop, toiletries. Unless there's anything else you need?"

"Nah, little Bell as a roomie is all I need, plus five hundred grand."

Emory chuckled. "Roomie and boyfriend. I really hope we know what the hell we're doing."

"We'll figure it out."

"Hopefully in time to make the first cut. If people don't love us, we're out."

"Yeah, true. See you in a bit. If I'm not done out here, go on in," I handed him a spare key. "Shower, put your stuff in the closet, whatever. You know which room is mine."

Emory winced. "Do you think we should try to have separate rooms?"

"No way," I said, then paused. "Unless you don't want to share my room? I'm just thinking we run the risk of getting caught if we're not playing the part of loving boyfriends the whole time."

"Agreed. I just feel bad making you sleep with me."

I wrapped an arm around his neck and ruffled his hair, the minty citrus scent tickling my nose. "As long as you don't snore like Trevor, we're all good."

"Be thinking of questions and logistics we need to hammer out," Emory said. "I'll bring dinner."

"Aww, already such a sweet boyfriend," I teased.

"I'm a damn delight," Emory said with a wink and made me laugh.

Those words stuck with me the rest of the day as I

worked in my shop—my dream career, my pride and joy, the way I kept myself from going insane—and by the time I set to work on my last appointment of the day, I couldn't help the smile that lingered.

Emory Bell *was* a damn delight.

I'd miss Trevor on this adventure, but I wasn't going to complain about getting to know Emory a bit better.

For a guy who didn't have a lot of close relationships, I'd take what I could get.

Maybe I'd never find love—wasn't looking for it, wasn't cut out for it—but having a couple good friends, a gorgeous old house, and my shop was just what my heart needed.

It would have to be enough.

CHAPTER 4

EMORY

My feet ached as I carried the last load of my belongings into Ivy's room at his new house after my shift. Okay, it was an *old* house, but he'd just bought it. It worked perfectly because it had the exact type of garage and space he needed for Ivy's Auto, which meant he'd been able to move from the area he'd been renting and set up his very own shop.

The Christmas House as Ivy called it—Trevor told me they used to call it that when they were kids, the house had a history and lots of stories of holiday magic swirled around it—was gorgeous. True, it needed a lot of work, but it was livable and I knew Ivy had big plans for making it into something special. Even though he was a complete and total Scrooge when it came to anything having to do with the holidays.

I couldn't help taking it as a personal challenge.

Not only would I do everything in my power to win *Once Upon a Christmas House*, I had every intention of bringing a little holiday cheer into Ivy's life.

Toeing off my shoes in his room—*my* room—I set to work unpacking, putting my things into drawers, bathroom cabinets, and hanging my clothes in the closet. When my stomach growled toward the end of my chore, I took the world's quickest shower—not letting my anxious, horny brain picture Ivy naked right where I stood —and headed down to the kitchen.

I could see Ivy working in the shop from the window over the sink. Sliding my feet into his unlaced work boots, I clunked out to the shop and walked through the back door.

"I'm not going to take advantage of him, Trev," Ivy said and I realized he was talking to my brother. "He's a big boy. We both know what we're getting into."

"I just don't want him hurt," Trevor said on speaker phone. "He's always seemed to have a thing for you—I don't know if he likes you or is just in awe of you—but I don't want him getting his hopes dashed."

"We're faking boyfriends to win some money and get my house fixed. Period. He doesn't think I'm asking him to marry me." I watched as Ivy washed his hands. "He knows I don't do relationships."

"So, you don't care that people think you're all of a sudden gay?" Trevor pressed.

"Were you going to care when *we* were going to fake it?"

"No, but I'm not gay."

"Okay?"

"I just don't want it causing problems for either of you," Trevor said.

"Let me play devil's advocate here," Ivy said. "What if I was gay, would that be a problem for you?"

"What? Of course, not."

"What if—hypothetically—I fell for Emory?"

My gut twisted.

Oh, god.

That.

That was my dream.

Obviously, I knew it wasn't going to happen.

But it was what I wanted so damn bad I could taste it.

"I don't know. I'd be worried he'd get hurt. It would be weird to see you with my baby brother. I wouldn't care if you were gay, but I don't think I'd want you with Em."

Whatever Ivy was going to say in response was cut off when my phone beeped.

Ivy jerked his head toward the door and I pretended to just be walking in.

"Hey, did you want to eat?" I asked, hoping he couldn't tell I'd heard the conversation.

His cheeks darkened and he studied me as if trying to decide what I'd heard. "Yeah, let me grab a shower—I'll take one out here since I'm filthy. Eat without me if you need to. We'll get busy soon, promise."

"What?" Trevor squawked.

"Get your head out of the gutter. We're making plans," Ivy said. "Unlike you thinking you can charm your way through anything—"

"Let's be honest," Trevor said, a grin evident in his words. "I usually can charm my way through anything. What do you need plans for?"

"A story about how we got together? Learning a bit about each other? Logistics for the challenges and making people believe we're a real couple worthy of winning the money?" Ivy was definitely getting frustrated with Trevor.

"Plans, shmans," my brother said. "Where's the excitement in that?"

"Some of us prefer to be prepared."

"I guess it's a must when you don't have my natural charisma," Trevor joked.

"Hey, how are you feeling?" I asked as Ivy rolled his eyes. I wasn't exactly sure how to take my brother's earlier reaction toward me and Ivy being fake boyfriends. Why had it been *fine* for him to fake a gay relationship with his best friend, but he didn't like me doing the same thing?

Ivy pointed over his shoulder and mouthed, "Shower," as I listened to Trevor tell me about today's doctor's report and his challenge to himself to leave the hospital at least one day before they thought he would.

I nodded and kept talking to my brother as Ivy went to the little shop bathroom and started his shower. Soon, a clean scent of sandalwood and sea salt filled the air. I closed my eyes, breathing deeply, and savoring the image of a naked Ivy in that tiny little shower.

Fuck.

Why did my blood have to boil for Ivyrson Gregory?

Why not the nice guy I worked with occasionally?

Why not my old roommate?

Why not *anyone* but my brother's straight best friend?

You don't know *he's straight.*

I thought back to Ivy's ramblings about not needing labels and not caring who someone loved. He was adamant *he* couldn't love anyone, but he didn't indicate anything regarding his sexuality.

Yeah, the hookups I was aware of had all been with females, but that didn't mean he didn't hook up with guys. Didn't mean he didn't find guys attractive and just opted for sex with females because it was expected.

All I knew was I needed to keep my damn attraction to him under control and not ruin whatever chance we maybe had to win the competition.

"Emory?" my brother called through the speaker and I knew I'd spaced out for way too long.

"Huh? Yeah, I'm here."

"I gotta go. I've got another round of physical therapy and I need to show them I'm ready to head to the rehab place."

"Good luck. Keep us updated. We'll visit."

"You better. Love you."

"Love you," I said.

"Hey, Em?" Trevor asked.

"Yeah?"

"Don't go getting yourself hurt or thinking you can steal my best friend." His words attempted to be light and joking, but I knew he was at least partly serious.

"Chill out, Trev. I'm a big boy. I know this is just a game. Ivy's always been your best friend and that won't change. I'm still just the tag-along little brother."

Trevor was quiet for a moment. "Yeah, okay. Love you."

The call disconnected.

Did I need to try to figure out whatever was going on with Trevor?

Or should I just let it go since it wasn't like anything was going to happen with Ivy and me?

If the man was into me, maybe it would be a different story. But he wasn't. We'd compete in the game, hopefully win, then I'd move out, and we'd all go back to the way things were before Trevor's accident.

Easy.

"Looking cute, little Bell," Ivy said from behind me as he ran a towel through his hair.

"Huh?" Had the man seriously just said I looked cute?

"In my boots. Maybe we make that one of our *things*," he said.

"Things?" Clearly, I'd been reduced to muttering one word at a time.

Ivy gestured toward the door, turning off lights as we walked out of the shop. "I was thinking in the shower. Couples have special little things, right? I think we need some. You wearing my boots could be something. I can be all about how sexy and cute I think it is. Or you borrowing my clothes. We don't want to go overboard, but if we go into the game with these things in place, we have a better chance of looking like real boyfriends."

He held the back door open for me as I tried to breathe normally.

Ivy and I were going to have *things*.

This show was going to kill me.

Yeah, but at least you'll die happy.

Fuck that.

I wouldn't die happy. I'd die with blue balls and all emo over the fact I was so close to something real with the man of my dreams while knowing the only thing we truly shared was being fucking faking fakers.

Trying to keep myself busy, I pulled out the bags of deli sandwiches I'd picked up on my way home.

Home.

No.

Ivy's place wasn't *my* home. Not for real.

Ivy wasn't my home. No matter how right it felt to settle into things with him.

"So," I said, handing Ivy a bag. "Me wearing your boots and clothes is a *thing*. What else?"

"You like coffee?"

"Do birds fly?"

Ivy cracked a smile. "Most of them. So, I make a mean cup of coffee." He gestured toward his countertop where a two-cup coffee maker sat. "How about we make it a thing that I fix you coffee each morning?"

"I like that," I said. "Makes us look cute and caring *and* I get kickass coffee. Score." Nudging my glasses, I huffed in annoyance when my knuckle smeared something on the lenses. "What else?" Putting down my sandwich, I took off my glasses and held them up to the light.

"First, those are disgusting," Ivy said, taking my frames from my hand and moving to the sink. "For real. Emory Shae," he admonished, sounding like a parent, "you should be ashamed of yourself. These things might as well be little petri dishes you wear on your face. Damn man, I work with greasy tools all day, but your glasses look like you're the one smearing oil." He ran my glasses under hot water, cleaned the lenses with soap, dried them, buffed them, and held them up to the light. "Better."

As he slid them back onto my face, the warmth of his body way too close, and the warmth of my frames from the hot water sending shivers through me, I cleared my throat. "Um, maybe that's our other thing. You clean my glasses for me."

Ivy stepped back, seemed to consider my words, and

shrugged. "Yeah, that works. Cute, caring, and definitely needed."

We fell into an easy silence while we ate.

As I gathered our trash, Ivy grabbed a notebook.

"What do we need to prepare for?" he asked, writing *Once Upon a Christmas House* at the top of the page.

"First, we need to destroy that paper when we're done," I said.

"For sure." He scribbled the word *Meals* on the first line. "What else?"

"Our history? How we met? Birthdays? Memories? Chores? Sex?"

Ivy's brows shot up.

I chuckled and rolled my eyes. "I meant like are you going to need to sneak out of town and find a hookup during the show?"

He pointed the pen at me. "We'll come back to that, but the short answer is no. The long answer is hell, no. Now, what else?"

"PDA—do we do it, how much of it, practicing it. Favorites. Date ideas."

Ivy continued down the page, my suggestions filling the lines as he scratched the words.

"Do we talk about our future or is this kinda just new and for the moment?"

He finished writing. "Okay, let's start with these." Glancing around the kitchen, he curled his lip. "You wanna sit in the living room?"

CHAPTER 5

IVY

EMORY HAD KICKED MY BOOTS OFF WHEN WE walked through the door, but I couldn't stop thinking about how cute he looked in them. He wasn't fashion model gorgeous, he was just an average guy with caramel brown hair and the deepest chocolate brown eyes I'd ever seen—and filthy glasses sitting on his pert little nose—but he'd come walking into the garage in my nicer pair of black work boots and my stomach had gone all weird. And I'd had this unexpected urge to keep him safe and happy.

Cleaning his glasses really was a necessity—they were disgusting.

But it was more than that—at least if I let myself be honest. Like I wanted to do nice things for him. Clean his glasses. Make him coffee.

What the hell was that about?

I'd never wanted to do nice things for anyone in my life.

Well, at least not since my dad tore our family apart when I was like twelve and my whole world went to shit.

I was probably just missing Trevor and wanting to make sure his little brother was taken care of. I appreciated Emory being willing to help me with the game. There was no reason not to enjoy building up our friendship now that we were stuck together for eight weeks.

Hopefully, eight weeks.

"Okay," Emory said as we sat side-by-side on the couch. "Meals."

"I'm thinking we split meals. Between bringing things home or cooking, we'll just take turns."

"You trust my cooking?" Emory asked, bumping my shoulder.

"You haven't died yet."

"Valid point. Are we okay with take-out more than homemade? I don't love to cook."

I shrugged. "I kinda like cooking, so I'll probably do more meals at home than carry-out."

"That works."

"Okay, what about our history?" I asked.

"I think it's best to keep it as close to the truth as possible," Emory said. "You and I have known each other basically since I was born because you and Trevor are best friends from elementary school. That's how we met. Recently, since I came home from college, we've spent more time together and one thing led to another, and now we're dating. Decided to submit an application for the show just for fun."

"Yeah, sticking close to the truth makes it easier. You know my birthday, right?"

Emory snorted. "Of course. The day before mine,

seven years apart. How many birthdays did we celebrate together from the time I was like five?"

"Your mom was always the best. Making sure Iris and I had a ride to your house, making sure I had a cake—not just sharing yours—it was like everyone in your family just automatically assumed we'd have a party together. Trevor and me playing while you and your friends did whatever it was you did," I teased. "And Iris stuck to your dad like glue. I swear, our father leaving the way he did fucked her up more than I'll probably ever know—I'm guessing it's why she dated such losers over the years."

"But she's got a good guy now, right? The baby's dad?"

"Yeah, he seems legit. I never thought I'd be okay with her moving away—and it's not like I *wanted* her to leave—but I know it's for the best and he'll take care of them. It's kinda weird, for the first time since I was twelve, I don't have to constantly be trying to protect her, take care of her."

Ohhhh. The thought hit me like a ton of bricks. Was Iris moving away the reason behind me feeling such a tug toward keeping Emory safe and taken care of? I'd always hated that I *had* to take care of my sister, even though I was grateful I was able to. Maybe I'd grown so used to being independent, responsible, and looking out for Iris, I automatically fell into wanting to do the same for Emory.

Even though it was a completely different situation.

And the way my stomach clenched and fluttered when I let my head think a little too long about how Emory looked in my boots definitely wasn't the way one felt about a sibling.

But yeah, I was sure my fucked-up past was

responsible for the weirdness I felt toward Emory all of a sudden. The fact I'd always been joined at the hip with Trevor and now I didn't have him by my side probably also played into things.

So, once again, dear ol' Dad wreaking havoc even all these years later.

God, I hated that man.

Hated what he'd done.

Hated the fact he'd screwed me up so bad I couldn't even hope to find someone to love and settle down with.

Thanks to him, it just wasn't in my future.

"Okay, so our birthdays aren't until summer. Shouldn't come into play during the show, but just in case it's good we know them and a few stories about them." Emory glanced at the list. "Memories?"

I laughed. "I remember little Bell tagging along after Trevor and me. Your brother used to get so pissed."

Emory's cheeks pinked and my gut flip-flopped.

What in the actual fuck was wrong with me?

I'd known this guy my entire life. Surely, I'd seen him blush before. Why was I having such weird reactions to him?

Maybe it's the house. You know the stories about the holiday magic here.

Huffing at that ridiculousness, I ignored the errant thought.

"I was such a little pain," Emory said.

"Nah, it built character for us."

"I remember sneaking out to your campouts trying to spy on you guys."

"I remember we never made it a whole night in the

tent, we always freaked ourselves out and went running inside to sleep on the couches." I laughed. "I would have given anything for my family not to fall apart, but having the Bells as my surrogate family saved me."

"We can completely leave it out, but maybe someday you can tell me what happened?" Emory asked softly.

My heart caught in my throat. "Yeah, maybe." It struck me right in the feels that Trevor hadn't told Emory my shitty past *and* Emory wanted to know more about me. I'd never felt like anyone wanted to know about me, not for real. But I pushed aside the warmth and willed my heart to return to its normal rhythm. Ivyrson Gregory didn't get emotional—there was no reason, there wasn't time, and it did no good. Besides, something inside told me, if I ever actually let go and allowed myself to *feel*, I'd never be able to rein it back in.

And I hated the idea of *feeling* all that shit almost as much as I hated Christmas. Sure, the good side of it all would be great, but the bad side would suck. Better to just avoid it all.

"I think we've got plenty of memories to use as needed." Emory nodded toward the notebook. "What about chores?"

I gestured around the house. "The Christmas House is clearly in need of a lot of things, but she's clean. And bare enough there's not much cleaning to do. Just the normal vacuuming, sweeping, dusting, bathrooms, dishes, that type of thing. Do we want to just split the chores?"

"Can I just say how much I love that you call it The Christmas House?" Emory asked, his eyes sparkling. "I know you hate the holidays, but the fact you call it that makes me want to believe you have at least a tiny bit of Christmas spirit in your heart."

A type of disgruntled growly sound escaped my throat. I wasn't mad—I knew Emory adored Christmas, his whole family did—I just didn't want him getting any kind of ideas in his head about me morphing into this holiday-loving, big-hearted, pillar-of-the-community type guy. It wasn't happening. I loved my job, I was good at it, I provided a useful service for Peppermint Hollow. But I also had no use for spirit or anything else in my heart. I wasn't a socialite loved by all. Period. Emory needed to understand that.

He snorted. "Okay, okay, baby steps. I can be patient." He wrinkled his nose. "I kinda hate dusting, but I have no issues with the others. Want to go by weeks or days? Or just pick the ones we prefer to do?"

"I'll do the dusting, it doesn't bother me," I said with a grin. "We'll make a list and each day or week we can check off what we've done. If it's not done, we'll do it."

"Perfect," Emory said. "When do you plan on starting the remodel?"

I shrugged. "Not planning on starting anything big until I can save up a bit of money."

Emory nudged me. "With your bigger shop—even without the additions you want to make—you should be able to bring in more income. And, if we win, you won't have to worry about money at all."

"True." My heart clenched. I wanted to win so badly, but I knew setting my hopes too high was just asking for a crash and burn. It wasn't as if anything in my life so far had been sunshine and roses—well, except for the Bells being in my life—and I knew better than to hope for anything good.

"Okay, what about sex?"

I choked.

Emory snorted. "How are you this dark, broody, I-hate-Christmas, hookups-around-every-corner type guy, yet you get all choky when I mention sex?" His big brown eyes blinked curiously behind his shiny lenses.

"First, I'm not all choky, I swallowed wrong." I pointed the pen at him. "Second, I don't have hookups around every corner. I don't *do* relationships, and I've had a lot of meaningless sex, but it's not like I'm hooking up daily. Hell, lately, not even monthly. And like I said before, I won't be needing to sneak off and have sex—it's not necessary, for one, I'm a grown man and I can control myself. Two, we're supposed to be a loving, committed couple. Season's Streaming seems to have a pretty open-minded viewership, so I don't think a same-sex couple is going to turn them off, but I'm not sure they're ready for an open relationship. I could be wrong—hell, maybe we'll lose to a throuple—but I think we're better off focusing on just being fake boyfriends and not worrying about sneaking in secret interludes."

A thought hit me.

Shit.

"Wait, do *you* need to be sneaking off for sex?"

Emory giggled. An honest to god giggle.

"Um, something you should know—in the interest of the show and our fake boyfriendship—I'm not super experienced in the bedroom department."

My eyes went wide as his cheeks went pink.

"I'm not completely a virgin," he hurried on. "I've gotten off with a few guys, just never done much more than that."

His jean-clad thigh was warm under my touch. "Being a virgin isn't a bad thing. And sex is anything you want it to be." Our eyes locked, but I quickly glanced at my hand on his leg. How had it gotten there? Why was I still touching him? A barrage of thoughts and images—all in some way related to Emory and sex—flooded my head. "But thanks for telling me," I said, quickly moving my hand. "That's the type of stuff that could make or break our little fake set-up."

"Me being a virgin?" Emory squeaked.

"No, I just mean we need to know shit about each other." I doodled the outline of an engine on the notebook. "So, we agree that we'll be committed to each other—no going out to hook up with others—for as long as we're able to stay on the show?"

Emory nodded. "I've survived twenty-three years, pretty sure I can make it eight weeks."

Twenty-three.

Damn, he was just a baby.

Not that my thirty was *old*.

I blinked away the thought. Seven years was nothing between two consenting adults. And even though it was all fake, Emory and I were both adults.

"Okay, we've got favorites, date ideas, PDA, and our future still to go. I gotta pee first, but I got peppermint stick ice cream, do you want a sundae?" Emory asked.

"Huh?" The change of subject yanked me from my stream of thought.

"Ice cream, do you want some?"

"Sure."

Emory stood. "Come help, we can talk while we create."

"Create? What are we creating?" I asked as I followed him to the kitchen.

"Scooping up plain ol' ice cream is boring. We're making sundaes." He pointed to the cabinets. "Bowls, spoons, napkins, and scooper. I'll be right back and we'll get busy."

I stood blinking after him. Emory had always been friendly but quiet around me. Trevor had laughed over the years and said if his little brother ever got comfortable enough, I'd see a different side of him. What I saw in Emory now wasn't so much *different*, he'd always been enthusiastic, caring, kind…effervescent was a word that came to mind when I thought of the younger man…but he'd always been that way mostly with his family and I'd just seen it because I happened to be around. Now, though, Emory seemed to have grasped onto the whole faking it thing and decided to get comfortable with me directly.

Not going to lie, I didn't hate it.

I wasn't looking forward to whatever holiday joy and junk he'd want to get us involved in, but chatting, making plans, and *creating* ice cream sundaes with him wasn't half bad.

He was so easy to be around—just like Trevor—but Emory had a completely different vibe than his brother, and I couldn't help but smile. I kinda already liked the feel of things with my fake boyfriend. Eight weeks of this wasn't going to be a hardship.

Not at all.

"Okay," Emory declared as he walked back into the kitchen. "Get both ice creams out, please." He rolled up his sleeves.

"Both?" I knew I definitely hadn't had ice cream in my freezer before Emory arrived.

"I got peppermint stick, it's my favorite, but I also got chocolate because I think the two go together well."

I handed him the two cartons.

"How many scoops do you want?" Emory asked, pointing to the peppermint stick.

I wrinkled my nose. "I think I just want chocolate."

"What? Nooooo," he wailed. "You have to be festive."

I cocked a brow. "Do I look festive?"

"Peppermint. Stick." Emory faced me with his hands propped on his hips.

"Never had it," I quipped, fighting back a grin at his indignation.

"That's not possible."

"I assure you, it is."

"Well, we can remedy that right now. And then you'll love it and we can bond over the fabulousness that is peppermint stick and chocolate sundaes."

"I don't think I like it," I hedged.

Emory yanked the lid off the ice cream and dipped a spoon in for a white and pink swirl of ice cream with tiny red specks. "Here, take a taste. I think you'll love it."

The spoon was at my lips, my mouth opening for the bite before I even realized Emory was feeding me ice cream in my kitchen.

Cold, sweet, and slightly minty goodness danced on my tongue, the tiny pieces of peppermint adding just the right touch of crunch.

"Well?" he asked, his big brown eyes hopeful.

Rolling my eyes, I huffed. "Fine, it's really good." I hated admitting it, but I didn't hate the glee on Emory's face. "One scoop of each."

"Perfect. Now, since I've proven I'm the ice cream master, can I just make your sundae like mine?"

I crossed my arms over my chest. "I'll trust you. Just no coconut or nuts, and I'm not a fan of butterscotch."

"Nope, I've got the perfect combo of marshmallow, fudge, and sweet peppermint—just a drizzle of each, not too much. Really, I've perfected this sundae over the years."

I nodded.

While Emory worked, he said, "Okay, favorites. Clearly, I like ice cream—sweets in general—what about you?"

"Red Vines—never Twizzlers," I said, lifting my chin in challenge.

"Whew, good thing you said that. Not sure I could be fake boyfriends with someone who liked Twizzlers."

"Damn straight," I said. "I like good dark chocolate. Like the kind with sea salt or orange. I had one not long ago that was blueberries and caramel bits in dark chocolate and it was delicious. I like sweets, but dark chocolate is my go-to."

"That's probably why you like the peppermint stick. It's sweet, but not super sweet. Next time, I'll get a really good dark chocolate ice cream to mix it with." Emory handed me the bowl. "This will put you on a sugar high for sure."

"Favorite food?" I asked as we made our way back to the couch, liking the thought of *next time*.

"I'm not picky, I pretty much like anything. My list of dislikes is smaller—oysters, calamari, coconut, sweet pickles."

I chuckled. "Team Coconut Haters, unite. But what did sweet pickles ever do to you?"

"Nothing specific, I just don't care for them. Dill pickles all the way."

"I've never tried oysters or calamari, but I'm guessing I don't like them. I'm a fan of pizza, never really met a steak I didn't like, love most vegetables, and I can carb load like no one's business on good pasta."

"Yesss, that all sounds so good. Big ol' burger?"

"Bring it on."

"Bread?"

"Should be a main food group, for sure."

"Last question and it will potentially end this relationship before it even gets started. How do you like your steak cooked?" Emory held up a hand. "I'm going to tell you now, there are only a couple ways you can answer this that won't have me packing right up and walking out that door." His eyes glimmered and he bit back a grin.

"On three, we both say how we like our steak. I may kick you out before you walk out if you answer wrong," I teased.

"One." Emory took a bite of ice cream, licking the spoon. "Two." My eyes were locked on his tongue dancing over the silver. "Three."

"Medium," we both said at the same time and threw our heads back against the couch with laughter.

"Thank god," Emory exclaimed. "Being friends with Trevor, I was afraid he'd turned you to the dark side with his love of well-done steaks and I wasn't sure I could handle *two* people in my life eating their steaks all wrong."

"No way, Trev can keep his shoe leather, my tongue wants all that flavor when I get meat in my mouth." The moment the words were out, I realized the unintended innuendo and groaned. "Still talking about steak," I muttered.

Emory cackled. "Good to know...you know, about the steak." He winked. "Okay, date ideas. We need some places we can go and not look like we have no idea what we're doing."

"True, but we're also claiming to be a fairly new relationship, so we can get away with not having go-to date locations." I took another bite of ice cream. It was almost too sweet, but the slight mint flavor offset the sweetness just right. "Movies for sure. Both neighboring towns have bigger theaters, and we've got the one screen showing older movies here."

"We've got the traditional little shops, the café, and the park here in town," Emory suggested. "Oh, there's bowling, too."

"And the mall, tons of restaurants, the carriage rides, walking tours, and museums in areas around us," I said. "I've never done any of those except the mall and some of the restaurants, but I know they exist."

"Okay, so, we've got plenty to choose from when we're not working, completing challenges, and getting the house ready for Christmas."

I took a last bite of ice cream before pointing the spoon at his smug little face. "I don't do Christmas."

"Well, it's a good thing your new boyfriend is a festive little fuck because I *do* do Christmas." Emory's eyes sparkled with challenge. "You can't expect to buy a place you used to call The Christmas House and *not* decorate it for Christmas."

"I can. In fact, that's exactly what I did," I grumped. "I don't have decorations. I don't want decorations."

Emory pursed his lips together and studied me. "Fine. I'll let it go. For now." He scraped the last bits of sundae from his bowl. "Do we want to be fun and easy and no strings in this relationship or do we want to be more serious, settling down, talking about the future?"

Grateful he'd let the idea of decorating for the holidays go, I took the subject change. "I think, if we want the best chance to connect with the viewers, we need to seem completely, totally in love and committed. So, serious, settling, talking about the future is my vote."

"Agreed. I don't think we need to push it, but if it comes up naturally, we go with it." Emory placed his bowl on the coffee table and stacked mine on top. "What about PDA—do we do it? If so, we'll *have* to practice a bit. Viewers will know immediately if we try to kiss or hold hands and haven't done it before."

"Yeah, I think the more lovey-dovey we can be, the better. Most of the audience is probably looking for that Hallmark-ish feel with cheesy holiday romance, so we'd be best to give them at least a bit of it."

"Agreed. I say we start with hugs and holding hands as it seems right." Emory bit his lip. "Kissing—maybe on the cheek to ease you into it? Sorry, I don't know your feelings on kissing—especially kissing a guy. I don't want to make you uncomfortable."

I took his hand in mine—in for a penny, in for a pound, right? "I don't do a lot of kissing. It's always seemed more intimate than what I'm looking for with something quick and easy." Standing, pulling Emory with me, I cleared my throat. "How about a hug and kiss on the cheek tonight. Practice kissing tomorrow so we're ready for the real thing?"

Emory nodded, those big brown eyes locked on mine.

Spreading my arms, feeling like the biggest dork because bro hugs with Trevor and hugging my sister was the limit of my hugging experience, I waited for Emory to walk into my embrace.

When he did, when his head rested against my chest and his arms wrapped around my torso, a weird flutter traveled through me. Hugs with Trevor had been quick—slaps on the back mostly. Hugging Iris had been brotherly. Hugging Emory was different. Like I pulled warm energy from his body, like I wanted to savor the connection for just a bit longer.

But Emory cleared his throat and stepped back. "Was that okay?"

I nodded, feeling foggy and disoriented.

"So, Operation Lovey-Dovey is a go. We'll make sure to be kinda touchy-feely any time the cameras are on."

"Probably should just commit to all of it twenty-four-seven so we don't have to worry about it looking staged *just* for the cameras," I suggested.

"Good idea," Emory said. "As long as you're okay with it, I have no problems with PDA."

"Yeah, not a problem," I said.

Emory yawned. "The email we got earlier said the crews would be showing up tomorrow for photos and interviews. I think we get to *meet* all the other couples and see the homes they want to fix up—like on a Zoom meeting or something." He stretched. "I think I'm going to go to bed and watch a movie. I switched shifts with Kari so I could have tomorrow to do show stuff."

Bed.

Shit.

"Um, you found space in the bedroom okay?"

Emory snorted. "Ivy, babe, you have five pair of jeans—four of them black—ten black shirts of varying sleeve length, a few black zip-up hoodies, three black leather jackets, what appears to be a third pair of black work boots, one black suit ensemble, a sweater, and a ski jacket in a closet that's larger than some people's apartments."

I cocked a brow. "And?"

He chuckled and patted my cheek. "Yes, dear, I found space okay. Even putting all of my stuff in the closet, there's still room." Emory danced his fingertips together under his chin with delight sparkling in his eyes. "Ohhhh, maybe we can decorate the house *and* brighten up your wardrobe."

"Nope," I said, trying to sound mean and firm, but struggling because Emory looked so damn giddy.

"Baby steps," he said with a wink. "We'll move from black to a nice dark gray at first. Maybe work our way to an aubergine or deep navy?" He tapped a finger on his chin. "Do you even own any gym shoes? Sandals?"

"Little Bell, we're not doing this show so you can redress me," I grumped.

"It's you or the house, maybe both," he quipped before yawning again. "But I'm exhausted."

"Wait, what's wrong with my clothes?" I glanced down at the black t-shirt I wore. It was old, thin, and had seen better days, but it was just a shirt I wore around the house.

Emory poked a finger through one of the holes, his touch bringing goosebumps to my skin. "Nothing is *wrong* with your clothes. You pull off the dark and broody man in black very well. I'm just saying there's nothing wrong with some color pops here and there." He started toward the stairs.

"I've got color in my ink, no need for color on my clothes too," I said, following him. "And I *do* have gym shoes—two pairs, in fact. I run from time to time and lift weights when I feel like it. Sandals aren't really my thing unless it's slides and socks—no one wants to see these toes."

"Ohhh, a challenge," Emory said. "That's a date idea. We'll go get pedicures so your feet are sandal-ready."

"It's November."

"Okay, we'll do pedicures so you know how good they feel and how nice your feet can look. Then in the summer, you can get one and wear sandals if you want." He paused at the stairs and patted my cheek again. "And it's not November just yet—did you plan on opening the door for trick-or-treaters?"

"Oh, shit," I said, realization of the date smacking me right in the head. "I didn't even think about it being Halloween. I didn't get candy or anything."

"That's okay. A lot of people probably don't expect a broody new guy in the old house to be handing out candy so soon after moving in. We'll focus on Christmas and then next year you can do Halloween."

I nudged at him. "First, everyone in town knows me,

it's not like I'm some stranger who just moved in. They know I'm not Mr. Socialite."

"Exactly."

"Second, I'd rather do Halloween than Christmas."

"Well, you've got time to get ready for next year. For now, I think it's best to focus on the show. I'm going to bed. We need to be up and ready for pictures and an interview by eight."

Suddenly struck by the fact I'd be climbing into bed with Emory Bell for the next eight weeks, I cleared my throat. "Yeah, sounds good. I'm going to finish up a couple things in the shop. I'll head up in a bit."

Emory studied me for a moment. "What side of the bed do you sleep on?"

"Huh? Oh, next to the closet."

"Perfect, I like the other side better anyway." Emory leaned in close, his minty citrus scent tickling my nose, and brushed a kiss over my cheek. "Good night."

For a moment I stood like a statue.

Until Emory giggled. "Yeah, definitely need to practice that. It's not a good look when I kiss my boyfriend and he looks like deer in the headlights. Tomorrow morning, Ivy." He patted my cheek. "You, me, freshly brushed teeth, and practice kisses. Be there or be square."

"Huh?" I shook my head, trying to clear the million and one thoughts sludging through it. "Oh, right. Up early, practice kissing, interview, pictures. Got it."

Emory cocked his head and tapped a finger on his cheek.

For the slightest moment, I wasn't sure what he wanted, but then a sweet grin lit up his face and I knew. Leaning in, I pressed a short and simple kiss to his soft cheek. The slightest hint of stubble against my lips wasn't as weird as I'd thought it would be.

Not weird at all.

Mumbling good night, I turned toward the back door where I spent the next hour wondering how I'd gone thirty years without ever anticipating a kiss.

Until Emory Bell became my fake boyfriend.

CHAPTER 6

EMORY

"YOU KNOW, IF YOU SPEND EIGHT WEEKS hugging the edge of the bed, people might start to wonder if you even like sleeping with your boyfriend." My sleep-rough words broke the predawn darkness and I reached out a finger to poke Ivy's back.

He grunted, but didn't move.

I hadn't slept well, which was to be expected.

New house.

New bed.

New fake boyfriend.

New reality show getting ready to begin recording.

Yeah, I could see why I tossed and turned all night.

But that was going to have to come to an end. I wasn't the type who could get by on a little sleep. I needed to be on top of my game at work and for the show if we were going to have a chance to win.

And I'd do well to remind myself that the show was the only reason I was in bed with Ivyrson Gregory.

We weren't real boyfriends.

We were putting on an act for a television audience. Period.

I wasn't going to give in to the potential thought of the way Ivy's eyes lingered just a little bit longer than necessary. Or how good my hand felt in his. Or the scent of sandalwood and sea salt that teased my nose when he leaned in to kiss my cheek. Or the heat of his bigger body, even all the way across the bed.

No, I wasn't going to think of those things because we were playing it up for a show. We weren't together. We weren't in love. We were nothing but friends hoping to win some money.

And I needed to remember that or my heart was going to end up crushed by the end of eight weeks.

Didn't matter that I knew Ivy had no opposition to same-sex relationships. Didn't matter that I got a curious-possibly-interested vibe from him—even if he likely hadn't recognized it himself.

Those things didn't matter because I was about to start an eight-week journey with a man I'd had a crush on for years. A man my brother considered a brother. A man who thought he couldn't *do* love. A man my complete opposite in about a million ways, but who made me feel safe and protected just by being in the same room.

And I needed to get out of bed, shower, brush my teeth, and prepare for kissing practice.

Fuck.

I was so screwed.

As I rolled from the bed, Ivy stirred.

"I'll get better at it," he said sleepily.

"Better at what?"

"Sharing the bed. Just never slept with someone."

I scoffed.

"Serious. Never fucked anyone in my own bed. Definitely never spent the night with someone."

"What about Trevor?"

"Never fucked him either," Ivy mumbled, but I heard the smile in his words.

I swatted his ass. "You know what I mean. All those sleepovers? Never slept in the same bed?"

"Nope. I always took the floor if we were in his room—I was used to it from all the nights sleeping on Iris's floor. If we camped out, we had separate sleeping bags. Most of the time we ended up in your living room on the two couches." He rolled to his back, his bent arm over his eyes, a smattering of dark hair visible on his chest, and a mix of colorful and dark ink etched on his skin.

I wanted to stretch out next to him and explore his tattoos, feel the warm weight of his body against mine, and pretend—just for a moment—all of it was real.

It.

Wasn't.

Real.

"Sleep however makes you the most comfortable, just know I don't expect you hanging off the side of the bed for me—it's not like I think you're going to get all handsy or put my virtue in danger."

Ivy grunted and ran a hand down his chest, disappearing under the blankets to...scratch his junk? Adjust his morning wood?

Fuck.

Launching myself from the bed, I beelined it toward the bathroom and spent way too long getting myself off under the hot stream of water. By the time I moved to soap and shampoo, my fingers were pruny, but Ivy's old house proved to have an efficient water heater.

Twenty minutes later, dried and dressed for the day, I stood at the kitchen window staring out at Ivy's Auto as I sipped hot chocolate. I yelped when big, warm hands landed on my shoulders, but the soft, minty breath at my ear was enough to calm my rapidly beating heart.

"Is this a boyfriend-ish thing to do?" Ivy asked.

Fighting the urge to moan and drop my head back to his chest, exposing my neck for his mouth, I forced a chuckle and gripped the mug. "Yeah, seems pretty on-brand—not that I've had much boyfriend experience."

"Thought you dated a couple guys in high school," Ivy said, rubbing his thumbs into my muscles and almost bringing me to my knees—this man had no idea what he did to me with his complete and total commitment to the whole fake relationship thing.

"The first guy I dated cheated on me. The second one…well, that's a story for another time." I didn't want to rehash that night at the party.

Ivy's stare made me squirm and, for a brief moment, I thought he'd push the topic, but he gave a tiny nod and moved on. "So, we doing this? I think we should have a couple goes at it before the crew shows up in," Ivy glanced at his phone, "thirty minutes."

"Um, yeah, sure," I stammered. I hadn't done a lot of kissing and I most definitely hadn't done *planned* kissing.

He turned me to face him completely, our eyes locking, and darted his tongue out over his bottom lip. "This is weird," Ivy muttered. "Isn't kissing supposed to be spontaneous and emotional? This feels like I'm preparing for that puff of air against my eyeball at the optometrist."

A giggle escaped me. "Gee, thanks. Glad to know I'm as sexy as the eyeball puffer."

Ivy smirked for a brief second before dipping his head and sealing his lips over mine. It wasn't the most intimate kiss, it wasn't the most skilled, and it definitely wasn't going to win any awards for sensuality, but it was the best kiss I'd ever had because Ivy's mouth was on mine.

He pulled away with a huff. "Okay. Okay. I think we can work with it. First one was like ripping off a Band-Aid. We'll get better. I think we need to work on being more spontaneous and just letting ourselves enjoy the moment."

"So, I'm an eyeball puffer *and* a bandage needing peeled off. Got it," I teased.

"You know what I mean," Ivy said. "Was it bad? I told you I haven't done a ton of kissing. I'd like to think I'm pretty good in bed—never had any complaints, plenty of satisfied customers—"

I cocked a brow. "Not sure *customers* is the best way to describe the girls you've slept with, but go on, tell me how much of a sex-god you are."

Ivy snorted. "I'm just saying, I can get a girl off no worries, but kissing is a completely new ballgame for me."

"We don't *have* to kiss on camera," I started.

"No, I think we need to get the audience horned up and on our side."

"*Horned up?*"

"Yep, sex sells. Kissing and touching will be the perfect foreplay to get the viewers wanting to see more—they'll want to keep us around if we give them bits and pieces each week—tease them, ya know?"

"It wasn't a bad kiss," I said, my lips still tingling from the earlier contact.

"Wanna try tongue?"

I choked on my next breath. "Huh?"

"We should try adding tongue," Ivy said. "Before the crew gets here and we're all sloppy the first time we go beyond just a peck."

Fuck.

I wasn't going to survive the eight weeks.

"Oh, um…"

"Do you not want to kiss me like that?" Ivy asked, his cheeks pinking. "Sorry, I didn't mean to make it seem like I think you're into me just because you're gay. If kissing isn't cool, we can—"

I wrapped my arms around his neck and pressed my mouth to his.

Ivy stumbled backwards slightly, caught himself as his arms came around my torso, and backed me up into the corner of the countertop. Groaning as his lips parted, his tongue flicking out to tease over my bottom lip, he brought a hand up to cup the back of my head.

I'd died and gone to heaven and never wanted to stop kissing Ivy.

He tasted of mint and I pulled myself closer as if I could slip into his skin.

Ivy's tongue danced with mine, slow and sensual—a beautiful exploration—and I lost myself to the sensation of feeling and tasting him.

A wash of emotion blanketed me as I reminded myself we were just playing a game. I wanted that connection, wanted the taste of his tongue on mine, wanted his rough hand cupping the back of my head.

Instead, I pulled away, attempting to control my gasping breath.

But Ivy pressed his forehead to mine and smirked. "Damn, little Bell, you can kiss. Maybe I've been missing out."

I snorted. "You're not half bad," I said, my words breathy as I tried to calm my rapid heartbeat.

"Guess we know how to entertain ourselves over the next eight weeks if need be," Ivy said.

I must have frowned at his words because Ivy tipped my chin.

"What?"

"Nothing," I said, moving away from Ivy's arms.

"No, something I said bothered you. If we're going to play this game, we have to be honest—communication will be key. They say that for real relationships—and for eight weeks, I think we need to consider what we have *real*."

I hugged my arms around myself, heat rising to my cheeks. "It's just I don't want kissing me to be a form of entertainment. I know it's a game. I know you're not interested in me. And I'm not at all saying I can't control any attraction I might feel. I'd just rather not be entertainment. Kinda feels like *for a good time, call*. For a good time, just make out with your fake boyfriend."

It was Ivy's turn to frown. "I didn't mean it like that." He tipped my chin again. "I'm serious. I've never been one for kissing, but if all kisses were like kissing you, maybe I'd be more into it. If and when we kiss, sure, it will be for the cameras if they're around—we're in this whole situation because of the show—but I want you to know I've *never* enjoyed a kiss as much as that one. Never wanted to make it a repeat thing." He kissed the tip of my nose. "You're not just a form of entertainment, little Bell."

My heart melted.

Did Ivy have any idea how confusing he was? I truly didn't think he was purposely trying to fuck me up. He was so convinced romance and relationships weren't his thing, and seemed so blasé about the whole situation. Wasn't the *straight* guy supposed to freak out about kissing the gay guy? Did Ivy see it all as only a means to an end with no reason to get worked up about it because he wasn't cut out for a relationship?

Which left me panting after him and longing for what would never be.

CHAPTER 7

IVY

KISSING EMORY WAS...

Eye-opening.

Good.

Confusing.

Really good.

A revelation.

Maybe a mistake.

Like *really* good.

As I poured myself a cup of coffee—trying to focus on our upcoming interview, photos, and meet-n-greet—I willed myself to stop thinking about how good he'd tasted.

How much I wanted to kiss him again.

Wanted to feel his lips against mine.

I was sure I'd missed out on some good kissing with the girls I'd slept with. But kissing had always seemed too emotional, too much of an intimate connection. Yeah, I realized burying myself in someone else's body was pretty damn intimate, but kissing always felt like *more*.

And if kissing Emory was anything to go by, I'd been right all along.

I wanted to ignore the doorbell. Wanted to yank Emory up the stairs and spend the rest of the day kissing him. No show, no fake boyfriends, no playing it up for the viewers.

Just Emory and me.

And our lips.

Our tongues.

Fuck.

What the hell was wrong with me?

I wouldn't even be in this situation without the show. I couldn't just ignore the show.

And I couldn't put Emory in that situation.

He was my best friend's little brother. Trevor had already proven he was worried about Emory's heart in my presence. I wouldn't be the one to make Trevor's worries come true.

And Emory had offered to help out of the goodness of his own heart. No way would I accept his help in winning the show under the pretense of a fake relationship only to switch things up because of a latent bisexual pull toward him.

Emory would likely be onboard. As bad as it sounded to even think it, Trevor always said his little brother had a thing for me. But I couldn't let Emory get involved when I knew damn well there was nothing I could offer him.

First, because I wasn't cut out for love and shit— thanks to dear ol' Dad fucking me over and ruining me for life.

Second, I'd never really given much thought to my sexuality. Was it fair to Emory to explore a curiosity just because I found myself attracted to him when we were living together for eight weeks?

No, it wasn't fair and I wouldn't do it.

So, we'd play the game. We'd be the best fake boyfriends ever. We'd hopefully win. And we'd enjoy the whole situation—maybe learn a bit about ourselves along the way. In the end, we'd have our money and we'd part ways with fond memories.

Easy.

I opened the door just as Emory slipped his hand in mine and gave a squeeze.

Why did that feel so damn right?

"Bell and Ivy," a red-haired woman with flashing green eyes and perfectly painted lips said as she stuck out her hand. "I'm Letty, Silas's assistant producer. We'll be spending a lot of time together over the next eight weeks if you're lucky." She winked.

My gut twisted as Emory and I both shook her hand. I wasn't sure if I liked Letty or not, but it wasn't like I had any control over who was assigned to us.

"The camera crew," she said, gesturing toward the three people behind her, "and I will stay in our buses when we're not following you around, but you're definitely going to be sick of us." She laughed at her own joke.

"Come on in," Emory said, taking over as a gracious host when I clammed up at the thought of having these people all up in my space for two months.

Emory offered the crew drinks, but Letty informed us we were to ignore them unless it was interview or photograph time. And the show provided the crews with food, drinks, and snacks, so we didn't have to worry about offering.

"Let's get our interview started, okay? Okay." Letty gestured toward the crew. "This living room is gorgeous, we'll set up here. I have to say," she said, turning to us, "I was thrilled to get one of the LGBT couples. First, you're gorgeous together. Second, our viewership is very into diversity and equality. I can't say we offer a ton of it just yet, but I feel like we're working our way toward it a bit more each year. I'm really hoping you two will get far—I think you have a real chance to win if you can get the audience on your side." She winked. "And that's where we come in."

Emory and I sat down on the couch, Letty taking the loveseat. But she glanced around. "No, the lighting is wrong. And you two lovebirds need to be cuddled up." She laughed and winked.

I had a feeling that wink and obnoxious laugh were going to be on my last nerve before the end of eight weeks.

Emory and I switched places with Letty, our bodies pressed together as we took our place on the loveseat. The assistant producer pulled a chair from the kitchen into the living room and perched on the edge of it.

"Okay, while the crew sets up, let's dish a bit about how this will go," she said.

Did the woman know how much she winked?

"First, let me tell you," Letty leaned in close and lowered her voice, "*I'm* aware of the little secret—Silas felt he *had* to let me in on it—but no one else is. And my game plan is to play it as if everything is real and true. You boys okay with that?"

We both nodded.

Letty flashed a smile, a smear of lipstick staining one gleaming white front tooth. "Perfect. And I've got to say, you two are just so damn adorable. If I have my way, we'll play this game right, and you'll consider me your magical Christmas romance elf after I bring you together for real."

I snorted. "Something you need to know...I don't like the holidays. As in, I hate holiday anything. I'm in this to win it, but I'm not into the holiday magic and Christmas miracles or any of that."

Letty beamed. "Ohhhh, a Christmas challenge. I like it."

Wink.

I groaned. "No, that's not—"

Emory put a hand on my leg. "We're willing to do what it takes to win. Ivy isn't one for holiday cheer, but we're committed for the long-haul. I like the fact you know our situation, but you're on our side."

"Emory, sweetie, don't think too much of me. I'm on your side because it's the way to win. Winning means advancement for me." Letty smiled, but it was more ferocious than sweet. "I'm in this for *me*, but if the two of you being together and happy and winning is the end result of me getting to move ahead, I'm all for it."

"We're good," one of the camera crew said.

"Perfect." Letty grabbed a notebook. "Okay, we'll start with some easy questions. Don't worry about messing up, we can edit things together. The show starts tonight with a preview of all the couples and then it's hard and heavy for eight weeks. Our crew here will be constantly sending footage to our editing and formatting team. That team will work around the clock to put clips together for the show.

If everything goes as planned, all the teams around the country end up sending their pieces to the main hub of the show and we put it together for a weekly episode. You two will pretty much go about your regular daily lives and just throw in some interviews and challenges. Our teams, however, will be working their asses off for two months. It should be fun, but it will also be exhausting. In the end though, if the show is a success, we all win. Well, except for the couples who lose." She threw her head back in laughter.

Gathering herself, she cleared her throat and dabbed at her eyes.

Letty seemed to be a mixture of professional shark and a bit of a slightly unhinged loose cannon.

"Okay, what questions do you have for me before we get started?" she asked.

"The cameras won't be on twenty-four-seven, right?" Emory asked.

"Correct. We'll have morning and evening interviews. We'll be recording all challenges, of course. We'll likely try to get clips of you at work. Pretty much anywhere in the house is free game except the bathroom and the bedroom —we'll always ask for permission if we need clips from those areas. We're intrusive, but not *that* intrusive. One thing I'm looking forward to is the silhouette filter we've got. We can record certain...um, steamier...times with an operatorless camera set to a filter that will only allow viewers to see shadowy outlines. I think it will be a nice way to get some viewers hooked on your romance," she coughed and winked, "*and* still provide privacy for this adorable new love match."

"Can we ask that the edits don't make us out to be..."

Emory paused and shrugged, squeezing my hand, "I don't know, I just don't want the edits to paint us in a negative light."

Letty nodded. "My job is, number one, to get my team through to the very end and have the audience love them enough to name them the winners. Yes, I'm in charge of making sure there's enough drama, intrigue, romance, and," she threw me a wink, "holiday magic to keep the viewers coming back for more, but I won't make you out to be anything but the dear Bell and Ivy I hope our audience will adore."

I appreciated her honesty. While she was there for herself, we all had the same goal of making it to the end—it helped to know where she stood and that she was on our side, even if only for personal gain. Her win would be our win, our win would be hers. Letty maybe wasn't the most enjoyable person to be around, but I could put up with her if I knew she was working to get us all to our end goal.

Relaxing into Emory's side—what? We were playing it up for the camera—I settled a bit more into the interview. Plus, I'd quickly realized two things. One, Emory was more physical than his brother. Two, maybe I was starved for touch, or maybe Emory just calmed things inside me, but I didn't mind being close to him. Something about it just felt right. Having him around was definitely not a hardship.

"Let's get this started, okay? Okay," Letty said as she motioned toward the cameras.

We started with questions regarding what we'd do with the money—me talking about expanding on my life-long dream of owning and operating an auto repair shop,

Emory expressing a desire to invest, help others, and save some for when he decided what he wanted to do with his life.

I showed Letty Ivy's Auto. I hadn't even thought of the show being promo for the shop, but when Letty mentioned it, I wondered if I'd pick up any new customers —Peppermint Hollow was a small town, but we were surrounded by bigger populations who might see the show. She asked questions regarding the expansion I wanted to do on the business—both on the physical building and hiring more labor as I got busier.

Emory chatted about his general studies degree, how he'd not yet figured out what he wanted to do with his life, and how he thought he'd like to find something that highlighted his organizational skills, love of numbers, skills with schedules and computers, and ability to lead. Letty laughed that the show might lead to job opportunities and I could tell Emory hadn't thought about that either.

As we walked back toward the house, Letty asked about the shop. "Do you do all the scheduling and billing and whatnot?"

"I do. In the beginning, when I wasn't super busy, it was easy. Part of my plan for expanding is to hire someone to run the business part while I do the mechanic part— that's what I really love, I don't love the administrative side," I said.

"Maybe you could try out a temp worker for eight weeks," Letty said with a wink.

"I'm not really at a point where I can pay for a new hire just yet, that's why I'm hoping to win so I can take that step," I said, wondering what part of *I really need to win* she wasn't understanding.

The woman just smiled smugly. "Right, right. It's too bad you don't have a boyfriend who's good with numbers, schedules, computers, and organization living right under your nose." She charged ahead up the steps. "Let's take a look at the house."

I glanced at Emory and he smiled. "She's something else, huh?" he whispered.

Rolling my eyes, I huffed out a laugh.

"I wouldn't mind at all, you know," he said.

"Mind what?"

"Helping in the shop. Even if it's just to get things more organized—or to help in whatever way you say you need it most—before you hire someone."

"I wouldn't be able to pay you, that's not fair."

Emory took my hand. "That's the great thing about having me as a boyfriend," he whispered for just me, glancing over his shoulder to check on where the camera was. "I'm living here rent-free for eight weeks. Might as well be useful."

"You're living here to help me win this game. That's useful." I frowned. "And it's not just about being useful. I think I'm going to like having a roommate."

Emory shrugged. "I'm just saying—and I get it if you don't think I'd be a good fit—I'm good with that type of stuff. Getting your shop organized and running smoothly sounds like a fun little task and I'm willing. If you're interested. If not, no big deal."

Nodding, I held the door open for him as we all trooped back into the house. "I'll give it some thought." Not going to lie, having Emory's help with the front-of-house work in the shop would be huge. I didn't want to take advantage of him, but I also didn't want to lose out on his offer.

Letty followed us around the house while we took a little tour, me pointing out parts of my new home I loved and parts I planned on repairing or revamping if I won the house remodel.

"Okay, I wouldn't be doing my job if I didn't do some research on my contestants and their lives. I looked into this house," Letty said. "It's got quite the history, but I'm sure you're aware."

"I've loved this house since I was a kid," I said, feeling a bit off-kilter because I wasn't sure where Letty would go with her information.

"We used to call it The Christmas House," Emory said. "Well, Ivy did and I joined in."

"That's so sweet," Letty said. "It's really too bad you don't like Christmas. This house used to be the envy of all when it came to holiday decorations."

"I mostly loved it for the house, not the decorations," I said stubbornly.

"He loved it for the decorations, too," Emory said. "He just doesn't like to admit it." He cuddled into my side and glanced up at me—damn, the kid was good. "If I have my way, we'll be back to Christmas House status within a year or so. The beauty of this house was a huge part of our childhoods."

He wasn't wrong. The Christmas House had been a childhood favorite of mine. It wasn't until my dad blew up our lives that I swore off anything and everything related to the holidays and convinced myself I hated all things Christmas.

Didn't mean I couldn't still love the house and all it meant to my growing-up years.

"So, *you* like the holidays and decorating?" Letty asked, her words clearly egging on our differences as we continued to meander through the house.

"I love them," Emory answered. "Lights, decorations, music, cookies, all of it." His big brown eyes blinked innocently up at me. "I've got my work cut out for me, but I think we can find that Christmas spirit again. We just need a little holiday magic."

I groaned. "The holidays are what you make them to be. I have bad memories of them. There's no holiday magic and I don't *need* Christmas spirit."

Letty tittered. "You do know there are quite a few stories of old about the holiday magic of this house, right? Folks finding their fortunes, couples falling in love, and a lot of unexplained tales of good things happening—with the only viable explanation being Christmas magic."

"Magic and viable don't go together," I groused.

"Ivy just hasn't had the chance to experience the spirit of the season for a very long time," Emory said, cuddling closer to me. "We have time."

I wanted to roll my eyes. Wanted to huff out a frustrated breath and head to the shop to tinker on a car. Instead, I played the game, ruffled Emory's hair, and pressed a kiss to his temple. "We'll see."

"Bell and Ivy—a true opposites-attract, grumpy-sunshine love story, huh?" Letty asked with a wink as we headed back to the living room.

Her words poked at something deep inside. I knew I wasn't made for love. Knew I couldn't be *the one* for anyone, even if it was something I wanted.

And I didn't.

But Letty's comment about Emory's and my love story had me thinking.

Thinking that maybe—if I was cut out for a relationship—*maybe* Emory and I could make something work.

I'd never thought much about my sexuality.

I hooked up with women because it was easier.

Expected.

I wasn't looking for love.

But Emory?

If I was looking, would he be someone I'd take a chance with?

Not that his sweet ass deserved someone like me.

Not that I would put him through my messed-up outlook on relationships.

But Emory was so easy to be with. So easy to like. So easy to...

Stop it. Everything is easy because you're both faking it. Nothing about this is real other than your desire to win a bunch of money. He's cute, he's easy to be around. Enjoy that, but don't go making it out to be more than that. He's your best friend's little brother. Off limits. And you don't do relationships, so just knock it off.

The thoughts running through my head helped to bring me out of whatever weird Emory-induced swirl I'd had going on and we resettled ourselves in the living room.

The second we sat down, Letty swooped in like a vulture. "Let's get to the swoony bits, okay? Okay. Tell the viewers a little about how you met, your relationship so far, and what you love about each other. Can I say that?"

She tittered—so, lipstick teeth, tittering, and winking, those were her things. Got it. "Is it *love*? Is it okay to celebrate the season by falling in love with love?"

Barf.

Emory gripped my hand, pulling me away from thoughts of jamming forks in my ears if I had to listen to Letty for much longer. "Well, Ivy and I have a history. We're the perfect example of a May December romance— seven years isn't a huge gap, but we grew up with him being best friends with my brother and me being the annoying little twerp following them around everywhere."

I bumped his shoulder. "You weren't *that* annoying, at least not to me—Trevor was maybe a different story." The words were true, I'd never minded Emory being around as much as his brother had.

"Awww, so it's a forever type of love?" Letty asked, her eyes all dreamy.

"We've known each other for forever," Emory said. "We didn't really find that spark until I came home from college. When we were ten and three or eighteen and eleven, we weren't thinking of love or anything like it."

Letty waggled her brows. "What about fifteen and twenty-two? Was teenager Emory getting all hot for the older Ivyrson?"

Emory tensed next to me. "While I'm not going to lie and say I didn't have a crush on Ivy from about age fourteen on, I don't want what we have now to be dirtied up by insinuations of something inappropriate between an adult and a minor." He cleared his throat, but a firm confidence exuded from him. "And while we're on the subject, even if it gets edited out, I want it made clear that Ivy and I are here because we want to play the game and win. We're not here to be fetishized. We're not here to help others feel good about themselves just because they watch a same-sex couple on a streaming holiday channel."

Letty, blinking like an owl, opened and closed her mouth a couple times, gave a nod, and moved right on. "Understood, heard, and appreciated. So, Bell and Ivy." She quickly segued from Emory's chastisement. "I have to say, the show *loves* the holiday feel of your nickname."

Damn, I was proud of him. Squeezing his hand in support, I tried to focus on what Letty was saying.

"When did the Bell and Ivy label become a thing?"

I shrugged. "Emory's older brother is my best friend. We met in second grade. We've been Bell and Ivy ever since—my given name is Ivyrson so Ivy was an easy shortened form. Bell and Ivy just stuck." Putting my arm around Emory and kissing the top of his head—was it easier to be cuddly and more intimate with him than anyone else I'd ever spent time with simply because it wasn't real? Simply because it was all for show? "When Emory and I submitted our application to be on the show, it just came naturally to keep the nickname." The lie flowed right off my tongue and I didn't even feel bad about it. Emory and I weren't the same Bell and Ivy as Trevor and me, but the name still fit.

"And where is this relationship? It's been building over a lifetime," Letty said, all swoony, "is the forever going to continue?"

Emory squeezed my thigh. "Wouldn't it be nice to know that? Ivy and I like where we are right now. A year from now? Five years? Ten? Who knows. But he's been my dream guy from the first time I realized I liked guys and I'm not going to take what we have for granted.

Relationships are hard and take a lot of work, but there's no one I'd rather put in the effort with than him."

Fuck.

If I didn't know he was faking it, my heart would have gotten all mushy.

And I didn't do mushy.

Instead, I nuzzled Emory's cheek. If he could play it up, so could I.

"You two are just so damn sweet," Letty said. Maybe it was the hearts in her eyes making her wink so much.

One of the camera crew interrupted. "It's time for the Zoom."

Letty clapped her hands together. "Perfect. Let's meet the other contestants."

Over the next two hours, we sat on a virtual call from the comfort of our dining room—Emory and I sharing a laptop and Letty tuning in from her phone. We heard from Silas—and I swore his eyes bore straight into us, like he was daring our fake relationship to fail—the various people in the same position as Letty, and several other important members of the crew. I had a feeling the folks doing the most work over the next eight weeks weren't the ones we'd just met.

"Okay, we're going to do a little meet and greet," Silas said. "Everyone spent today touring their homes and doing interviews. What you see today will be very similar to what the audience sees streamed tonight as a preview—it's also been a chance for our editing and formatting crews to work out a few kinks."

For the next hour and a half, we *met* our competition.

Couple number one was Julie and Mark. They were teachers who met online and lived in the Midwest. They were attractive people who seemed really nice if a bit bougie.

Couple number two was Mike and Joanna. A retired couple who had been married fifty years and lived in upstate New York. Mike walked with a cane and I wondered about his ability to complete challenges.

Couple number three was us, Bell and Ivy. A photo of Emory and me flashed on the screen and I couldn't help but think we looked really good together—would the audience like us? The tour of our house reminded me just how much I loved the place and hoped to fix it up sooner rather than later if we could pull off a win.

Couple number four was Bridgette and Claire. The two women had kept an online relationship going for a year and recently met in real life. They were super cute and I immediately envied the adorable little bungalow they had in a Chicago suburb.

Couple number five was Chad and Heather. They claimed to be friends-with-benefits living together in an older home out in Oregon where they ran a health food store.

I felt Emory tense beside me. Was he thinking the same thing as I was about the friends-with-benefits part? Should we have gone that angle? I hadn't even known it was an option.

Couple number six was Jackson and Andy. *Another* damn friends-with-benefits couple, the men lived in South Carolina in an apartment home overlooking the water. Jackson was a photographer and Andy was a model.

Seriously? The submission page had made it sound like participants *had* to be in a relationship. On one hand, maybe the lax rules were the reason Emory and I had been allowed to continue after Trevor was taken out. One the other hand, would Emory and I have had a better chance if we only had to play it as friends-with-benefits?

The seventh couple was Shawna and Theresa, bisexual females who had recently gotten married and lived in Florida. They were definitely in the honeymoon phase of their relationship and I had a feeling they'd be a favorite of the audience.

Couple number eight was Cody and Jackie. Also bisexual, they'd both left same-sex relationships recently and gotten married spur-of-the-moment. They were very hipster and lived in San Francisco where Cody owned a bicycle shop and Jackie ran her own small business selling handmade crafts.

The ninth couple was Marian and Stanley. He was a preacher in Iowa and she was a housewife. They did their interview in front of a patriotic background and wore buttons supporting their political party. While I wanted to give them the benefit of the doubt—and I was sure there were those in the audience who would be huge supporters—I was immediately irritated by the vibe I got from them.

"Whoever got them sure drew the short straw," Letty whispered and I was grateful she was still muted.

The tenth couple was Rae and Mallory. The two women lived in Texas and were very active in their community for LGBTQIA equality, especially trans rights. Rae ran a non-profit that strived to protect trans youth and Mallory taught preschool.

"And," Silas said as the video ended, "there you have it. The ten original couples of *Once Upon a Christmas House*." He glanced off-screen briefly before smiling and holding up a finger for us. "Excuse me just one moment," Silas said right before muting the audio.

While he put on a show of looking angry and gesturing with his arms, I thought through the couples we'd been introduced to. It seemed as if Season's Streaming had purposely gathered together a fairly diverse group of people to compete—we didn't know everyone's gender identity, sexuality, religion, or political affiliation, but there definitely seemed to be a decent amount of intersectionality throughout the contestants.

"The network is telling me we've got a surprise," Silas said. "Now, I want it known that I wasn't aware of this addition and I'm not in favor of it." His words were made to sound authoritative, but it was easy to see he was playing it up for the cameras as much, if not more, as Emory and I would be. "It appears we have one more couple to add to the show."

The screen filled with shocked faces from all of the couples.

"Yes, yes," Silas said. "I can tell you all know what that means. There will be a double elimination at some point during the show. Well, I don't like it, but let's go ahead and meet our eleventh couple."

The final couple shared was Sarah and Dean, newlyweds and new parents living in North Dakota with a super cute baby and an old farmhouse that looked like it would blow over with the next storm. Dean was a goat farmer and Sarah had recently left her job as an administrative assistant to stay home with the baby.

I almost felt bad for them being added in as the last-minute addition and made to look like they were ruining the schedule of eliminations.

Almost.

They were still our competition and I wasn't going to let feeling bad for them stand in the way of winning.

The virtual meeting wrapped up with well-wishes and fake smiles.

Letty and the camera crew checked in with us to make sure we knew where each camera was placed throughout the house and made plans to film us at breakfast and at our jobs the next day.

We wouldn't know about the first challenge until right before it was given.

We said goodbye to the crew and Letty and quickly retreated to the bedroom.

"Oh my god, that was a lot," Emory said once we were tucked away from the cameras throughout the house.

"I know we talked about just ignoring the cameras for the most part, but I'm glad we can escape here at least some of the time," I said, flopping down on the bed. "Letty is a trip. And what's up with the friends-with-benefits couples we met?"

"Yeah, I was surprised by that. Thought it had to be actual couples, but maybe they're counting it as couples since they're living together and have an intimate relationship—I mean, I'm assuming that's what the *benefits* part indicates." Emory shrugged. "I really do think they should have gotten a throuple for the show, but maybe none applied."

"Do you think we screwed ourselves over by claiming to be in a committed relationship while others went the friends-with-benefits route? Would we have had a better chance if we weren't having to pretend to be in love?"

"Maybe," Emory said. "Maybe not. People love love,

especially this time of year. Think of all the Hallmark type holiday romances people gobble up. They want to see love and romance and happily ever afters. Friends-with-benefits isn't super romantic—unless they're going to end up playing up the friends-to-lovers angle—and seems like an easy way out." He grabbed a pair of boxer briefs from the drawer. "We don't really have any room to complain since we're doing our own little bit of faking it, but we have no idea if any of those couples are the real deal or not. Looks like the show wasn't super strict on checking out the supposed requirements—they seemed to shoot for diversity over specifics. Clearly, the ones with the baby aren't faking—at least not that part. But any of the others could be faking just as much as we are."

"I don't think the preacher and his wife are faking it. Or the retired couple. The rest? Who knows. We just have to play it up as good or better."

"Agreed. I think our best option is to either approach it as if everyone is faking it and we have to do it even better *or* look at it as if everyone is the real deal and so are we. Or a combo of both—like, we're the real deal but we're playing it up even more for the cameras."

"Yeah, we really have to win over the audience and focus on the challenges." I said. "Your little speech was really good."

"It was easy because it was the truth."

"No, I mean the part about having a crush on me way back then and not taking what we have for granted," I clarified.

Emory sat on the edge of the bed. "Yeah, I know. It was the truth." He took my hand. "Look, I know you're not into me."

I started to protest. Started to correct him that I wasn't into *anyone* beyond quick and easy sex, not just him, but Emory stopped me.

"We've talked about the importance of communication throughout this game and I want to be clear with you. I know we're faking things—even if we're pretending not to be faking," he smirked and shook his head at the ridiculousness, "but what I said about our history and not taking what we've got right now for granted, I meant that. I like what we've got going on, it's been fun so far and I was ready for something different." He cleared his throat. "I'm not trying to make things weird, just want you to know."

Emory left the room, heading into the bathroom presumably to take a shower.

And left me with a jumble of thoughts and not a single clue what any of them meant.

CHAPTER 8
EMORY

WEEK 1

Your challenge this week is to interact with your neighbors. New to town? Old friends? The level of interaction is up to you, but our Season's Streaming viewers will be giving points and voting based on how much effort you put into the challenge.

"Thoughts?" I asked Ivy the next morning when we read the weekly challenge as the camera crew rubbed sleep from their eyes and set up to record breakfast.

Ivy, looking sinful in his work clothes, wrapped his arms around me and pressed his chest to my back. In a low voice he said, "Pretty sure our neighbors would be good friends with Marion and Stanley if you get my drift. Not sure we want to get too involved with them. Now, kiss me, the camera is rolling."

As if kissing him was a struggle.

Not kissing him was the real problem.

My damn lips and heart were in for a real crash and burn when the game was over and our little fake relationship ended.

But I could definitely enjoy it while it lasted.

Turning my head, I nuzzled my nose against his cheek and let Ivy drag his lips over mine in a simple, easy kiss.

I ignored the pang in my heart that whispered tantalizing promises of how good this could be if only it were real.

"If we're going to get more points for more effort, I say we go big or go home with the neighbors. Have you met them? Are they going to come outside with hate-filled posters while burning the rainbow flag?" I hadn't experienced *a lot* of homophobia in my lifetime—Peppermint Hollow wasn't the most liberal, and I knew plenty who were praying for my soul to repent and stop liking dick, but I'd never been fearful of living authentically in the little town. Despite that, I knew people's hate ranged from micro-aggressions to severe violence—maybe not in our town—but I didn't want to walk into a dangerous situation.

I also knew we wanted to do what we could to win the game.

"More along the lines of disdainful looks, promises of thoughts and prayers for sinful souls, and accepting a certain news channel as gospel right alongside the good book," Ivy said as we sat down with coffee, bagels, and fruit.

"Then I say we play nice, maybe offer to bring dinner, and visit for a bit."

Ivy wrinkled his nose. "I've been here for a few months and we're just going to waltz over with enchiladas and pick up new besties?"

Laughing as I chewed a bagel, I couldn't help but think about how comfy cozy it was to share a moment with Ivy.

We were just eating and chatting, but it was somehow more special than any of the time I'd ever spent with other guys.

"I'll check in with them today before I head to work, see if we can set something up. Don't stress, I'll take care of it." Catching the movement of one of the cameras out of the corner of my eye as I gathered my dishes and stood, I leaned down and pressed a kiss to Ivy's cheek, figuring I might as well enjoy it while I could. "Enchiladas actually sound really good."

The day went well—albeit somewhat weird with a camera following me around the café—and I found myself on the neighbors' doorstep in the early afternoon.

Mr. and Mrs. Sheffield were slightly leery of the cameras—and let me know they weren't thrilled with how much of a distraction the show was to the whole town—but the salesman side of Jeffery Sheffield wasn't going to turn down the chance to throw the name of his used car lot into conversation, so they agreed to dinner.

I offered our home, but I got the idea the two were the type to think they'd maybe catch the queer bug if they stepped foot into the place, so we agreed to Ivy and I bringing the food while the Sheffields hosted.

It wasn't an evening I would have planned voluntarily and I wasn't exactly looking forward to it, but if it earned us points and got us closer to the $500,000 and Ivy's house getting remodeled, I could deal with it.

Stopping by the shop on the way to the house, I allowed myself a moment to admire Ivy bent over the engine of a car as he tinkered with a repair. The man was fine and I realized I'd never smell grease, oil, and rubber again without thinking of the time I had the hottest fake boyfriend in town.

"I'll head to the store to get ingredients for the enchiladas if you're interested in making them," I said. "If not, I'll pick up some frozen ones and throw them in the oven."

Ivy curled his lip. "Frozen enchiladas? You still living at college?" he teased. "Nah, I'll text you the items to pick up. Once I'm finished here, I'll shower and start on dinner."

As I headed toward the door, Ivy grabbed my arm and pulled me close for a kiss. It was just a quick one, nothing steamy, but it made my heart flip-flop.

It's just for show.

Don't get wrapped up in this man.

Ivy's breath tickled over my ear and heat swirled through my chest.

Too late.

The man was a damn good fake boyfriend and his act made me wish like hell he wanted a real relationship.

The camera didn't follow me to the store and I enjoyed the little break as I gathered the supplies Ivy had texted.

By the time I left the ingredients on the counter and headed upstairs to shower, Ivy had already preheated the oven and cleaned up from his day in the shop.

The bathroom smelled of his sandalwood and sea salt scent and I had to finish my shower with a blast of cold water to convince myself jacking off to images of my fake boyfriend wasn't necessary *every* time I found myself alone in the bathroom.

The savory, spicy scent of enchiladas filled the house by the time I dressed and headed downstairs.

"I'm not great with wines, but I looked it up and found that enchiladas pair well with white wine," Ivy said, holding up a bottle of Riesling. "If our neighbors don't drink, we can split it."

"If I split that bottle, I'll be wasted."

Ivy cocked a brow. "Lightweight?"

"Beyond."

"Good to know." He gestured toward the oven. "Those will be done in about twenty minutes and we can head on over."

Our phones buzzed with the special tone for Letty. She'd texted to say it was interview time. I thought the impromptu interviews were going to be the part I hated the most about being on the show, but we headed toward the living room to sit for the questions.

"So, early audience interest shows they like you, but they aren't completely sold on you," Letty said, frowning. "We need to up the cuteness and likability."

"Always great to hear you aren't likable," Ivy groused.

"I think you'll be one of the teams that grows on people, we just need to get you past the first couple weeks and give it a chance to happen."

Letty signaled the camera to start rolling and launched into her questions. "So, Emory, tell me about your love of Christmas and where it came from."

"I've always loved Christmas. My parents made it a really great time each year. The commercialism and hectic nature of the season can get to me sometimes, but I like the decorations, music, food, and gifts." I bumped Ivy's shoulder. "I know this one doesn't like the idea of holiday magic or the spirit of Christmas or whatever, but I feel it this time of year."

"So sweet," Letty gushed. "Pretty sure a lot of people can relate." She turned her gaze toward Ivy. "You have a different take on the holidays, Ivyrson. Tell us about that."

Ivy tensed and, for a moment, I thought he would refuse to answer. Instead, he shifted and took my hand like a life preserver—be still my heart. It was all for show, right? "I didn't always hate the holidays, but I had a bad experience during my younger years and it left a bad memory. I don't like the greed and toxicity on display this time of year."

Letty pushed a bit longer, but Ivy wasn't interested in answering, so she moved on. "Now, Emory, I know you've got a brother—he's in the hospital, is that right?"

"Yeah, my brother Trevor was in a bad accident right before the show started and he's got a long recovery ahead of him."

"And Trevor is your best friend?" Letty asked Ivy. When he nodded, she went on. "What about siblings for you?"

"Older brother I don't have contact with and a sister who recently moved away with her new husband and baby." Ivy's body language screamed he wasn't willing to divulge much more and Letty seemed to catch on.

"Is Trevor a fan of the show?" she asked me.

"He better be," I said. "We're counting on his vote whether he's recovering or not," I teased.

"How does big brother feel about his best friend dating his little brother?" Letty asked, waggling her brow.

Ivy squeezed my hand. "We're all close. Loved each other like family before and love each other like family now. Trevor knows Em and I are good together."

My chest squeezed.

If we were *really* trying this relationship, would Trevor be on board?

Letty, hearts in her eyes, sighed and scribbled something on her notepad and signaled to the camera to stop recording. "Okay, that was good. Ivy, I think we can play up the traumatic past in order to get folks hooked and wanting to keep you around to delve deeper."

"My past isn't a hook," Ivy said, bristling.

Letty tapped the pen against her chin and pursed her lips. "I think, if you're wanting to stick around, you'll agree that anything and everything is a hook." She checked the time. "Now, go enjoy dinner with your neighbors."

"You okay?" I asked quietly, hating the cameras at that moment.

Ivy shrugged. "She's not wrong. I just don't want to relive it."

I pulled him into a hug. "It's in your court. I'll play it the way you want to."

Ivy hugged me close and nodded against my head. "Thanks. Let's get the kitchen cleaned up and head on over."

I washed the dishes as Ivy pulled the enchiladas from the oven.

Once he had the casserole dish packed in towels and placed in a basket, he moved behind me to rinse his hands.

"Dear god," he mumbled. "How can you even see out of those?"

"Huh?" I asked, trying to nudge my glasses up with my shoulder as my soapy hands scrubbed at a spoon.

Ivy gripped my chin and turned my face toward him.

"Your glasses. They're a mess again." He eased them off my face, ran them under hot water, and grabbed a paper towel.

Once he had them cleaned, dried, and buffed to a shine, Ivy, with his back to the camera, gave me a look before he slipped the frames back on my face. Leaning in, he kissed my cheek. "Trying to be more likable," he whispered. "Kiss me."

His finger tipped my chin and my breath caught when his lips brushed over mine.

Ivy got my votes for being likable.

For damn sure.

Fuck.

I liked him fine.

Just fine.

Ivy situated the basket on his arm a moment later and held the door open for me. As we walked down the sidewalk toward the Sheffield's place, he flipped the keychain a million miles a minute.

"They weren't *that* bad when I talked to them," I said. "But if you're worried, we don't have to do this."

"No, it's fine. We need the points. I'm just worried. I don't want them to be rude. I can take it, I just won't stand for them saying anything to you."

"You don't have to protect me," I said. "I've had rude things said to me plenty of times. Plus, I think Sheffield is hoping to get some business for his car lot, I doubt he's dumb enough to piss off the audience if he gets too homophobic."

"True," Ivy said, the keychain clicking between his fingers.

The evening with the Sheffields turned out to be fairly

pleasant—well, as pleasant as an evening can be when you know the people you're spending time with aren't on board with your relationship, fake or not.

The couple gave a few side-long glances when they deemed Ivy and I were sitting too close—which made Ivy jut his chin and scoot even closer, which I thought was adorable. But they didn't say anything.

The enchiladas were delicious and the wine paired nicely.

A glass or two into the meal, Mr. Sheffield was regaling us with stories of deals he cut on cars, Mrs. Sheffield was simpering over her husband as if he was the best thing since sliced bread, and Robby Sheffield—their teenaged son who had come home from work just in time to join us for dinner—was looking at Ivy and me like we hung the damn moon.

Mr. Sheffield sputtered a bit when Ivy told him in no uncertain terms we would not be leaving Mrs. Sheffield to do the dishes to join him for a cigar. After an awkward pause where Mr. Sheffield glanced between his wife, his son, and Ivy and me, the man recovered quite nicely and made himself as useful as one can when he'd likely not been in the kitchen for more than breakfast or grabbing a beer.

Mrs. Sheffield, very obviously not used to the elder male in her house doing anything to help, smiled gratefully at Robby and us as she set to work making coffee while we washed, dried, and put away dishes.

When we moved to the living room for coffee and dessert—I found out quickly that not only did Mrs. Sheffield make a mean sugar cream pie, it was something Ivy had never had and he absolutely loved it. The

Peppermint Café's sugar cream pie wasn't *as* scrumptious as Mrs. Sheffield's, but I made note to bring one home for Ivy as a treat sometime soon.

See, I could be a good fake boyfriend.

"So, you're the mechanic next door, right?" Robby asked from his spot next to his father on the couch. In the split second it took to recognize that look in the teen's eyes, I knew two things. The kid was gay—but definitely not out to his parents—and he had the hots for Ivy.

You and me both, kid. You and me both.

"Yeah, Ivy's Auto is mine. Used to run it from a garage on the other side of town, but I bought this place since it was pretty damn perfect for my shop."

Mrs. Sheffield's eyes went wide at the use of profanity, but there was no way I'd expect Ivy to temper himself. Not because he wanted to be disrespectful, just because he wasn't one to change who he was. Not for anyone.

That was one of the things I'd always appreciated about the man.

"Did you go to school to be a mechanic?" Robby asked.

"Yeah. Started tinkering with engines and shit when I was in my teens—rebuilt my first car. Went to trade school to get my certification. I take trainings each year to re-certify—people want to know a mechanic knows what they're doing. I specialize in older cars, but I'm trained in diagnostics and repairs on newer cars—I just like the older ones because they're where I got my start. The computers in the new ones make it easier in some ways and harder in others."

"Robby here has dreams of working on motorcycles," Mr. Sheffield said with a harrumph. "Leave it to a young and dumb kid to not appreciate the chance to take over the family business."

Robby's cheeks pinked. "Just don't see myself selling cars the rest of my life."

"Gotta do what you think you'll love," Ivy said. "Family business or not, if you're not going to love it, it's not for you."

The teen's eyes glowed with admiration and puppy-love as he gave Ivy a small smile.

The elder Sheffield wasn't as infatuated. Not by a long shot.

"And what about you, dear?" Mrs. Sheffield asked me. "What do you do?"

"I haven't figured out exactly what I want to do yet," I said.

"Well, don't waste too much time," she advised.

"Em is one of those people who is talented in so many areas that trying to settle down with one profession isn't easy. He's so good at everything he does." Ivy put a hand on my knee and I felt it all the way to my toes. "He'll figure something out—maybe a whole lot of somethings."

I was pretty sure hearts grew wings and fluttered above my head as I smiled at the best fake boyfriend ever. "Until then, I'm happy at the Peppermint Café and looking to help Ivy in the shop as needed." I wasn't going to give up on that idea—I really did think I could probably help him, even in just a short amount of time.

"Are you hiring?" Robby asked. "I could maybe work a couple hours a day—"

"You've got school, homework, and sports—those come first—" Mr. Sheffield started.

"Dad, I know. I'm just saying I could maybe pick up

some tips and tricks of the trade while I clean the floors or empty trash," Robby said, fighting to hold back an eyeroll and wanting *so* damn badly to work for Ivy.

"After the holidays, I'm going to look into hiring on some staff—especially if we win the game and I have money for expanding," Ivy said with a wink. "I'll keep you in mind for an hour or two a day—just miscellaneous type stuff in the beginning at least."

"Yes, sir," Robby said. "I'd appreciate it."

We chatted for a bit longer. When Robby excused himself to get some homework done—his eyes lingering on Ivy's arm around my shoulders as he gave a wave and headed up the stairs—we opted to head home.

"Thank you for having us," I said.

"Sorry it took a game show challenge to get our asses over to meet you," Ivy said, shaking Mr. Sheffield's hand.

"Well, we aren't thrilled with the distraction that darn show is bringing to town," the older man said. "And I can't say I enjoy the detour from more traditional—"

Mrs. Sheffield elbowed her husband. "We're definitely going to be watching the show and cheering our new neighbors on," she said as we moved to the kitchen to gather our belongings. "Oh, Ivy, dear. I wanted to tell you just how much I love the addition of the ivy on the side of the house. I've seen old photos and the house always looked gorgeous with the thick greenery growing—I've missed it. Ever since you moved in and got it growing again, I've just loved looking at it."

"What ivy?" he asked.

The older woman gestured toward the side of our house facing hers. "On the stone wall facing us. So pretty.

And how ironic that the man named Ivy has the green thumb touch to bring back the ivy."

He just grunted.

"Oh, one other thing," Mrs. Sheffield went on, clearly not recognizing Ivy's discomfort and confusion. "I meant to ask if you've had time to explore your new home. My grandmother was great friends with one of the previous owners and I always *loved* the stories of holiday magic filling that old beauty."

Ivy cleared his throat. "Um, no. I haven't had time to explore much. Hoping to do more of that if we win and get to move ahead with the remodel. If not, I'll do little bits here and there as I do repairs."

"Well, the attic is the place to start if I remember the stories right. The whole house is chock full of the spirit of Christmas, but the attic holds most of the goodies. The older the decorations, the more magic they seem to have if my grandmother's stories were to be believed."

Ivy chuckled. "Well, Christmas really isn't my thing and we won't be decorating."

"Says Ivy, not me," I interjected.

"So, the decorations—old or not, if they're even still in the attic—likely won't be making an appearance this year," Ivy plowed on.

"Oh, that's too bad," Mrs. Sheffield said. "Everyone always loved when that house was decorated. Candles in the windows, soft glow of lights. I remember one year, the owners let people walk through—she'd put up over thirty Christmas trees throughout the house."

I gripped Ivy's arm when he looked as if he might black out. "Thanks again for a nice evening." Steering Ivy toward the door, I grabbed the basket just as he fished his keychain from his pocket and began to flip it at a high speed.

When the door closed behind us, he cursed. "This town better not think I'm putting up thirty Christmas trees and letting a bunch of people traipse through my house."

"Shhh," I said with a giggle. "Cameras."

"What's she talking about with the damn ivy?" he asked. "I'm not a plant person and I definitely haven't done anything with ivy on the stone wall facing her house."

I hummed a bit of Jingle Bells before shrugging. "I'm going to say something you don't like," I started.

Ivy clapped a hand over my mouth. "Don't even. There's no holiday magic in that house and, even if there was, it has nothing to do with me moving in."

"I don't know," I sing-songed. "The regrowth of ivy vines when a man named Ivy—who just so happens not to believe in the magic of Christmas—moves in? Sounds pretty *Peppermint Hollow gets its very own Hallmark-ish holiday story* to me."

"Shut it," Ivy said, throwing his arm around me like I'd seen him do with Trevor a thousand times over the years. It was a friendly gesture. Nothing more. So, why did I feel safe, protected, and cuddly tucked away under his arm? Why were my stupid brain and heart wanting so badly for this to be real?

I shoved away the thoughts and continued humming Jingle Bells until Ivy good-naturedly threatened to strangle me. We chatted about mundane things as we walked the rest of the way home—probably much to the disappointment of the camera crew who was always hoping to pick up some juicy tidbit.

"Hey, can you come upstairs for a bit," I said, hoping I sounded mysterious and sexy enough to make the cameras and the audience think something secret and steamy was going to take place.

In reality, I just wanted to talk to Ivy for a bit without ears around.

He gave me a look, but dropped his keys on the counter and put the casserole dish in the sink before following me up the stairs.

Shutting the door to the bathroom, I turned on the vent so the cameras wouldn't pick up anything other than murmured words.

"So, how did you think that went?" I asked.

"Not the way I'd pick to spend an evening, but I guess it wasn't terrible." Ivy shrugged as he washed his hands. "I'd probably be willing to send people to Sheffield's car lot if they needed a deal on a decent car. Hopefully, he'll suggest my shop if he talks to anyone needing repairs. He's old-fashioned as hell and way too bigoted for my taste, but I think he's smart enough to know when two small businesses can help each other."

"What did you think of Robby?"

"Nice kid. Kinda sucks he seems to be between a rock and hard place with his parents. Hopefully he'll figure out how to take steps for himself as he gets older and not so reliant on them."

"I didn't want to talk about them on camera," I said. "I think Robby has a bit of a crush on you."

Ivy scowled. "Really? You think he's gay?"

"Gay, bi, pan, whatever, but he definitely looked at you with stars in his eyes."

"Probably just because I'm older and doing something he wants to do."

"That's definitely the case, but he also had that look in his eyes. Believe me, I know what a crush on Ivy Lane Gregory looks like," I said.

I've been looking at that same look in the mirror since I was his age.

"Damn, that sucks then. I'm guessing he doesn't think he can come out—not with parents like them." As usual, completely oblivious to the fact anyone might have the hots for him.

"I think meeting us, seeing us together maybe gave him hope. Maybe just knowing we're together and making it work—even if it's fake, he doesn't know that—made a difference for him and will help in the future."

Ivy was quiet for a moment, but he nodded. "Yeah, I like that. Kinda makes me feel bad we're faking it, but it's all worth it if it helps the kid in the end."

"Agreed. Now, I want to get cleaned up before our nighttime interview. I've got an early shift in the morning."

Later, after we'd both showered—I wondered if Ivy jerked off in the shower as much as I did...it wasn't like I could beat one off in bed these days...and if he did, who did he picture? I wasn't deluded enough to think he imagined me the way I imagined him, but sometimes I let myself fantasize. Anyway, clad in t-shirts and flannel pants, we headed downstairs to meet with Letty.

"We'll get the final results at the end of the week. Numbers are constantly coming in as folks watch the online segments and the end-of-week show. And any numbers gathered are sealed until then, only Silas has any access and it's limited. So, keep it up. Assume the worst and play the game with every ounce of effort you've got," Letty said.

She pointed to the camera and wiggled to get comfortable in her seat. Her lipstick looked freshly applied and I wondered if she ever took her mask off.

"So, dinner went well?" she asked.

We chatted a bit about dinner, our neighbors, Ivy's enchilada recipe, and what we'd be doing for the rest of the week.

"Well, we've got a surprise for you," Letty said.

We both froze.

Surprises from *Once Upon a Christmas House* weren't something I thought of as happy or good.

"We've opened up for the audience to send in challenges of sorts. This one is Truth or Dare. Let's play, okay? Okay." Letty said with a wicked grin, a smear of lipstick staining her teeth. "Emory, Truth or Dare?"

My heart nearly pounded out of my chest. "Um, truth."

"Perfect." She reached into a little cup and pulled out a slip of paper. "Have you ever been in love?"

"Easy," I said with a shrug and sigh of relief. "No."

Ivy tensed beside me and Letty's eyes went wide.

It took about half a second for me to realize my mistake.

I took Ivy's hand. "Not until this guy right here."

Did my voice sound as fake and cheesy to them as it did to me?

Fuck.

"Everything changed when we got together," I went on. "I'd been looking for love and couldn't ever pin it down, then I came home and Ivy was here. Our past, our present, it all clicked—and now I get to look forward to our future. With not only a friend I've known forever, but the man I love."

Ivy gave my hand a squeeze. Whether to tell me I was doing well or to get me to shut up, I didn't know, but I stopped my flow of words by pressing the back of his hand to my lips.

"So sweet," Letty said with a sigh before turning predatory eyes toward Ivy. "Okay, Ivyrson, Truth or Dare?"

"Dare." His answer was clipped and tight.

"Total transparency, based on *Once Upon a Christmas House* rules, once you choose a dare, you either complete it or lose points. I should have stated that earlier. This will be your one freebie to switch if you want." She cocked a brow and waited.

"Dare," Ivy said through gritted teeth.

"Perfect." She reached into a different cup and pulled out a slip of paper. Smiling like the damn Cheshire cat, she clicked her tongue and hummed. "Oh, our audience is goooood. Ivy, you've been dared to let Emory decorate the house for Christmas."

The whoop of excited laughter was out of my mouth before I could catch it.

Ivy turned a scowl my way and I dissolved into giggles.

"I'm sorry," I said, trying to pull the laughter back in. I bit my lip and tried not to go up in flames—or more giggles—at the look on Ivy's face.

"Fine," he bit out. "Emory can decorate, but—"

"No buts," Letty cut in. "The dare is to let Emory

decorate. Period." She turned to me. "Looking forward to it, Emory." She leaned close and pretended to whisper. "Since the decorating came from a dare, there's a bit of money to spend on it if you need to hire someone to hang lights or something similar."

I rubbed my hands together. "Sounds great. I can't wait to get started."

Ivy groaned.

I had to wait a couple days to start the decorating project thanks to work, but I found two college freshmen home from school for the holidays to help me hang the lights and willing to split the money I'd been given to pay them.

The next few days went as smoothly as could be expected when you've got cameras following you ninety percent of the time and your fake boyfriend is grumpy as all get-out about the holiday decorations you're slowly bringing down from the attic.

Ivy wanted nothing to do with going shopping with me for lights, so Mom and Dad tagged along. We spent a nice November day together, eating lunch, playing with Sassy and Stella, and shopping for lights. I wanted to see what was in the attic before I started buying a lot of decorations, but I knew new strands of lights were going to be a must.

We wanted to go see Trevor, but the first time we called to check about visiting, he was in therapy. The second time, he was zonked from therapy. Leave it to Trevor to push himself and make a challenge out of conquering physical therapy and rehab.

The day of the first elimination, I made it up to the attic and really started exploring. Over the years, the home had changed ownership a couple times and each inhabitant seemed to have sprinkled a little of their own touches in the décor they left behind.

I hated that Ivy and I could very easily be voted off the show before I even got the chance to hang the lights and decorate the beautiful old home with all the treasures I found in the attic, but I tried to stay positive.

Ivy needed the win for his shop and his home.

I wasn't destitute, but my half of the prize money would allow me to take a bit more time to figure out what my future held.

And selfishly, I wanted seven more weeks with Ivy.

Part of me hoped the fact I was getting to decorate would entice the audience enough to let us stay, but I didn't know what the other contestants were up to. Maybe Ivy and I were boring people to tears and viewers couldn't wait to get rid of us.

"Will this part be shown before the vote?" I asked Letty as I toted another armful of decorations down to the living room.

"No, we'll put this together for next week's opener if you survive the cut tonight," she said.

"Gee, thanks for the vote of confidence," Ivy groused as he washed his hands at the kitchen sink. We planned to eat and then we'd join the live elimination show.

"I'm just saying," Letty said as the cameras rolled. "We've got to be prepared."

"We aren't out," Ivy said. "People are too excited to see Emory make my home look like Christmas threw up to vote us off just yet."

"We'll see," Letty said, tapping a pen.

"What the hell is that?" Ivy asked, pointing to a vintage Santa face made of tin and faded paint.

"Santa?" I said with a cheeky grin, waving the gigantic face in front of Ivy.

"Hell. No. That thing is creepy as fuck. Put it away."

I turned the Santa and studied it.

To be fair, it *was* creepy as fuck.

"Okay, okay, this one will go back upstairs."

"Don't bring anything back down."

"Bossy," I teased, putting the Santa behind my back and pressing a kiss to his cheek. "Don't get too grumpy," I whispered. "We have a game to win."

Ivy wrapped his arms around me and nuzzled our noses together before kissing me soundly. "You like when I'm bossy," he growled.

Holy.

Fuck.

Now, I needed to run up to the attic to put the creepy Santa away *and* get my dick under control.

Because, yes. Yes, I very much would like it if Ivy wanted to get all kinds of bossy, even if I knew he was just playing his part.

"Maybe I do," I quipped, not missing the flash of *something* on Ivy's face before I quickly made my way up the stairs to stow creepy Santa back in the attic.

"Bring down another box," Letty called from downstairs.

"That's not necessary," Ivy echoed.

Smiling, I grabbed a huge box and said a quick thank you that it wasn't terribly heavy as I headed back down the stairs.

"We've got time to record some footage. If you're out,

we'll toss it and you can take everything back upstairs," Letty said. "If you're safe, we'll use this for next week."

I rubbed my hands together. "Let's see what we've got."

Ivy groaned.

Cracking open the box, I dug into the old newspapers and blankets used to wrap up the fragile items.

"Oh my god, look at this," I whispered as I removed a vintage nutcracker from the cloths.

"Hell. No. *Again*." Ivy shook his head and pointed a finger at the antique wooden figure. "Look at that thing. It looks evil and its eyes look like they're watching me."

"It's an inanimate object, chill out," I said, giving his leg a squeeze. I could really get used to this whole PDA with my fake boyfriend thing. "Do you really hate Christmas or just any piece of décor you deem creepy?"

Walking to the fireplace, I positioned the nutcracker on the raised brick.

"It's watching me. Like its eyes follow me," Ivy groused as he moved around the room.

"Ohhhh, look at this old quilt." Letty pulled a rolled-up, vintage quilt from the bottom of the box and gently spread it on the floor. "No way," she breathed.

"What?" Ivy and I both asked at once.

"Come look at this thing."

As I studied the quilt, goosebumps broke out along my neck and arms. "Whoa, is this for real?"

The large, old blanket was made in what I thought of as a traditional quilt pattern, mostly reds and greens with a few golden-hued squares of cloth mixed in. The stitching was a mix of reds, greens, golds, and silvers—the metallic threads having lost much of their sparkle over the years. All along the edges of the quilt were stitched vines of ivy—which would have been coincidental enough, but on the bottom right corner, in big loopy letters was the name "Ivy."

"It's got your name on it," I said.

"It's got the word ivy on it," my fake beau protested. "Not the same thing. The whole damn blanket is decorated with ivy, they probably named the pattern after the plant or something."

"It's written as a name, with a capital I. It. Has. Your. Name." I hooked my arm around his waist. "I don't know whether to be in awe or creeped out or a little bit of both."

"It has nothing to do with me," Ivy argued. "How could it? That blanket has been here for years and years. I just moved in."

"Holiday magic," Letty and I answered in unison.

"Bullshit," Ivy said.

"Believe it or not, but I, for one, definitely do. This house is full of Christmas magic. First, the ivy growing on the wall outside, and now your name on the quilt." I gently picked up the quilt and moved to situate it on a vintage wooden ladder propped in the corner. "Does that look okay? I kinda like the way it just drapes over the rungs."

"Looks great," Letty said. "Let's see what other treasures are in here."

We unwrapped the cutest little set of dishes. Two bowls, two plates, two mugs, all decorated with a little house, snow, and tiny stars.

"These are adorable. We can use them during the

holiday season," I said, holding up the mug. "Look, the house is almost a replica of yours."

"Probably lead-based paint," Ivy grumped.

"Grinch," I said, swatting his butt as I took the dishes to the kitchen. After a good washing, they'd be perfect for holiday season use.

"Okay, time for one more. What else is in there?" Letty asked.

After digging and unwrapping through several old cloths, I uncovered a vintage snow globe. "Oh my god, Ivy, it's your house. Just like on the dishes. Look, it's a perfect little miniature of The Christmas house."

Ivy took the snow globe and studied it, a far-away look glossing over his face. "Guess it is," he said with a glance toward the cameras. "And it's *our* house." He swirled the snow globe in his hand, flecks of glitter and fake snow tornadoed around the little house.

At that exact moment, a warm whoosh of air traveled through the house, fanning the candle flames, and making the fire pop and crackle in the fireplace.

Letty and I stared at each other, wide-eyed.

"How you gonna explain that, Mr. Grinch?" Letty asked.

"Old, drafty house," Ivy said with a shrug. He handed me the snow globe. "Definitely not *magic*."

Letty's phone buzzed and she hustled us to the table. With the laptop open and the cameras rolling, we watched through the elimination episode. It was truly surreal seeing ourselves on the screen—there were several times I found myself shocked the cameras had caught certain things, and then amazed they *hadn't* recorded other happenings.

So far, I wasn't upset with the way the footage had made Ivy and me look. If we made it through the cut, we could definitely step it up in the PDA department—some of the other couples seemed to be making out non-stop and dropping innuendos left and right.

Would the audience like those types of things or would they vote to see those couples go? Did Ivy and I pass as a real couple? Or did the teams who entered as friends-with-benefits have more chemistry than us?

Damn.

This shit was nerve-wracking.

"Okay, we're back," Silas said with a blindingly bright smile. He was definitely the type who would not only produce the show but host it as well. "I know the scoring process seems a bit confusing and we've had a lot of online questions about it, but I can promise you it's accurate and fair. These couples earn points throughout the week based on challenges—attempted and completed—viewer-submitted challenges, and online votes coming in from the audience." He gave a wink. "Which is why these teams are counting on our viewing audience to tune in and cast votes. You're their best chance at staying in the game. Just make Season's Streaming and *Once Upon a Christmas House* your go-to and follow these couples to the end. Now…on with the votes." Silas moved to a stool next to a big display screen. "I'm going to read the names of each couple who is *safe*. When I get to the end, there will be two teams who haven't been named. This week, those teams will get a chance to plead for votes and save themselves. Here we go, in no particular order."

"Our first safe couple is Mike and Joanna, our retired

couple from upstate New York." The screen lit up with the couple's name.

"Safe couple number two is Julie and Mark. Our teachers from the Midwest." Again, we watched the display light up with their name.

Jackson and Andy, photographer and model from South Carolina.

Cody and Jackie, the hipsters from San Francisco.

Bridgette and Claire with the little bungalow outside of Chicago.

Marian and Stanley. Ugh, the two waved little flags with their political party when their names were announced.

Fuck.

I was truly nervous.

Had we really not made the cut?

Shawna and Theresa, the newlyweds from Florida.

Shit.

We had to make it through this cut.

Sarah and Dean, the new parents in North Dakota.

Damn it.

Were we going to lose to a fucking goat farmer?

"And our final safe couple is Rae and Mallory." The two women from Texas.

Fuck.

Ivy took my hand.

"Well, we've come to the hardest part. Chad and Heather, you're up for elimination. Ivy and Bell, you're up for elimination." Silas pouted a bit and I'd never wanted to punch someone in the mouth so badly. "Based on your scores and the votes throughout the week, you've scored the lowest. *However*, both teams get a chance to sway the viewers and ask for final votes."

In a haze of shock and sadness, I took comfort in my hand tucked in Ivy's as we headed to the living room for our last-ditch effort to plead for votes.

Just as we reached the couch, Ivy turned me to face him and kissed me soundly. "We've got this. I'm not ready to give up." He leaned in and whispered. "Kinda liked having you around here this week, little Bell. Play it up. Beg if we have to. I want this win."

I nodded at his words as Letty whispered, "Keep that up. Let the audience see you kissing."

Ivy kissed me again. "We've got this," he repeated for the camera. "You've got Christmas decorations to put out, we're not done."

I chuckled. Not feeling super confident, but hoping Ivy was right.

Letty gestured for us to sit. "Okay, not the results we wanted, but you've got a chance to talk to the viewers. The stage is yours."

Swallowing unexpected tears, I snuggled into Ivy's side and pressed my lips to the back of his hand. He gave a squeeze and kissed the top of my head.

"So, we knew we had as much a chance of landing here as anyone else, but I've got to be honest, this sucks," I said, sniffling and swallowing thickly. "We'll be fine if we have to say goodbye." Was I trying to convince the audience or myself? "But we want this so badly. All of the contestants have their reasons for wanting to win, but selfishly, we really want to expand the shop and fix up this gorgeous old house. I'm not above begging," I bit my lip and batted my lashes up at Ivy, "just ask this guy." Yeah, it was suggestive. But I'd have no trouble begging Ivy for anything he wanted to do to me if we were a real couple, so I didn't feel too bad about the words. "We want your votes. I want to decorate this house. I want to hear from all of you—leave us comments and let us know what you want to see. We are who we are and we can't change that, but we got into this show to win and give the viewers what they wanted, so tell us."

Ivy pulled me closer. "You're all probably very aware that this type of endeavor isn't my *thing* really." He took a deep breath. "I don't love the holidays. I'm not the life of the party. I'm broody and come across as grumpy a lot. But from the moment Ivy and Bell committed to doing this show, I've been one hundred percent *in*. I love this house and I love my shop—I'll expand and repair with or without the money, but it would help a lot." He turned to me, tipped my chin, and brushed his lips over mine. "And I'm not going to lie. Competing with Em by my side this week has been amazing. I want more of it—more of the challenges, more of the time together, more getting to know him. Yeah, I've known him most of our lives, but this game gives everything a different feel and I want to stay in the competition." He gave a shrug. "So, if you're feeling it, we'd really like your votes so we can stick around and earn this win."

Ten minutes later, my heart beating a million miles a minute, we sat back down in front of the laptop. Silas's smug smile came back on the screen and his gaze seemed to bore into mine.

"Those were some interesting live interviews," he said.

Interesting?

Was ours not good enough?

What did Chad and Heather say?

The rhythmic sound of Ivy's keys flipping between his fingers filled my ears and his warm hand on my bouncing knee helped to calm me slightly.

"Let's get this over with, whatdya say?" Silas asked. "When we announce who will be leaving the show, their screen will immediately go blank. They'll return to their daily lives—we'd love to have the couple join Season's Streaming as viewers and voters for the rest of the show's run," he winked, "and we'll be sad to see them go."

An arm from off-screen appeared and handed Silas a device of some sort.

"Ah, where the magic happens," Silas said, waving the tablet for the camera. "The name of the couple saying goodbye is listed here. I'll tap this button, the name will display, and that couple will know they're out." He hovered his finger over the button, but then sighed. "Right after a quick break. We've got to pay our bills, you know."

CHAPTER 9

IVY

"Okay, we're back," Silas said and I willed my heart not to claw its way out of my chest. "When I click this button, the name of the couple on the screen will be the ones eliminated. I'll ask that each remaining couple celebrate with a kiss under the mistletoe—viewers, you'll get to see that on the *next* episode."

Feeling as if I might pass out, I held my breath and Emory's hand.

Silas made a big show of clicking the button.

The screen flashed with *Chad and Heather*.

It took a moment for my head to process whether they'd won or lost, but Emory's little whoop of excitement next to me pulled me from my maze of thoughts.

He stood and yanked me into a hug.

Realization that we'd made it through washed over me and I spun him around, laughing as his legs wrapped around my waist.

"Mistletoe," Letty whispered.

"We don't have—"

"Doorway," Emory said, his mouth on mine as we laughed and kissed.

When the fuck did mistletoe show up at my house? In my doorway?

For the moment, I didn't even care. I took long steps to the doorway between the living room and kitchen, tightening my arms around Emory. When I thought we'd reached a satisfactory distance to the green leaves and white berries tied up in a red ribbon, I gripped the back of Emory's neck and tilted his head for a longer, deeper kiss.

Fuck if I didn't love kissing him.

The adrenaline of squeaking through to play another week pumped through my veins, but the majority of my blood was making a beeline right toward my dick.

What the fuck?

It was just the excitement, right?

I hadn't had sex in quite a while, that had to be the reason for the way my cock strained behind my zipper.

Emory made a little whimpering sound.

Fuck.

That noise was like a white-hot poker spurring me on while also breaking me from the trance.

Shit.

We had quite the audience.

I broke the kiss and pressed our foreheads together.

"We did it," Emory whispered.

"We did. Seven more weeks." I winked and kissed his nose.

Emory seemed to come back to himself then and his cheeks reddened as he released his legs around my waist and slid down my body.

Yeah, having his warmth pressed against me wasn't the best way to calm myself. No big deal. We had to make viewers connect with us and cheer us on—sex sold, so our little make-out session would likely be helpful.

"We're going to let you celebrate for tonight," Letty said with a suggestive grin. "The living room cameras are on and the silhouette filter will automatically turn on in the bedroom if it detects anything that appears to be more than sleeping."

The waggle of her brows irritated me.

When everyone was gone, Emory bit his lip and stepped away. "Sorry."

"Don't be. We needed to look real—and we're excited to survive."

"I'm too pumped up to sleep. You wanna build a fire and watch TV or something?"

Or something flitted through my head.

Would I take things further with Emory if he wanted the same thing? Hell, yes—and did I probably need to question that? Maybe. Or maybe I could just go with the flow. Was it really that big of a deal? I was attracted to Emory and wouldn't mind taking things further, at least during our time together.

But that wasn't what we'd agreed to. Trevor would kill me if I hurt his little brother and hurting Emory was the last thing I wanted to do. Plus, even if we went into it *knowing* it was just casual and had to end at some point, I had absolutely nothing to offer Emory outside of good sex.

You've never had sex with a guy, how do you know it would be good?

Whatever. Those kisses were dangerous and I was

about to combust—there was no way we wouldn't be *scorching* together.

"You make coffee, I'll build a fire," I said, willing my dick to lose interest. With the taste of Emory still on my tongue and my blood pumping like lava, I refused to think about how good Emory and I could be together.

He was a virgin.

He deserved more.

He deserved better.

I wasn't just some horny teen who couldn't keep it in his pants.

We were here to win.

Nothing more.

I found myself angrily throwing logs into the fireplace a few moments later. Forcing myself to calm down, I listened to the sounds of Emory puttering in the kitchen as he brewed our coffee.

I'd miss having him around when this ended.

I wasn't made for settling down or loving anyone, but his company was definitely something I'd already gotten way too used to.

"Turn it on one of those cheesy holiday romance movies," Emory called from the kitchen.

"How about no?"

He giggled and my heart flip-flopped.

While I scanned our movie choices, Emory made enough noise to wake the dead as he finished the coffee.

"You need help?" I asked over the back of the couch.

"Can you come pour the coffee? I'm getting us some pie."

"Pie?" My stomach growled as I stood and walked toward the kitchen. Pausing in the doorway and checking to be sure Emory was otherwise occupied, I reached up and yanked the mistletoe from the little nail it hung on. Tossing it in the trashcan and covering it with a paper plate, I joined Emory at the counter. "When did you get pie?"

"I brought it home from work. Figured we could either use it as a celebration or a commiseration." He sliced through a creamy sugar cream pie.

"Celebration sounds a lot better than commiseration," I said as I poured coffee in the Christmas mugs he'd found in the attic. "Did you wash these? Seriously, do we know they aren't made with lead paint?"

"They aren't *that* old. There was a pretty modern price tag on one of the mugs, you're probably older than these dishes," Emory said with a cheeky grin.

"Ouch." I held a hand to my heart. "As long as we aren't going to get lead poisoning."

"The only thing we're risking is being filled with the holiday spirit," Emory teased.

"Oh god," I groaned, partly because of his continued good cheer and partly because my dick decided to get raunchy and think about all the other ways I could *fill* him.

Fuck.

Maybe I should have taken the option of sneaking off for a hook-up from time-to-time. Getting Emory as a roommate and competing with him on the show seemed to have woken—and shifted into high gear—my sex drive and an until-now-buried attraction to men—or at least an attraction to Emory. Never before had I experienced such horny thoughts and a desire to take someone to bed.

Our bed.

Double fuck.

This needed to stop.

We settled on the couch, sitting close because the cameras were always rolling in the living room. Comfortably enjoying our pie as the coffee cooled, we watched a few commercials and then I flipped through the guide to see what was available.

Opting to just let the current movie play while we ate, I reached for my coffee and took a sip. "Damn, that's good. Where'd you get it?"

"Get what?"

"The coffee."

"From the pantry. Why?"

"I didn't realize I had...whatever that is," I said, sipping the coffee again.

Emory frowned. "It's just the regular Folgers you have in there."

"No, this is like some sort of flavored stuff. Chicory maybe?"

He shook his head. "Nope, just the same coffee we've been drinking since I got here."

"No. Try it." I nodded toward his mug.

Emory picked it up and took a sip, his eyes going wide over the rim of his cup. "That's good."

"Right? I told you, it's not regular coffee."

"But it *is*," he insisted. "I made it. I know it was from the Folgers container."

"Did someone put a different coffee in it?" I wondered aloud, not sure *why* someone would do that.

"No," Emory said with a confident shake of his head. "I opened that coffee up right before I made it. Even if someone had wanted to replace our coffee—no clue why they would, but whatever—there was no way for that to happen."

"Then why is the coffee all flavored, *Todd*?" I said, my voice mimicking Margo from a traditional Christmas comedy movie—I maybe didn't like the holiday any longer, but the movie was a damn classic.

"I don't *know*, Margo," Emory shot back.

Our eyes caught and we busted out laughing. Trevor, Emory, and I had watched that movie just about every year since Mr. and Mrs. Bell had decided we were old enough.

"You know what this means, right?" Emory asked once we'd stopped chuckling.

I eyed him suspiciously. "Folgers changed their coffee? I bought the wrong kind?"

He shook his head with a smug grin, his eyes twinkling mischievously.

"The mugs are full of lead and that's what we're tasting?" I asked, suddenly realizing where he was going with his ridiculousness.

"Nope," he said, popping the *p*. "These mugs are filled with holiday magic and they make our coffee taste like an old-fashioned drink folks who lived in this house long ago probably enjoyed."

"Nope," I parroted back, doing my own *p* pop. "Probably didn't get washed well enough and we're drinking some sort of residue. Gross. I'll make the coffee next time and you'll see."

Emory bit his lip, his cheeks pink as he tried to contain his smile. "Okay, Grinchy, you do that. But I guarantee you, I washed those mugs perfectly and the coffee isn't flavored. It's. Holiday. Magic."

I pretended not to hear him as I sipped the coffee. It truly was delicious, but there *had* to be a logical explanation for the distinct flavor.

"Um…Ivy?" Emory asked softly over the rim of his mug.

"It's not magic—"

"No, not that…I mean, not the coffee at least," he whispered, placing his mug down on the coffee table and standing to move closer to the fireplace. "Ivy."

"What?"

"Come here," he whispered.

I moved to stand next to him as he studied the snow globe with the little replica house inside. Emory was so close his nose almost bumped the smooth curve of the glass. "Oh my god, do you see that?"

"I see a snow globe with a house that looks similar to mine."

"Look at the living room window," he whispered. "There's a light coming from it."

"Yeah, the painter was really talented."

"No, Ivy." He huffed. "That window wasn't lit up like that when we saw it the first time."

"Sure it—"

"No. It wasn't. And look at the front door. There was no wreath on it, but now there is."

I stood next to him and moved closer to inspect the little house tucked into the snowy landscape of the globe. "I'm sure it was just something we missed."

"Quick. Turn off the lights in here."

"What?"

"Turn them off. Let's see if the little house changes."

Humoring him because I knew there was no way the

snow globe house was going to change, I turned off all the lights downstairs.

Emory stared at the little house intently for at least five minutes while I gathered our plates and mugs.

When I returned to the living room, he frowned and pushed his smudged glasses up his nose. "I swear the lighting wasn't like that when we first saw it."

I took the glasses from his face. "Probably can't see shit because of how dirty these are. I swear, do you just smear your fingers over them all day long?"

Emory squinched his eyes, his little scowl looking adorable. "They're not *that* bad. Plus, you've been keeping them cleaner than they've ever been."

"Go on upstairs and take a shower. I'll wash them and be right up after I check the doors."

He glanced back at the snow globe and sighed. "Okay, good night."

Was he disappointed about his holiday magic theory falling through? Let down because we'd both gotten a bit worked up during that kiss and now we were ending the night a lot more platonically than my dick—and maybe his—wanted? If that was how he was feeling, I wished I could have told him I was feeling the same.

I locked the back door and moved through the living room to make sure the front door was locked as well. Avoiding the damn creepy-as-fuck nutcracker on the hearth as I spread the embers out so the fire would burn down quickly, I beelined toward the kitchen—seriously, I could feel the fucker's eyes on me—and cleaned Emory's glasses.

As I made my way through the living room to head up

to bed, refusing to look at the nutcracker, my eyes caught on the little snow globe.

What.

The.

Fuck?

The living room window glowed much softer now, but the upstairs window shone brightly.

As if a light were on.

Upstairs.

In the bedroom where Emory had gone to get ready for bed.

No.

Nope.

I refused to believe it.

My mind was playing tricks on me.

Probably lead poisoning.

Emory was taking a shower and probably hadn't even turned on the bedroom light.

I moved quickly, taking the stairs two at a time, forcing myself *not* to think about the stupid snow globe.

The thought of Emory in the shower came to mind.

Nope.

That wasn't much better.

Not *any* better, in fact.

Rounding the corner into my room—*our* room—I found the lamps on, the room awash in light, and the scent of Emory's citrus mint shampoo floating on the air.

Ignoring the lamps, I quickly turned off the one on my side of the bed and shucked off my clothes to pull on a pair of lounge pants and a t-shirt. I normally slept in just underwear, but with the cameras and sharing a bed with

Emory, I'd decided to change things up for the duration of the show.

"Did the snow globe change?" Emory asked when he walked into the room with damp hair and his t-shirt clinging to his wet skin.

"Didn't pay any attention to it," I said, handing him his glasses as I lied as smoothly as possible.

His face fell, but he shivered. "Brrr, is it just me, or is it cold in here?"

Climbing under the covers, I paused to take stock of the room. "Yeah, probably should have turned the heat up. Want me to go click it up a few notches?"

"Nah, once I get warm under the blankets, I'm sure I'll be fine."

"You sure?"

"Yeah." Emory placed his glasses on the night table and gave me a wink. "Plus, we could always cuddle." He crawled into bed and leaned close to whisper, "For the cameras."

"You think they'll turn on?" I asked, glancing around the room.

"Maybe. Kill two birds? Give the audience something to talk about," he continued in a low murmur, "and get warm?"

"I'm game." I hoped my words sounded as nonchalant as I meant for them to. I could cuddle for a bit, warm up Emory, give some good footage, and then sleep. No big deal.

Except my heart was beating a thousand miles a minute and my dick was saying it was a *very* big deal he most definitely wanted to be involved in.

Nope.

Cuddling *only*.

I opened my arm for Emory to snuggle close. Cuddling with a person was the same no matter the gender, right? I could do this. I wasn't a cuddler with the women I'd slept with, but for five hundred thousand, I'd be the best cuddler in the whole damn world.

The moment Emory tucked his chin and buried his face in my chest, his arm wrapping around my torso as I turned slightly to face him, I knew without a shadow of a doubt that cuddling with Emory Bell was different than anything I'd ever done.

And I never wanted to stop.

Holding someone in my arms wasn't something I'd had a lot of practice with. But holding Emory immediately felt...*right*.

Shit.

No.

I couldn't feel this way.

It wasn't what we'd started out to do.

Wasn't what we'd agreed on.

Wasn't anything *close* to what I needed or wanted in my life.

I had plans.

For my house, my shop, my future.

Those plans had never once included getting involved with *anyone*, let alone Emory-fucking-Bell.

But his body curled into mine, his warmth seeped under my skin, his scent filled my nose, and everything clicked into place.

Obviously, I'd have to ignore the way my body and heart responded to having Emory so close—*mine, mine,*

mine—but maybe it was okay to open myself up to the feelings for just a moment.

Let myself think about what it meant to feel like my entire body had just tied itself in knots around the one and only person on the entire planet who was made just for me.

He was an absolute perfect mix of lean, hard contours and soft, warm curves. The rigid press of his hipbone, the weight of his knobby knees, those things contrasted with the soft curve of his ass, the gentle slope of his shoulder, and the plump arc of his lip. He smelled good enough to eat and his soft little snores against my chest had me smiling despite thinking I'd *never* get any sleep this way.

I want him.

I want him in my bed every night.

Want to touch him—not for the cameras, not for the money— want to make him shiver and moan and come apart in my arms.

Holy.

Fucking.

Shit.

Where the hell had that come from?

Maybe for the cameras? We up the ante and put on an even more entertaining show for the audience? Could be fun. We both get something out of it. Increase our staying power with the viewers.

No.

I was assuming way too much.

Emory's feelings toward me, for one.

Not to mention that I had no desire for my first experience with a guy to be recorded on camera.

Too late for that.

Well, any *more* than the kissing and cuddling.

Unless Emory asked for more, we'd stick to the PDA plan as it was. Cuddling in bed at night would be a bonus I'd look forward to all day.

And at the end of eight weeks, if everything went as planned, we'd be five hundred thousand dollars richer and well on our way to making our futures better.

Sure, I'd go back to being alone, but that had been the plan all along.

And I was fine with it.

Emory shifted, nuzzling his nose into my neck, his soft breaths tickling my skin.

Fine.

Everything was totally fine.

At some point, I must have finally fallen asleep because I awoke sometime later with my rock-hard cock aching, a furnace burning between us, and Emory's cute little ass pressed against me as the sun barely peeked into the bedroom.

Cracking an eye, I glanced around and noticed the red glow of the recording light from two cameras. Yeah, they were supposed to be the silhouette filter ones, but knowing they were on made things even more awkward.

Waking up with a hard-on wasn't new.

Waking up with my dick ready to pound nails and wanting to explore Emory's perfect ass was definitely an unfamiliar experience.

Emory snorted and groaned, rocking back against me before rolling over and curling into my chest.

Then he froze.

"Good morning," I whispered gruffly, figuring the cameras would pick up at least a mumbling. Lowering my voice more, grateful we didn't have to wear microphones for the show, I leaned close. "Cameras are on, so don't look freaked out."

"I am freaked out," Emory hissed.

"Why?" I asked with a chuckle.

"I've never...it feels...I want to..." Emory grunted, burying his face in my chest again. "I don't even know. I'm sorry, I didn't plan on mauling you through the night."

"At least we stayed warm, you're a toasty little thing," I teased. "Gonna kiss you now," I warned in a low whisper.

Without waiting for his response, I tipped Emory's chin and brushed my lips over his. Morning kisses in bed were a new thing for me and I didn't hate them.

Not at all.

Oh god.

The kiss had been a mistake.

Emory whimpered slightly and shifted his hips.

When our hard cocks brushed together, Emory gasped and froze.

What would the camera be able to pick up through the filter?

I gripped his ass and held him close, our throbbing morning erections pressed together for what seemed like an eternity of pleasure. With my lips at his ear, I reminded in a whisper, "Cameras are on, play it cool. I'm going to kiss you again then say something about having an early appointment. I'll shower and meet you downstairs."

"I'm so sorry," Emory choked out.

"Don't be. It's not like waking up like this isn't enjoyable." Not letting him get in another word, I kissed him, grinding our cocks together until I couldn't hold back the groan. "Damn, babe, gonna have to take a rain check—I've got an early appointment." Slapping his ass and chuckling when Emory whimpered, I rolled from bed, praying the camera filter didn't catch my tented pants, and made for the bathroom.

"You're an asshole," Emory called out.

I laughed and peeked my head around the doorframe. "Why's that?"

"Leaving me here to suffer," he said.

"Wanna join me?" Shit. What would I do if he said yes?

Emory glowered. "No, we don't have time. Hurry up so I can get ready too."

There. Perfect little thirst trap scene for the viewers.

I did feel kinda bad for little Bell though.

While I was in the privacy of the bathroom where I could jerk myself off—while most definitely *not* thinking about Emory's perfect ass and soft little whimpers—he was stuck out in the bed, on camera, until I was done in the shower.

I sped things along as much as possible, but the bedroom was empty by the time I emerged with damp hair and fresh boxers. Once I was dressed, Emory had stomped up the stairs, the scent of bacon wafting behind him.

"The cameras turned off after you left. Guess they figured nothing exciting was going to happen." He wrinkled his nose. "Seriously, I'm sorry about that."

"Seriously, don't be. Unless you were uncomfortable, it didn't bother me. We got some good footage and it wasn't a hardship in any way."

Emory snickered. "*Hard*ship."

I bit back a grin. "What are you, twelve?"

He shrugged. "I just don't want to put you in any

awkward positions. I know you're not attracted to me like that—"

I stepped into his space. "I maybe don't want a relationship because my past fucked me up." I cupped his face. "And I maybe only got into this game for the prize." Brushing my mouth over his, I savored his tiny moan. "I know it's not the point, but attraction isn't the problem."

The kiss was unnecessary and selfish. The flicker of hope and desire in Emory's eyes punched me in the gut.

"Not that we can or should do anything about it— we've got a good setup planned out—but I don't want you thinking I'm turned off by you or anything like that."

God.

The way his face fell, like I'd told him he'd won the lottery and then shown him the ticket was fake, nearly brought me to my knees.

"Yeah," Emory said, squaring his shoulders. "Sure. Okay. We keep with the plan. Can you go make coffee? I need some, but I don't want to be accused of tampering with it. Use the mugs we used last night. I want to prove to you it's not the coffee."

I slapped his ass as he headed toward the bathroom. "I'll wash the mugs this time. You'll see. Just a regular ol' cup of coffee."

Joke was on me though.

The damn coffee still tasted like chicory and was the best cup of joe I'd ever had. I had no clue what was going on, but it definitely wasn't holiday magic.

That wasn't even real.

Right?

We somehow skated through the next three weeks of challenges and cuts.

The comments for us on the show's page were all over the place, but they helped us realize the viewers were hooked on our romance. After a discussion with Emory in which we both decided it wasn't a hardship and it was worth it to earn the points, we definitely kept up the PDA and nighttime cuddling.

In fact, holding Emory in bed and waking up with him wrapped in my arms had quickly become one of my very favorite things in the world—so, maybe it wasn't all for show on my part any more, but I didn't mind having an excuse to feel him against me.

Yeah, I was so screwed when this game ended. I knew it was for the best—no one should get stuck with someone who is incapable of a healthy, loving relationship—but it was gonna hit me hard. At least I knew the pain was coming and could slightly prepare for it.

I wasn't sure what to do with the feelings I had for Emory—for two reasons. One, I'd never had these type of feelings for anyone. Two, never in a million years would I have thought I'd go for a guy. On one hand, it was throwing me for a loop. On another hand, it didn't seem to matter—Emory was just Emory.

And on the *other* other hand, it didn't matter because I didn't do relationships and Emory had only agreed to play the game—nothing more.

We never took the PDA past kissing and cuddling—and when the question came up in the interview room, we said we wanted to keep that portion of our relationship private. It was a risk—especially since we had zero access to anything the other teams were doing and no idea what the audience was saying about those teams—but going full-on display for the cameras wasn't something either of us were comfortable with.

In all honesty, I was about ready to bash the cameras—throw a sheet over them or *something*—and take things to the next level with Emory. But he seemed content to keep things the way they were, so I followed his lead. Although, he'd said enough in the past for me to know he had no idea I could possibly find him attractive—and to be fair, he'd known me as straight his whole life so it was a reasonable assumption—so I didn't even know if Emory would even consider the possibility of taking things to the next level. If he ever thought about it, I had a pretty good idea that he'd *never* pursue it with me.

God, I could just picture the blush on that gorgeous face if he ever had to ask me for something outside of our fake relationship.

And that was what I had to keep remembering.

This.

Was.

Fake.

Another thing we learned was the audience was a bit evil. They seemed to not only get off on the potential of *Ivy & Bell* getting off together, but also on making *me* suffer through all the holiday magic shit.

One of the challenges included me taking a daily picture of the ivy growing on the side of my house. To earn the points, I had to admit it was growing like crazy and hadn't been there when I first moved in. For bonus points, I had to begrudgingly concede that I wasn't doing anything to make it grow and that the spirit of the holiday season *might* be part of why the plant had started to overtake the entire side of my house.

A little white lie wasn't the worst thing to do for points.

Emory had had a blast decorating at the end of week one. I'd shut myself in the shop and stayed busy the whole day, but I could admit he and the guys he hired to hang the lights did a really good job. I wasn't going to say I *liked* the decorations—inside or out—but I could appreciate they'd been well done.

The viewers submitted some pretty raunchy challenges at first, but Season's Streaming made it clear they wouldn't be airing anything more than the filtered footage and definitely nothing that would impact their ratings in a negative way.

After that, the audience submitted more innocent type challenges. Emory and I had fun answering their questions and playing their games.

Letty was still annoying, but she also had a fierceness to her that made me glad she was on our side and wanted us to win.

The show's challenges had fallen into a pattern of *do something naughty* and *do something nice*.

The nice things were easiest. We helped at a soup kitchen, volunteered to wrap presents—although, my wrapping definitely needed major intervention—and cooked dinner together. Those things earned us points and the audience seemed to love watching us together. Probably helped that Emory was an absolute doll and up for pretty much anything with his sweet smile and big brown eyes sparkling behind those glasses.

We'd struggled a bit more with the *do something naughty* challenges.

I swore Emory kept hanging mistletoe for his part, but he swore the pieces of greenery that kept popping up weren't him. I'd started feeling bad about throwing them away, but they irritated the fuck out of me each time I walked through a doorway and saw one hanging.

When Letty asked about our naughty challenge during week three, I tried to argue my case that being forced to live in a house decorated in holiday cheer with a man who might as well have been a holly-jolly elf himself was one of the biggest challenges of my life.

Letty said I earned points for creativity, but we still had to complete an actual challenge.

So, we had a snowball fight.

It was probably the most fun I'd had in my entire life. Ending the day curled up in front of the fire with Emory and that damn chicory coffee—which, by the way, I tested and it tasted completely normal in all other mugs—was the perfect way to end a day. I didn't care if the cameras were on, if we earned points, or if the audience sent in votes—sitting with Emory next to me brought to light that I hadn't simply been happy in a very long time.

By the time we got to Week Five, Emory and I were closer than ever and I had a really good feeling about the outcome of the game. I'd even had a couple thoughts of asking him to stay as a roommate when the show was over. Sure, it would be an adjustment to have him move from my bed to his own—and I wasn't able to think about what it would be like if he had guys over—but my head kept saying it was at least a way to keep him around.

And I definitely wanted, much to my surprise, to keep

him around. Emory had worked his way into my life and awakened something in me—and I think it affected me more because he hadn't even been *trying*. He had no motive, no plan to win me over, he was just being his true self and he'd lodged himself so deep, I couldn't fathom not having him in my daily life.

But those were thoughts for another day.

After our first week drop into the bottom two, we'd hovered near the bottom one other time, but never ended up in the lowest again.

Week Five brought us to six couples left and the stakes soaring.

We'd said goodbye to Julie and Mark, the teachers from the Midwest. The audience seemed to think they were boring based on the comments we got to read after the couple had been sent packing.

Marian and Stanley had luckily gotten the boot. They'd had a fierce fan base cheering them on because of their outspoken political stance, but the votes just hadn't been enough.

Shawna and Theresa, the newlyweds from Florida, had left as well. They'd gone down on the double-elimination week with Mike and Joanna, the retired couple from upstate New York. Shawna and Theresa had actually left due to a medical emergency—so, not an *actual* double-elimination, but two couples said goodbye. From the audience comments, Mike and Joanna just couldn't keep up despite being sweet as could be. Shawna and Theresa likely would have been major competition if they hadn't needed to leave for reasons outside of their control.

The remaining couples were Jackson and Andy. The

photographer and model, friends-with-benefits from South Carolina.

Cody and Jackie, the hipsters from San Francisco.

Bridgette and Claire with the little bungalow outside of Chicago.

Sarah and Dean, the new parents and goat farmers in North Dakota.

Rae and Mallory, the two women from Texas.

And obviously Ivy and Bell.

After Week Five's vote, we'd be down to five couples all with the goal of being one of two to make it to Week Eight and survive the final cut.

"Let's get this started, okay? Okay," Letty said, bleached teeth blinding in contrast with her lipstick as we sat down for our interview. "Ivy, dear, do you *have* to?" She gave a nod toward my hand where I flipped my keychain.

"It's what he does, it's fine," Emory said. He was wearing worn jeans, a black hoodie from my closet, and my black work boots. I knew he'd just done it for the camera since we'd heard a couple comments from the audience about how sweet it was when he wore my things, but damn if I didn't like seeing him in my stuff.

Wouldn't mind seeing him out *of my stuff either*.

Letty pursed her lips, but didn't say anything more. "The audience has questions," she started.

"I'm sure they do," I muttered.

She pressed on. "Emory, it's assumed your answer to these questions will be the same for each, so let's see what Ivyrson has to say, okay? Okay." Tapping her notebook, Letty grinned. "Ivy, how do you explain the strange happenings around the house?"

"Just strange little happenings. Nothing more."

"The ivy suddenly starting to grow—out of season, no less—when you moved in?"

"It's been a warmer than usual fall, we got a good mix of sunshine and rain, plants do weird things." In reality, I had no damn clue how or why that ivy had started growing and I was ready to chop it all down the moment the show was over.

"What about these mugs?" She held my coffee cup up for the camera to see. "Rumor has it that your regular ol' coffee tastes different—almost as if it's a special brew—when it's in these mugs."

"Lead paint," I mumbled. "For real though, probably just something in the finish. Nothing magical."

Letty nodded. "The mistletoe appearing even though you keep tossing it away? The nutcracker? The snow globe?"

"The mistletoe is either Em or the crew. That one's too easy."

"It's not me…" Emory said just as Letty said, "The crew isn't here to interfere."

"The nutcracker is just creepy, nothing to do with holiday spirit or whatever."

"And the snow globe?" Letty pushed.

"Yeah, Ivy, what about the snow globe?" Emory said with a feisty grin.

Did I say I wanted him to stick around? Forget it. He was a damn little pain in my ass.

The snow globe was the one thing I couldn't explain.

I wasn't saying it was magical or anything—maybe cursed—but the damn little house windows lit up differently each evening and usually matched the lights we had on in the real house. And don't even get me started on the wisps of smoke I swore I sometimes saw from the chimney.

I shrugged. "Great design. They don't make them like that anymore." The keychain clinked against my palm.

"Mmhm," Letty hummed as Emory took my free hand. "Well, let's move on to some of the audience comments, okay? Okay." She handed us a card with several comments. "These are just a few of the ones we pulled in hopes of giving you a taste of what your fans—and non-fans—are saying."

Ivy and Bell are the absolute sweetest, not to mention HAWT. I'd totally pay good money to watch them in action. ~mamalikes2watch

These two started out like they'd never even kissed, but their chemistry has skyrocketed. Definitely have my vote. ~santahasabigold*ck

Ivy and Bell 4-ever. ~givemeromance

Watching Ivy and Emory is like watching a gay romance novel play out right in front of us. Fake relationship or friends-with-benefits to begin with (yeah, I don't buy they were together from the beginning), forced to spend hours upon hours together, fall for each other while holiday magic swirls around them. I can't wait to see how it will end. ~andrealuvsivy&bell

Ivy & Bell don't stand a chance. They're gone as soon as the losers get sent packing. Right now, they're just barely treading water. ~notafan

Don't even like this damn show, too many queers. Bring back traditional values. ~makeamericastraightagain

Anyone else notice how bad these two totally wanna bone? Are they getting it on in the bathroom? Really wish the cameras could catch everything. ~justhere4thep0rn

Don't get me wrong, I completely adore some of the other couples, but Ivy and Bell have my heart. ~luvmesumluv

What a crock of sh*t! This site lets you make up a name to attach to your comment, but it won't allow me to use the name I want. Says it's "derogatory." Whatever. ~givemefr33sp33ch69

Do Ivy and Bell have a "fan page" for specific kinds of content? *wink wink* Sign me up. I'd watch the f*ck out of that sh*t. ~ofwhore

Emory snorted. "Maybe we should think of a *fan page for specific kinds of content* if we don't win? Bring in the money another way?"

I chuckled, but hell no. I wasn't sharing Emory.

He's not really yours to share or not, is he?

"I'm sure you won't be surprised," Letty said, "but we have a little announcement to make. Let's get to it, okay? Okay."

Emory tensed and I groaned.

Season's Streaming appeared to fly by the seat of their pants—at least where *Once Upon a Christmas House* was concerned—and were constantly making changes and additions.

"Based on extensive analyzing of audience feedback—the good, the bad, the ones here for sweet romance, the ones here for drama, the ones looking for something spicier, *all* of it—we've decided to up the ante and provide a *Once Upon a Christmas House: After Dark* option."

Letty continued on as I picked my jaw up from the floor.

"After Dark activities still won't be shown on camera—any more so than the filtered footage we already show—but couples can pick the spicier challenges and earn points just for choosing them. The audience will still hold the votes, so the steamy part is mainly to give them a little more of what they want, get their imaginations going, if you will, and keep their attention and their votes."

"What happened to the network saying they absolutely wouldn't do that?" I asked, unsure of how I felt about the addition.

"Like I said, we've extensively analyzed feedback. No couple will be forced to opt into the After Dark—and some will opt in and fit the challenges to their specific situation depending on what they hear from their fans. Everyone will still be able to play their game the way they want. After Dark just adds a facet the fans seem to want."

"And these After Dark challenges, they can be on a case-by-case basis? It's not all or nothing?" Emory asked.

"Correct." Letty gave a firm nod. "Now, I'm going to give you a head's up about a future challenge because you'll both need some time to think. You're each going to be responsible for planning a date for the other. It has to be something you think they've never done, something they'll enjoy, and something you can do together. If it's something neither of you have done, bonus."

My mind immediately started whirring as to possibilities.

"Let's wrap this up, okay? Okay," Letty said with a wink. "We'll end with an audience challenge. Over the course of the show so far, we've heard bits and pieces of Emory's dating history and it seems like he hasn't dated much. We also know Ivy hates Christmas. Your challenge from the audience—and this was unanimously voted on from between two options—is to tell each other the *why* behind those things."

My heart clenched and I immediately wanted to say no.

I didn't want to share those things with thousands of people. Hell, maybe millions...I had no clue how many were watching this damn show.

But Emory brushed his thumb over my knuckles. "We'll agree to this, but it will be a private conversation. No cameras. *Maybe* a brief recap in an interview, but we'll let you know." He gave my hand a squeeze. "This isn't something Ivy and I have ever delved into and we'd prefer to keep it between just the two of us."

Letty cocked her head. "If we can get a short statement summarizing the *why* for each of you, maybe a muted scene of the conversation, I think we can make that work."

As she signaled the camera crew to wrap it up, I wondered just how I'd get through telling Emory about the shittiest Christmas I'd ever had.

CHAPTER 10

EMORY

"You look good," Ivy said as he clapped Trevor on the shoulder in my parents' den when we went to visit the day after the audience issued their challenge.

"Thanks, man," Trevor replied, smiling fondly at Sassy and Stella as they sniffed us. "Been hitting it hard, helps to see progress."

Ivy was right, Trevor looked good. Strong, healthy, like he was in good spirits. I'd been somewhat worried the pain and recovery from his accident would bring him down, but he'd had great therapists and my parents had enjoyed having him back home.

The dogs glanced between the three of us as if waiting to see if this was a playdate, a walk, or a boring sit-down visit. Trevor chuckled. "Bed, girls." He gestured toward their big bed in the corner of the den. "We'll play later."

I wasn't sure I ever wanted to have children, but I knew my brother looked at his dogs as his babies. He treated them like gold and I loved to see the three of them so happy, but I worried for him when the day came they were no longer with him. He'd be devastated.

The dogs obediently moved to their bed, went through their usual find-a-comfy-spot routine, and flopped down curled together. They were well-trained and had been the best dogs ever since Trevor got them as puppies.

Trevor, propped up in a recliner, eyed the little camera I held. "What's that for?"

"Audience challenge," Ivy grumbled. "We agreed to show some muted footage as long as we got to record it ourselves and didn't have to do the whole conversation for the viewers to see. We'll give a brief—very brief if I have anything to say about it—recap and get our points."

Trevor narrowed his eyes. "Damn, that sounds ominous. What do they have you doing? PS- I gotta say, the audience seems to be a really weird mix of people getting all swoony over your *romance*," he rolled his eyes, "and people getting boned up over putting you guys in uncomfortable situations."

"You're watching?" I squeaked out.

My brother looked at me. "Of course, I'm watching. Why wouldn't I?"

Ivy's keys had started their clinking. "Figured you weren't happy about the whole thing from the beginning, wouldn't want to watch us fake our way through."

Ouch.

There it was.

The reminder I needed.

No matter how much chemistry had been building between Ivy and me this past month, everything was still fake. He didn't see me as anything more than Trevor's little brother. And I had to be okay with that because that was all we'd ever agreed to. I wouldn't be that gay boy fawning all over the straight guy and making a fool of myself.

We're not one hundred percent on that straight thing though, right?

I pushed the thought away. I'd ignore the ache in my heart. I'd stop fanning the flame of hope about Ivy and me. The way he tucked me close every night in bed? Just for warmth in an old house and giving the cameras some sort of footage to apply the filter to. The sexy way we flirted most mornings when we woke tangled together and achingly hard? More snippets for the crew to use in hopes of us moving forward a bit more each day. The way he grabbed me and kissed me, told me about his day, snuggled with me on the couch? All just habits we'd fallen into to win a game.

A game.

That's all it was.

It wasn't real, no matter how real it felt.

No matter how much I wanted it to be.

"Nah, I've been watching." Trevor eyed the way Ivy's hand immediately took mine when we sat down after setting up the camera. "You two are laying it on pretty thick."

"We're in it to win it," Ivy said.

"The others—"

"No, we can't discuss the others," I said. "We could be disqualified if they find out we're getting information about the other teams."

"Shit, I wasn't thinking," Trevor said. "Sorry." His eyes lingered on our hands where Ivy absently ran his thumb over my knuckles. "So, what's this new challenge?"

"We have to tell each other about our pasts. Why I don't date much and why Ivy hates Christmas," I said.

Trevor's eyes went wide. "And you want me here for that?"

"You already know my story," Ivy said. "And Em didn't want to have to tell his story more than once."

Concern clouded Trevor's face. "What story?"

I sighed and Ivy squeeze my hand. "So, part of why I haven't dated much is because of some shitty things in my past. You know a little about them, but not everything."

"I swear to god, if someone hurt you, I will beat them to death with this damn crutch," Trevor said through gritted teeth.

Ivy rumbled beside me.

"Not the way you're thinking…probably would have, if not for you two," I said. Running a hand through my hair, I huffed out a frustrated breath. "This is harder than I thought it would be."

"It's just us," Ivy said. "Tell us what feels right to tell. We're not judging."

"So, the first guy I dated in high school cheated on me for like an entire year. I was crushed and embarrassed when I found out. Felt like a total fool." My cheeks pinked at the memory. "The feeling of never being good enough— of being the guy who gets cheated on—has stuck around ever since."

"You're not—" Trevor started, but Ivy held up a hand and stopped him.

"My sophomore year, I started dating this senior named Joe."

"Fuck that guy," Trevor said. "I never liked him."

"Yeah, well, you had good instincts. Clearly, I didn't." I

sighed. "He constantly wanted sex. I had absolutely no experience beyond kissing, but he pushed and pushed for more. In hindsight, I'm sure he was getting it from someone else because there was no way he would have let me stall for so long."

Tension poured from Ivy.

"We ended up at a party. I hated it the moment we got there. It was so loud and crowded." The sweat, the heat, the stale beer, the pounding music washed through my memories. "Joe was drinking and getting meaner and more persistent as the night went on. I spent most of the time avoiding his advances by dancing in large crowds, but he eventually separated me and pushed me upstairs." I drew in a calming breath, trying to get the scent of Joe's beer breath and sweat out of my nose. "I was so dumb and so scared. Part of me was gloating that an older guy wanted anything to do with me—it wasn't like I didn't want to do some of the things he was pushing for—but when he got me alone in that dark room, it was like ice water washed over me. I knew immediately I didn't want those things with *him*, didn't want my first time to be rough and mean." Ivy's keys were the only sound filling the room and he squeezed my fingers in his warm grip. "I told him I was going to puke. He was pissed, but pushed me toward the bathroom and told me to hurry up, he had plans for me." I shrugged. "I don't know if you remember it, but I called you."

Trevor's eyes went wide. "You said you were freaking out because there was alcohol and wanted me to come get you."

I nodded. "I ran out of the house and down the long driveway."

"We found you by the mailbox," Ivy said, his thumb caressing circles on my knuckles.

"Yeah," I said. "So, I kinda swore off guys until I found someone who wouldn't force me into something I wasn't ready for. Spent the rest of high school with just friends. That's how most of college was too." I wasn't about to tell them I spent all those years lusting over Ivy because he was the only guy I wanted to climb like a tree *and* felt safe around. "Last year of college, I decided to give dating a chance. But I didn't have much experience and *safe guys* were a mixed bag, so dating was kinda blah for me."

"I think you're doing great," Ivy said, my head and heart clinging to his words whispered close to my ear.

"I'm sorry I didn't push to figure out more," Trevor said. "I should have taken care of that asshole."

I shook my head. "Nah, it wouldn't have helped me. I was just happy to be away from him and feeling solid on my feet again. But that's the whole story as to why my dating life has been lackluster—until I found the best fake boyfriend a guy could ask for," I teased and elbowed Ivy.

"Right back at ya, little Bell," he said with a smile, but it didn't reach his eyes and I noticed he threw a glance toward my brother.

Trevor's eyes bore holes into us.

"So," I said, hoping to relieve the tension. "There's my story. Now it's Ivy's turn."

He cursed and let go of my hand, leaning forward with elbows on knees, the keychain clicking a steady rhythm.

"Ivy." My hand going to his back. "You don't have to do this. We can get points a different way."

"No, you did it, I'll do it." He took a deep breath, shuddery under my hand as I rubbed circles.

Trevor didn't look as unsure about his best friend's story as he had about mine, but I knew that was because he knew Ivy's story. But my brother did watch us like a hawk while Ivy gathered himself.

"Just let me talk, okay?" Ivy asked. "I'd rather not answer any questions, just want to get it out and be done with it."

"It's your story," I whispered, wanting to pull Ivy into my arms and hoping my hand on his back gave a bit of comfort.

"Looking back, their marriage wasn't good. I can recognize that now. Hell, it's part of why I know I'm not cut out for love—I never really saw it. But as a twelve-year-old kid, I didn't realize anything was wrong. They didn't really fight. There wasn't any violence. Just disconnect, apathy, and probably dislike. I think they'd gotten together more as a hookup with no interest in anything else, but Mom got pregnant with Irvin and their parents demanded they get married. They definitely didn't marry for love—but as a kid, I didn't know that."

Ivy took a deep breath, his keys never stopping.

"Irvin was eighteen and I was twelve that Christmas. I think Iris was five or about to be. Mom was always pretty distant. Not abusive or neglectful, just not involved. Her mind was always elsewhere—when she wasn't working, she was *out*. After…after, if she wasn't working one of two jobs, she was asleep. She slept a lot after. I don't think she loved him—I know he didn't love her or us—but I think, after that Christmas when it all went to shit, she resented him. Regretted her choices. Hated that she was stuck with Iris and me."

I wasn't going to interrupt, but I wondered if Ivy was

going to actually say what his father had done. I knew the guy had left. I remembered weeks and months after that Christmas when Ivy and Iris were at our house more often than not. Whispered snatches of conversations about Mr. Gregory being gone. But I'd been about the same age as Iris and didn't have the understanding to know what was going on or even ask any questions.

"We didn't just lose a dad, we lost a brother too, ya know?" Ivy snorted. "Irvin tried to contact me—several times, in fact. I think he's actually talked to Iris. But he left too. Dad didn't offer to take Iris and me, but he told Irvin he could come if he wanted since he was eighteen and had a job to help with rent. My brother was six years older than me, we weren't super close, but I sometimes wonder what life would have been like if he'd stuck around and helped me instead of fuckin' off to live with Dad and…" Ivy paused and drew in a shaky breath. "His new family. He served my mom with divorce papers right there in the living room with the little electric heater running and gift wrap strewn everywhere. Looking back, I know he wasn't mentally well and it was likely for the best he left—but who does that? He smiled, handed her an envelope of paperwork, and said, 'Thought these would fit real well since it's the happiest time of the year.' Then he told Irvin, Iris, and me we had half siblings and a stepmother. He knew it would be a hard transition, but he hoped we'd all be able to be happy and get along. Come to find out—and I only gathered this from sneaking Mom's diary and reading it one day several years later—Dad had a whole other family in a town not too far away. He'd been seeing this woman for about ten years and had three kids with her. Two younger than me and one younger than Iris.

From what Mom wrote in the diary, she wasn't surprised. She wasn't even upset about the divorce. Mainly, she was shitty she got left with us." Ivy huffed out a breath. "And it wasn't like an open relationship thing. I think Mom knew he was cheating and just didn't care. Dad worked a lot of business trips so it was easy to sneak around. Mom had her own fair share of side relationships, so they were both fucking around."

He switched the keys to his other hand.

"So, yeah, that's what's in my head when I think of Christmas and the holidays. Plus, every other shit thing that seems to happen around this time." Ivy ran a hand through his dark hair, the ink on his skin a blur. "The first like five Christmases were terrible. Couple of them, Mom didn't even get out of bed all day. I used money she gave me to get Iris gifts and stayed up late making sure she had some gifts from Santa. Several Christmases, Mom opted to work. I know she needed the money and she always made sure we had food, clothes, and the bills were paid—but she provided the money, she didn't do the shopping or paying the bills. It's like she just checked out. I didn't have a choice, I became Iris's caretaker—it was exhausting, but no one else was going to do it. Then, Mom got sick not long after I turned eighteen. Sounds horrible to say, but it was almost a blessing when she went so quickly. She died just before Christmas. Then it was just Iris and me for a long time. One Christmas, we lost power. Another year, the pipes burst. Then there was the Christmas I slipped on the ice and broke my arm. Last Christmas, Iris announced she was getting married and moving away—I'm happy for her to have found a good guy and they're building their little family. But the only good

Christmas memories I ever had are overshadowed by Dad leaving us for his other family and every shit Christmas since then. If it hasn't been a disastrous holiday, it's been lackluster at best."

He stopped, drew in a long breath, and then gave a shaky laugh.

"Holy shit, that was a lot to unload all at once. Never told anyone all of that." The keychain clinked over and over. "Um, do the girls need to go o-u-t?"

Sassy and Stella perked up their ears, glancing between Trevor and Ivy as if willing their dad to give the go-ahead.

Trevor eyed Ivy and nodded. "Yeah, they'd like that. Take them around the block if you want."

Ivy gripped my knee and gave a squeeze. "I'll be back, keep this one in line." He grabbed the dogs' leashes and clicked his tongue. "Let's go, girls."

Sassy and Stella thundered toward the door and Ivy followed.

Soon, the door clicked shut and I was alone with my brother.

"Damn it, Em," Trevor grumbled.

I ran my hands over my face. Did I lie? Pretend I didn't know exactly what my brother was talking about? "I know. It wasn't on purpose," I said.

"This was exactly what I was afraid of," Trevor started but paused. "Actually, no, it's not."

Cocking a brow, I waited.

"I definitely hadn't planned to see him looking at you like that."

"Like what?"

It was Trevor's turn to cock a brow. "Seriously? You don't see it? I've been watching you two for weeks on the show and you're good. Real convincing. I think it's why so many are hooked on your story and keeping you until the end. But seeing you two together right in front of me was more than I was ready for."

I waved him off. "It's just habit now." No, I wouldn't let my heart get excited.

"It's more than that. You still look at him like he hung the moon, no doubt about that—you've got those same puppy dog eyes you've always had when it comes to Ivy—but he's different. I've never seen him look at anyone the way he looks at you. Never seen him so protective or connected—it's..." My brother clenched his jaw.

"Why are you so against us? Not that I think there's an *us*, but you've hated the idea since the beginning. If he *did* like me, if we *did* get together, would you hate it so much?"

Trevor shook his head. "Before I saw you two sitting there in your own little bubble, I would have said yes. I would have argued that you'd end up hurt. That Ivy doesn't do relationships. I would have felt like I'm losing my best friend, my little brother, or both."

"And now?"

"Now." Trevor paused and swallowed. "Now, I realize you're two of the biggest knuckleheads I've ever met and you both need to be honest with yourselves and each other."

"I really don't think he feels any kind of way about me other than a friend and hoping we can pull this off to win the game," I said, forcing the pitter-patter of my heart down a notch. I'd spent way too long reminding myself this was all fake, I wasn't going to let Trevor get my hopes up.

"Bro, I've known him for almost as long as you've been alive. He looks at you like he wants to eat you alive and wrap you in bubble wrap to protect you from everyone but him." Trevor shook his head. "Never would have guessed it—and maybe it's just you that's got him hooked—but all those girls in the past never stood a chance with the way he's tangled up in you."

"You really think so?" I whispered.

"I do."

"I can't—" I took a deep shuddery breath. "I can't mess up what we've got. We're close to winning. I can't change the rules now."

"I think you owe it to yourself and to him to tell him how you feel. You two decide what to do from there. But you've gotta be true to yourself and open with him. If I know Ivy the way I think I do, he'll *never* make the first move. In part, because he doesn't want to hurt you by getting all mixed up in his *I don't do love* mess. Also, because he doesn't want to change the rules. *And* because he's never fallen for a guy before, so he's out of his comfort zone. Hell, he's never *fallen* for *anyone* before. That's how I know he's gone for you—I've *never* seen him this way."

The door opened and Sassy and Stella galloped into the den to say hello. Trevor made them both sit, gave them each an ear rub, tossed them both a treat, and told them to go lay down.

I stood and stretched. "Gotta pee. Anybody need anything?"

"Grab some waters," Trevor said.

My mind raced a million miles a minute on my way to the bathroom. After washing my hands—and trying not to obsess over what Trevor had said—I grabbed waters and headed back to the den.

Ivy looked guilty and Trevor looked smug when I returned, but they quickly covered up whatever they'd been talking about and moved the conversation to neutral topics.

Trevor's recovery and therapy were going well. He'd started some work-from-home tasks to stay busy outside of appointments. Much to the doctor's surprise—but not to any of us—Trevor was about a week and half ahead of schedule. The doctor was pleased and said my brother was the perfect example of how to make therapy work for your recovery.

I didn't have a lot to say about work, but I told a few funny stories about some of my regulars and mishaps that happened each day. I was more interested in adding to the conversation when Ivy started talking about what he wanted to do with the shop.

"Little Bell has offered to help me get things up and running," Ivy said, taking my hand as if it was the most natural thing in the world.

"He's good at that kind of shit," Trevor said with a grin. "Schedules and organizing and numbers. Let him at it, he'll have things running like a well-oiled machine in no time."

Ivy talked about some things he'd been tinkering with on his car, the mouse nest he found in a car's undercarriage, and the potential jobs he could have Robby do if he hired the kid part time.

By the time we ate dinner with Trevor and my parents, I was ready to get home and anxious to talk to Ivy. I had no clue what I was going to say, but Trevor was right. I owed it to myself and to Ivy to be honest.

When we walked through the back door to the kitchen, Ivy huffed out a little chuckle. "I guess I might as well just give up on taking that shit down every time it pops up, huh?" He nodded toward the mistletoe. "I'm not saying it's holiday magic, but *someone* is damn determined to make sure we make out in every room of this house."

Moving to stand under the greenery, I pulled Ivy with me. "I'm not gonna complain."

Desire flashed across Ivy's face and he cupped the back of my neck. "Can't say I have anything to complain about either." His words were husky as he dropped his mouth to mine, his tongue tracing over my bottom lip and delving in to tease against mine when I opened for him.

Heat flamed in my belly. I wanted this man. Sexually, romantically, in any and every way I could get him. As our slick tongues glided together, Ivy's strong hand gripping the back of my neck, bits and pieces of what I wanted to say flitted through my head.

Be honest.

Tell him how you feel.

Don't mess this up.

Recalling the cameras spaced out around the house, I broke from the kiss and moved my lips to Ivy's ear. "What if I said I wanted to take this further than kissing for the camera?"

Ivy pulled back and studied my face, his cheeks flushed, breathing heavy. "Further how?" he asked in a low, gruff voice.

I glanced toward one of the cameras before whispering, "I want you, Ivy. I'm not trying to make things weird. I know you're not looking for a relationship. But we're together right now and even if it has to end, I don't want to say goodbye and know we never took advantage." Okay, that wasn't the complete truth. Damn it. I wanted to tell him exactly how I felt about him, but the words just couldn't overcome the fear. Not yet.

"Sex?" Ivy murmured.

"Whatever you want."

Ivy eyed the camera, ran a hand through his hair, and yanked me toward the stairs. Once in our bedroom, he closed and locked the door, and pushed me into a corner where we'd decided the cameras couldn't catch much. "You want to have sex? With me?"

For a moment, my world fell away. "I mean, if it's not something you want—"

Ivy gripped my wrist and pressed my palm against his erection. "Does this feel like something I don't want?" he growled against my lips. "I don't know what to make of it —maybe I should have been making out with guys long before this—but you get me all worked up like no one *ever*."

"You're just horny and missing out on sex," I said, wishing like hell I'd have the courage to make this more about my feelings for him instead of just the physical.

"No, little Bell," Ivy crooned against my ear. "If I was just horny, the thought of sex with *anyone* would turn me on. But the only person I want to get naked with right now is you." He huffed out a laugh. "Is that absolutely blowing my mind? Yes. Am I in the mood to question it? No."

"What do you want to do?" I asked, my cock threatening to burst behind my zipper.

"Everything? Baby steps? Something in between?" Ivy asked, a flash of uncertainty crossing his face. "I've never done this."

"You've gotten yourself off, right? You've gotten off with others," I said. "We can do that. Not saying I have much to go on, but I can promise my best effort." I bit my lip, suddenly petrified I'd screw something up.

Ivy cupped the side of my face, his eyes intense as he studied me. "We'll learn together."

God, my heart.

This man.

Tell him this is more than sex for you.

And have him balk because he's convinced he can't do anything involving a real relationship or resembling love?

No, thanks. Not at that moment.

Shifting from the corner, I grabbed t-shirts and tossed them over the cameras.

"You want to stand or lie down?" I asked, taking Ivy's hand.

"For what?"

"I want you in my mouth," I murmured at his ear, thrilling at the groan rumbling through his chest.

"Fuck, Em," he growled.

Taking control of the moment with a fake-it-til-you-make-it confidence, I pushed Ivy to the edge of the bed and hooked my thumbs under the waistband of his jeans. "Can I take these off?"

Ivy nodded. "Yeah. Fuck, you can do whatever you want." He palmed the back of my head and pulled me in for a long, slow kiss. My brain and cock short circuited as they fought to savor and begged to charge ahead.

I made quick work of the button and zipper, pushing

Ivy's jeans and underwear down his long, sinewy legs as his rock-hard cock bobbed. "Sorry if this—"

"Shut up," Ivy said as he kicked the jeans to the corner and stripped his shirt over his head. "If it involves my dick in your mouth, it will be amazing."

Chuckling, I pecked his lips before trailing kisses across the colorfully inked skin of his chest. I wanted to spend time exploring the designs, teasing his dark nipples, licking my way down his torso, but my cock strained in my jeans, already leaking. There'd be time for exploring later.

Hopefully.

Oh god, what if this was a one-and-done? What if it was horrible? What if Ivy freaked out?

"You don't have to do this," Ivy said.

His words pulled me from my thoughts. "I want to." *I've wanted to do this for years.* I dropped to my knees.

I'd given blow jobs.

They'd been few and far between.

And no promises on how good they were.

But this was Ivy.

Every single ounce of anxiety and anticipation pressed down on me.

Until he ran his ran his fingers through my hair, cupped my cheek, and gently removed my glasses.

His soft touch reassured and spurred me on.

With my hands on his hips, I nuzzled at the soft skin of his lower belly where red and black ink swirled. The hitch of his breath was a shot of courage. My thumbs ran over his V-lines as I flicked my tongue over his leaking slit.

Ivy hissed, his hand running through my hair again

before caressing my cheek with the back of his fingers. "Fuckin' gorgeous," he murmured.

Forgetting my anxiety, pushing aside how badly I wanted to tell him how I felt, I spread my lips around his plump cock head and took him deep. The sandalwood and sea salt scent I'd come to associate with Ivy tickled my nose as the unique flavor of his skin and pre-cum mixed on my tongue.

Ivy groaned as I bobbed my head up and down his shaft, his fingers loosely carding through my hair. When I cupped his balls, he grunted, gripping my hair tighter as I sucked him.

Losing myself in the moment, I savored the flavor of him bursting on my tongue. Before I knew what was happening, Ivy pulled from my mouth and grabbed my arm, pulling me to stand. "As fucking amazing as that is," he said, "I want more. Get naked before…"

"Before what?" I froze.

Ivy shook his head as if in awe, trying to understand something. "I was going to say *before I change my mind*, but that's not going to happen. Just get naked before I embarrass myself and come all over the place with nothing to show for it."

He helped me strip from my clothes and I stood shivering as his eyes and hands roamed over me. "You're gorgeous, Em. Lie down."

As if in a dream, my own Christmas miracle, I lay down on the bed, my cock smearing pre-cum all over my belly. Ivy kneed his way onto the mattress and moved to lie between my spread legs. "This okay?" he asked.

I nodded, the heavy warmth of his frame pressing

down on me was most definitely okay. The hot throb of our cocks coming together took my breath away.

"Words, Em. Is this okay?"

"God, yes," I choked out. "So good."

Holy.

Fucking.

Shit.

I was in bed, naked, cock-to-cock with Ivy.

Ivy.

Fucking.

Lane.

The one guy I'd swooned and lusted over for years.

My brother's best friend.

It was a dream. It had to be. Soon, I'd wake up and find I'd jizzed myself and it had all just been a dream.

"Wanna feel you come for me," Ivy murmured, rocking his hips and rutting his hard cock against mine. "Fuck, Em, you feel so good. Never felt this good."

His words went to my head. I knew Ivy liked sex with women—I'd heard him talk about it enough when he and Trevor were in the throes of their horny teen and young adult years—so hearing him say nothing had ever felt so good sent my ego soaring.

"Kiss me," I whispered. "Touch me." Absorbing his shiver as my nails raked down his back, I cupped Ivy's ass and pulled him close.

He growled, sealing his lips over mine and thrusting his tongue into my mouth in the same rhythm as his rocking hips. When his hand reached between us and stroked both our shafts, thumbing over our leaking cock heads and smearing our pre-cum together, I moaned.

Arching my back, I thrust my cock into his big, rough hand, our dicks hot and throbbing.

My hand cupped his balls, thrilling to find them drawn up as tight and ready to explode as my own. "Fuck, Ivy, I'm so close. Make me come," I begged against his lips.

"God damn, Em," he panted. "Fuck." A groan rumbled through his chest when I applied pressure to the sensitive strip of skin behind his balls. "Fuck, do that again."

We thrust and teased, stroking and rutting as we lost ourselves in the primal dance of two bodies seeking release. Then Ivy shifted, pushed my knees apart, and braced himself up on his hands to loom above me. His eyes raked over me, fiery as they took in my legs open for him, our leaking cocks pressed together. "Wanna see you come, see you covered in me," Ivy said.

He rocked his hips and my tight hole pulsed with need. This was good. This was enough. But god, how I wanted him driving into me. Pulling my eyes from Ivy's, I glanced at the mirror where I watched his long, lean body thrust over and over. The slick, hot friction of our cocks rutting together built into an inferno.

"Jack yourself," Ivy demanded.

With a whimper, I gripped my dick and stroked. Ivy caught my chin and kissed me, fucking into my mouth before he whispered, "Let me see you come."

That was all it took. Release barreled through me and I cried out as long, thick ropes of white painted my stomach. Ivy groaned and shifted to his knees, fisting his cock and pumping, his eyes never leaving mine as he stroked.

With a grunt, his head thrown back, Ivy shot his load

all over my chest, mixing with my cum in a pattern I couldn't help but swirl my fingers through.

"Fuck." Ivy huffed out a breath and lowered himself to press our chests together. "Fuuuuck," he moaned.

"Is that a good fuck or bad fuck?" I asked, trying to sound light and easy, but my heart threatening to claw its way out of my chest.

Please don't let this go bad.

Please don't let this go bad.

Please—

"Fuck, little Bell, that was amazing," Ivy mumbled into my neck. "Plus, two birds, one stone."

"Huh?"

"We scratched an itch—a rash I didn't even know I had which is still blowing my mind—*and* gave the audience more of what they wanted. Cameras might have been covered, but they'll get the gist."

Tell him, you idiot.

Pushing aside the thought, ignoring the way my heart ached for something more than a show with Ivy, I ran my fingers through the back of his hair. "Yeah, hopefully got us some more votes," I mumbled. "Letty's gonna be pissed we covered the cameras."

"Let her be pissed."

"I need to shower and we probably need to look at info for the next challenge."

"Go for it. Once I get feeling back in my legs, I'll do the same. I'm calling it an early night tonight, got an appointment first thing." Ivy shifted from on top of me to my side, his face still buried in my neck, hand absently running up and down my arm. "You still gonna help me tomorrow?"

"Yep, I've got breakfast shift and then I'm all yours."

Ivy hummed and trailed his hand down to my hip.

By the time I dragged myself to the bathroom for a quick shower—my head a jumbled mess of *what the fuck happens now* and *what did any of that mean*—and returned to the bedroom, Ivy had cleaned my glasses. He smiled as he kissed my nose and slipped them on my face.

While he showered, I ran downstairs to fix a bowl of ice cream. Doubling up on the scoops because Ivy would *say* he didn't want any and then take bites of mine, I couldn't help but smile and hum Christmas songs as I worked. After checking the doors were all locked, I made my way through the living room. Giggling at the creepy nutcracker—the thing really did look like it was watching you—I paused at the little snow globe. The tiny house—like the real one—was dark except for the glow from the upstairs window.

"I don't know how this whole Christmas magic works, but keep it up, please," I whispered. "That man is everything I've ever wanted all rolled into one gorgeous, fucked-up package. I just need him to realize we're better together than apart."

A rush of warm air in the room sent shivers through me and I grinned before taking a big bite of ice cream. A draft? Maybe. But I was choosing to believe it was the holiday spirit giving me a thumbs up.

"Em?" Ivy called from upstairs.

We spent the rest of our evening tucked into bed, eating ice cream, pacifying a shitty Letty, and planning for our next challenges.

CHAPTER 11

IVY

THE MORNING AFTER EMORY TOTALLY BLEW MY mind, we woke up tangled together like normal. But there was something new and different between us.

Trying my best to ignore the weird twist in my heart *and* my best friend's words from the day before, I ran my hand down Emory's bare chest and kissed his neck. This could be easy and fun, no strings, no worries, no big deal.

Except you know *it's something more, just admit it.*

I couldn't admit it.

Couldn't even let myself go there.

I had no idea how to *do* something more than easy and fun.

I especially had no idea what to do with the thought of falling for a guy.

Not just *a guy*, my best friend's little brother.

"We good?" Emory's sleepy voice asked as he shifted his perfect little ass against my morning wood. "Didn't get weird over night? You're not freaking out?"

"Surprisingly, no," I answered. Freaking out over the

feelings swirling in my gut? Yeah, for sure. But I could keep ignoring those. Right?

Freaking out about being wildly attracted to Emory?

No.

Honestly, I'd never given a lot of thought to my sexuality, but finding myself so damn drawn to Emory hadn't thrown me for a loop as much as I would've guessed. Maybe because I'd known him for so long. Maybe because we'd had time to bond long before anything got physical. Maybe because the need to fake a relationship forced us into a more intimate connection than I likely would have ever let happen for real.

And now I found myself completely obsessed with Emory Shae Bell.

To the point I wanted him around at all times.

Not like crazy stalker obsessed. I just enjoyed his company. Things were so easy between us.

Good.

Things were good.

I was content in a way I hadn't been in...well, ever since my dad left.

Which meant a ripple of unease teased at the edge of my mind.

Nothing ever stayed good.

Something always happened.

Which was why I had to ignore the fluttery, romantic feelings toward Emory and any hint of giving things between us a shot.

I knew better than that and I wouldn't put Emory through the shit of getting involved with me.

"Wanna give the audience something to talk about?" Emory asked, pressing into me again.

"Not gonna turn that down," I murmured before sucking on his earlobe. Sliding my hand down his abdomen, I slipped under the waist of his underwear. "Can I take these off?"

Emory shimmied the boxer briefs down his legs before groping behind him to yank at my underwear. "Touch me." His breathless words were punctuated by desperate thrusting and I loved how quickly things could go from simmering to boiling hot between us.

My hand wrapped around his hard cock and we both moaned when my throbbing dick pressed between his ass cheeks.

"Do you wanna..." Emory panted.

"Yes," I gasped. "Not now, but yes." My cock leaked into his crack. "Fuck, yes."

"Make me come," Emory demanded, his bossiness sending a jolt of desire straight to my dick.

Glancing at the cameras, recalling Letty demanding we uncover them last night, I rolled on top of Emory just enough to reach the drawer and fumble around. The first bottle I found was eucalyptus menthol rub from the last time I had a head cold.

Fuck no.

Cuticle cream.

What? I worked with my hands in grease all day, sometimes my cuticles got nasty and needed some attention.

Where was the damn lube?

Chapstick.

Nope.

Lotion.

I'd take it.

Grabbing the bottle, I pulled the covers up over our heads so the cameras wouldn't get anything but filtered shots of moving blankets.

Snapping open the lid, I squeezed a glob of lotion onto my hand before coating my cock generously. I'd had sex with a girl like this my first time and I knew getting off without penetration could be just as good if not better.

Not that I didn't want to be inside Emory.

God, it had quickly become a repeat fantasy for me, but I didn't want our first time to be audience fodder.

So, you're planning on there being more than one time? Continuing things after the show?

"Keep your legs together," I whispered, smearing lotion between Emory's thighs just under his ass. Tossing the lotion to the side, I took hold of my cock and pressed into the tight juncture of Emory's legs. The fleshy globes of his ass surrounded me as I pressed forward, the head of my cock sliding across his taint and bumping against his balls. "This okay?"

Emory groaned. "Fuck," he panted. "Yeah."

"Try to stay quiet unless you want a soundtrack of our bedroom noises to go viral," I murmured. Reaching for his dick, I wrapped my hand around his hot, throbbing flesh and stroked in time to my shaft thrusting between his legs.

Emory whimpered, his sex sounds—and knowing I was one of the only men to ever touch him like this— spurred me on. "Fuck, Ivy." Reaching back, his hand gripped my ass, pulling me deeper, his legs clenching tightly around me.

The thought of pressing into his tight hole had my rhythm faltering and my cock leaking pre-cum on every pass along his balls. With one hand clutching at his chest, teasing a pebbled nipple, and the other stroking his dick, I rocked into him over and over.

As his balls drew up tight and the tingle started at the base of my spine, I pressed my lips along his jawline. "Kiss me."

An act I'd avoided with women had suddenly become something I adored with Emory. Capturing his mouth with mine when he turned his head, I teased his lips open and feasted on his tongue, swallowing his whimpery moans as he got closer to his release.

Knowing we didn't have long to savor this new development between us—the game and our situation weren't going to last forever—and hearing my brain and dick chanting, "Do. All. The. Dirty. Sexy. Things."—all while *knowing* it was for the best to take a step back and slow down, my synapses glitched right as images of sucking and fucking Emory flashed in my head. My orgasm barreled through me and I groaned into Emory's mouth, my cock pulsing my load onto his balls, taint, and thighs.

Emory's body tensed and his dick throbbed in my hand, his warm, slick release spurting over my fingers as he came, shuddering against me.

We lay together, panting and breathing harshly until I *had* to move the covers from our heads in order to catch my breath and get fresh air.

"Fuck," Emory whispered.

"Agreed."

"Sheets are gonna need washed."

I laughed. "Correct."

"We good?"

"So good."

"We should get up. We've got five hundred thousand dollars to win," Emory mused.

"That we do."

But we just lay there in our lotion-y, sticky mess, our skin damp with sweat, our hearts beating in the same erratic rhythm as we savored the high and slowly came back to earth.

"Are we doing this just for the viewers?" Emory asked quietly.

I could have lied. It would have hurt, but it would have been easier. Instead, I pressed a kiss to his neck. "It's not just for the viewers, at least not for me."

Had he not been pressed against me, our breathing in sync after mutual orgasms, I likely would have missed the tiny sigh escaping his lips. Relief? Dismay? I couldn't tell.

"It's not for me, either," Emory murmured.

Why did that tidbit thrill me so much?

I wasn't supposed to want Emory to feel any sort of way about me.

Because I wasn't supposed to feel any sort of way about him.

Unbidden, Trevor's words from the day before came roaring to mind.

"How long have you been in love with my little brother?" he'd asked with an intensity I recognized as protective and apprehensive mixed with amused and excited.

I'd started to protest, glancing over my shoulder at where Emory had disappeared to use the restroom and grab waters, but the look in my best friend's eyes told me there was no use.

"I don't know, man," I'd sighed. "It wasn't something I planned. Didn't see it coming. But it happened and I don't know what the hell to do with it." My entire body melted with the words, like five hundred pounds had been building up pressure inside me and admitting I felt something for Emory was the release valve.

Not that admitting it solved anything, but still.

"What do you mean, you don't know what to do with it?" Trevor had asked. "You lean into it. You let him know how you feel. You don't give up this chance to find love."

"I don't do love—" I'd started.

"Bullshit. Maybe it's not something you've done before, but I've seen the way you look at him. You don't need perfect, madly in love parents with the best marriage ever for you to fall in love with someone. If I didn't think you could love him, we'd be having a very different conversation right now. But I know you and I see it in your eyes. You're in love with him. Whatever you do, don't string him along, don't make him doubt himself, and don't wait too long. Because I love you, but I will hurt you if you hurt him."

"I thought you were against anything happening between him and me?"

"No, I was against my little brother getting his heart broken by a life-long crush and unreciprocated love," Trevor had said. "Seeing you two together changes all of that. But get your head out of your ass and listen to your heart."

His words played on a loop in my head as my hand trailed up and down Emory's chest. Trevor wasn't *wrong*, but he also didn't get it. He hadn't grown up the way I did. Hadn't experienced the lack of love between my parents even before my shithead dad walked out on us for a whole other family.

That kind of shit did things to a person.

I wouldn't get Emory tangled up in my shit.

Even if it meant enjoying what we had for the time being and then saying goodbye when the game ended.

Emory deserved more.

He deserved better.

Not to brag, but Emory and I sailed through Week Five's vote. The show said goodbye to Bridgette and Claire, the couple with the little bungalow outside of Chicago. The comments we were allowed to see said the women just weren't making an impression anymore and were too forgettable.

And damn, if that didn't give us a kick in the ass to make sure we were memorable.

The remaining couples were Jackson and Andy, friends-with-benefits from South Carolina.

Cody and Jackie, the hipsters from San Francisco.

Sarah and Dean, the new parents and goat farmers in North Dakota.

Rae and Mallory, the two women from Texas.

And Ivy and Bell, obviously.

"Ready for your challenges for Week Six?" Letty asked as the cameras started rolling. She grinned widely and winked, but only really managed to look like her eye had a twitch and smeared lipstick on her teeth. She was really pretty and a major personality, but she desperately needed to figure out a lipstick that worked better on her mouth. "Let's do this, okay? Okay."

We had a partial idea of the challenges coming our way since Letty had given a head's up, but the After Dark *spicier* challenges were a wild card.

"The *Once Upon a Christmas House* challenge this week is to take each other on a date you think the other would enjoy—bonus points if it's something that person has never done," Letty explained.

This would be easy since we'd had time to think about it. I knew for certain I was taking Emory to get a massage because it was something neither of us had done before—I wasn't super pumped, but it couldn't be *that* bad if people got massages all the time and enjoyed them.

I wasn't one hundred percent sure, but I had a pretty good idea of what Emory had planned. I figured we could make a full day of it and I was already looking forward to spending the day with him.

You two could spend every day together if you'd just admit you've fallen for him and tell him how you feel.

Except doing that would set us up for the inevitable break up.

Why? Are you your father?

Fuck that shit. I wasn't a cheater. I wasn't the type to get into a loveless marriage and then leave my kids behind.

I pinched the bridge of my nose trying to stop the thoughts, my keychain clacking away.

To be fair, it wasn't like your dad planned any of that. He and your mom likely never should have gotten married.

Yeah, well, he shouldn't have cheated and run off to his new family either.

Emory's hand warmed my thigh where he touched and gave a little squeeze.

"We've got some ideas, I think." I heard Emory's words and realized I'd spaced out. Good thing they could edit that shit.

"How about the After Dark challenge? Let's do this, okay? Okay." Letty made a big production of opening an envelope. "The After Dark audience challenges you—if you choose to accept it—to do something *spicy* you've never done together."

My mind immediately filled with a conglomerate of all the sexy things Emory and I had never done together.

"So, let's talk about the way this is going to work, okay? Okay," Letty said. "The audience has submitted a few ideas and we've categorized them into Spicy, Spicier, and Spiciest. You're both going to add a few suggestions to the categories. You'll each draw from one category of your choice—the spicier the category, the higher the point values. After you each have one challenge, you'll decide together which category to draw from for your third." She held up a hand. "Now, we'd like to remind you that no contestants are required to participate in *any* challenge and After Dark is no exception. You can choose to earn points and votes through our regular challenges only, or you can spice things up with the After Dark challenges. However, once you commit to the challenges, you will be expected to complete them barring any religious constraints, physical limitations, or medical conditions."

Letty handed us each small cardstock pieces and a marker.

"You can each write one suggestion for each category. Spicy, Spicier, Spiciest. We'll give you five minutes, okay?

Okay." She smiled and winked. "Oh, and no one will know if the items you draw out were suggested by the audience or one of you—unless *you* wrote the challenge."

Holy shit.

There were so many things we could do.

What was already in each category from the audience?

What would Emory write?

Should I go with something super simple to make the points easy to get? Or go for something I *really* wanted to do with Emory that would make the points totally worth it?

Dying to glance over at what Emory was writing, but knowing Letty was watching like a hawk, I quickly scribbled one thing on each card, folded them, and dropped them in the Spicy, Spicier, and Spiciest buckets before handing the marker back to Letty.

Emory followed suit about thirty seconds later and snuggled into my side when I put my arm around him. "This is nerve-wracking," he whispered.

"We can stick to the regular challenges," I offered.

Letty motioned to one of the crew to grab the buckets, but she cocked a brow in our direction. "Well, boys, what will it be? Are we getting spicy with After Dark or sticking to the tamer challenges?"

Emory took my hand and kissed my knuckles. "Spicy?" he asked, those big brown eyes blinking at me innocently from behind his lenses.

I grinned and kissed his nose. "What the hell, might as well."

"Let's do this, okay? Okay," Letty said. "Three picks. Here we go."

CHAPTER 12

EMORY

"EMORY, YOU PICK FIRST," LETTY SAID.

I glanced at Ivy, wishing we'd had time to discuss our picks beforehand. He just nodded and gave me a little grin.

I reached into the bucket labeled *Spicy*.

Opening the folded piece of cardstock, I read, "Dance naked together." Feeling like a kid caught reading a dirty word, I snorted and my cheeks burned. "Well, that should be fun." I winked and hoped my voice wasn't as breathy as it sounded in my own ears.

"Spicy," Letty teased. "Okay, Ivy, your turn. Spicy, Spicier, or Spiciest?"

With his eyes locked on mine, Ivy reached into the *Spicier* bucket.

My breath caught in my chest when he opened the folded paper and a brow shot up. "Well?"

"Watch porn together," he read, his voice like gravel.

"Well, things just got *spicier*." Letty fanned herself and laughed obnoxiously. "Okay, gentlemen, one more pick.

Which will it be? Remember, the spicier the bucket, the higher the points."

Ivy and I turned to face each other. Did he have visions of naked dancing and porn galloping through his head the same as me?

"Whatdya think?" he asked.

"I'm onboard with any of them, but one from all three would round things out nicely," I said with a shrug, trying not to seem too anxious and excited about the challenges we were now committed to. "Can't say I'm not curious what *Spiciest* might hold."

"Let's do it," Ivy said, putting his arm around my waist and pulling me close as he pressed a kiss against my head.

"Going for the Triple Spice," Letty exclaimed. "Here we go, okay? Okay." She gestured for us to draw.

"Go for it," I said with a nod toward the bucket.

Ivy reached into the bucket labeled *Spiciest* and handed me a folded card.

I took a deep breath, bit my lip, and opened it up. "Do something sexual that's outside of your norm."

The possibilities were endless, but in reality, none of the challenges were going to be super hard. Dancing naked was maybe outside of our comfort zone, but only because it wasn't something we'd done together. Watching porn together would be easy—unless Ivy wanted to watch straight porn. *Something sexual outside of your norm* was likely meant to get super creative, but I hadn't done a whole lot in the bedroom and Ivy had never had sex with a guy, so finding something outside of our norm was going to be a cinch.

But the audience didn't need to know that.

"Well, it looks as if you have your challenges. Let's go

out there and win this game, okay? Okay," Letty enthused, lipstick staining her teeth as she winked dramatically.

The camera crew packed up.

Letty reminded us of the cameras around the house and insinuated she'd march over here and uncover the bedroom cameras herself if we covered them again, and then we were alone.

I slipped into Ivy's work boots and his hoodie and followed him out to the shop. As he got busy on an oil change, I brought paperwork and the laptop into the bay to chat with him as we both worked.

"Did you put in any of the ones we picked?" I asked.

"No, you?"

I shook my head. My suggestions had involved a shower, getting off in his car, and toys. "What did you put in there?"

Ivy threw a smirk over his shoulder. "I'll never tell."

"You realize these challenges are going to be pretty easy, right?"

He chuckled. "Yeah. Pretty sure the audience thinks they're making us get super creative when in reality pretty much anything would meet the requirements."

"Right," I said with a snort. "So, I already called for our massages and pedicures."

"I figured you were going to go with pedicures," Ivy said, his ass looking delicious as he bent over the hood of the vehicle he was servicing. "When are we going?"

"Tomorrow." I waved the appointment book. "You've only got two on the books, so we'll get those in and out and then make a whole day of our dates."

"Sounds fun. Maybe end the day dancing naked?" Ivy waggled his brow.

"Can we dance to Christmas songs next to the tree?"

"No."

Laughing, I slid off the workbench. "You're no fun. I'm going to finish these in the office and then look at some of those applications we got. I've got a couple hours at the café, but I'll be home around five. Wanna do dinner at six?"

"Sounds good. You want to cook or have something delivered?"

I wrinkled my nose. "Um, is that even really a question?"

After a long day of working on shop things and bustling around the café, I was grateful to get home knowing we had pizza, breadsticks, and a two-liter of Coke being delivered.

I finished my shower before Ivy came in to get cleaned up.

With nothing pressing to do, we spent the rest of the evening cuddled up by the fire watching two of the few Christmas movies Ivy would admit to enjoying.

He just shook his head when I pointed out the snow globe house was lit up differently than it was the night before, insisting it was just the way the fire cast shadows.

He made out with me on the couch, our kisses tasting of cola and red sauce, but just rolled his eyes when I gestured to the mistletoe that continued to magically appear in doorways no matter how many times he griped and tossed the greenery in the trash.

With visions of massages and pedicures dancing in my head, we settled into bed late that night. Just like breathing, I shifted comfortably into Ivy's embrace and sighed into his chest.

I love this.

I love him.

You need to tell him.

Trevor's words came back to me. My brother was right. I did need to tell Ivy how I felt—tell him what we were doing meant more to me than just faking it for the cameras. I'd admitted the sex we'd had wasn't *just* for the cameras, but I hadn't been honest about the depth of my feelings and wanting more with him.

How would Ivy react?

I was pretty sure I knew, and I couldn't blame him. He'd been nothing but up front and honest from the very beginning. He wasn't in this for anything more than winning the game. He wasn't looking for love. He didn't *do* love. Hell, he didn't even do relationships.

The fact the man I'd thought was straight my whole life was attracted to me enough to bring me into his bed and give me the best experience of my twenty-three years as we competed our way through the game was beyond what I'd ever even hoped for.

I wasn't sure I wanted to push my luck by telling Ivy I wanted more.

Drifting off to sleep, I told myself to just enjoy the ride and prepare my heart for picking up the pieces when it came to an end.

Our massages were absolute bliss.

Lavender scented the air. Soft music played. The sound of a bubbling fountain soothed. Ivy cocked a brow at the robes, but he shucked out of his clothes and wrapped himself in the cottony softness as if he'd given himself over to being pampered.

Mila and Anton were a husband and wife massage therapist team and they earned every single bit of their fee and tip. With the heads of our heated beds pushed close enough Ivy could take my hand in his, Mila and Anton applied warm massage oil and went to work on our backs.

Over the next hour, I floated blissfully in and out of consciousness, my awareness tethered to Ivy with the caress of his thumb against my knuckles. I loved that Mila and Anton kept Ivy and I connected even when we rolled to our backs. For me, the best part of the whole experience—outside of just the extreme relaxation and spending time with Ivy—was when they worked on my feet, my hands, and my head. Seriously, top-level feel-good shit right there.

As we got dressed at the end of our session, Ivy agreed he liked the hands and head, but his favorite had been his neck and back. Which probably made sense because he was often bent over cars for long periods of time.

"I feel all doped up," Ivy said, his eyes heavy. "Like I could take you home, wrap us in a blanket, and sleep for eight hours straight."

"Nothing stopping us once we're home." I quickly sent the short snippet of our massages I'd had Mila take on my phone to Letty for the crew to edit into show footage. Ivy and I had refused when the show wanted a camera person to go to the massage with us.

We tipped Mila and Anton in the little jar they placed in the room, pulled on our jackets, and headed out with the bottles of water they'd instructed us to drink.

"Wanna get smoothies before I embarrass myself at the

pedicure place?" Ivy asked nodding his head toward the new little health spot in Peppermint Hollow.

I chuckled as we popped into the smoothie place. As we waited for our smoothies—mine an Orange Pineapple Mango Vitamin C Immune Booster and Ivy's a Strawberry Pineapple Banana with Greek Yogurt—I caught two separate people eyeing us.

The first was a lady and her husband who both gave us the stink eye, huffed while mumbling something about people needing to find God, and stuck their noses in the air as they walked on by with their purchases.

The second was a woman with a baby on her hip. She blushed when she realized she'd been caught watching us. "I really hope you guys win," she said, smiling as the baby cooed and screeched in greeting when I waved to the cutie. "My boyfriend and I have been watching from the beginning and you've been our favorite the whole time. He wants to make an appointment for an oil change at your shop."

Ivy gave his usual nod with a brief smile. "That would be great, we'd love to have you." He wasn't one to be overly effervescent when talking to people he didn't know.

I pulled a business card from my pocket. "Be sure to call and set something up. Thanks for watching—we appreciate your votes."

Her order was called and she gave a quick wave, boosted the baby on her hip, and grabbed her drink before darting out the door.

"You just ignore that first couple," the guy behind the counter said. "She's an old biddy and her husband is just as bad. They go to my church and we're about over their hatefulness." He placed our smoothies on the counter.

"Now, I know you can't talk about the show, but I want you to know that most of this town is cheering for you. You've been doing us proud every week and we're rooting for you to win that money."

We thanked the guy and walked out.

"Does it bother you?" I asked.

"What?"

"The people who hate on anyone different than them? Aside from the nasty looks I'd guess you sometimes get about the tattoos, you probably haven't ever dealt with hateful looks and comments about the person you're with." I sipped my smoothie. "Sorry about that. I guess it's something we knew would be an issue when we started this, but today was kinda the first time we saw it. I feel bad pulling you into it—I hope it doesn't fuck up your reputation in town."

Ivy snorted. "First, my reputation in town has been that of the broody, holiday-hating, quiet mechanic for years. Before that, I was the sad, angry kid from the fucked-up family. Being seen with you—people assuming I'm bi or whatever—isn't going to hurt my reputation. Plus, you know I've never been one to worry about what people think of me. That old lady's comment almost makes me want to take you to the center of town and make out to see how many homophobes we can pull out of the woodwork."

I chuckled. "We could...or we could just go get our pedicures and not try to stir up trouble."

"Boring," Ivy teased. "But okay."

We walked a bit farther. "I guess it's nice to know that more of the town is on our side than against it," I said.

"I'm going to feel really bad if we don't win and let them down."

"Is it kinda weird to know that everyone in town knows our business and what we've been getting up to?" Ivy asked, wrinkling his nose as he took a sip. "Don't get me wrong, I know I just said I don't give a damn what people think about me—and I don't—but knowing that old guy behind the counter has watched a filtered shadow of us in the bedroom and just made our smoothies is kinda surreal."

"Agreed. Hell, that guy's probably posting in the comments section right now that we both got pineapple in our smoothies."

Ivy threw his head back and laughed. "That man was older than your parents. You think he knows the significance of pineapple and sex?"

I joined in with his amusement. "You never know. And just so you know, I got pineapple because I like it, not because I'm making assumptions about anything."

Ivy bumped his hip against mine. "I like pineapple too. But we both know where naked dancing is going to lead," he whispered in my ear as we walked into the nail place.

Great.

Having a boner while getting a pedicure was going to be a new experience.

Hmmmm, should I let Letty know so we could earn more points?

Five minutes later, I bit my lip as I eyed Ivy's shapely calves sprinkled with crinkly dark hair and colorful ink. We both had the legs of our joggers pushed up and our feet soaking in warm water as we sipped our drinks.

"I could fall asleep," Ivy murmured, his eyes closed

and head leaned back as the massage chair worked up and down his back. "You may have created a monster—I'm thinking I need a foot rub every night."

"I gotchu," I said, smiling dreamily as the warm water bubbled around my ankles. "We can trade off. Don't forget my hands."

We fell silent as our feet soaked. Just as I thought I'd drift off to sleep, our nail techs rolled their stools over and turned off the foot bath water.

For the next thirty minutes, they clipped, trimmed, filed, and exfoliated. Ivy's feet weren't in great shape, but I knew they'd definitely seen worse. He wiggled in his seat as they used a pumice stone on him and I couldn't help but tease him about being ticklish.

"Shut up," he groused. "I don't think anyone has ever touched my feet like this until today." He turned wide eyes my way. "Maybe we can get extra points."

We both cracked up laughing and I took pictures and video to send to Letty.

By the time the nail techs had lotioned us up and treated us to hot towels, our smoothies were gone. We declined any color on our toes and slipped our buffed and shiny nails back into our socks and shoes before paying and making our way out the door.

"Well," I hedged.

Ivy tossed his cup in the trash and threw an arm around my neck. "Fine. I can admit the massages were great and the pedicure was nice. If it wasn't almost Christmas in the Midwest, I'd be willing to wear some slides because my feet look pretty decent for the first time in thirty years."

I pumped a fist. "Score. Now you know you like

massages and pedicures. When this is all over, you can keep it up. Self-care is important." The words were forced around the huge lump in my throat, but I meant them. I wanted Ivy to take care of himself when we went our separate ways.

He didn't answer for a long while, just tightened his arm around my neck as we walked. Finally, he mumbled, "Yeah, maybe."

With our muscles feeling like Jell-O, we made our way home.

"Dance then movie in bed? Or nap and then dance later?" I asked.

"If I get in bed for a nap, I'm probably never getting out," Ivy said. "I say we dance and then take food to bed for a movie and early night."

"Perfect. You get a song ready and I'll put food together. I think dancing in the bedroom is best since the cameras down here aren't filtered."

"Yeah, last thing I want is to broadcast this perfect ass of yours for the world to see," Ivy teased, swatting at my butt as I walked toward the kitchen.

"Never know, might bring in new business for the shop." I swayed my hips, laughing as I walked to the kitchen.

A bit later, I made my way upstairs balancing a tray filled with apples, peanut butter, mixed nuts, granola bars, protein drinks, and waters.

I found Ivy perched on the side of the bed, stripped to just his underwear, scrolling through his phone. "Looking for a song," he muttered.

The air was damp and scented with Ivy's signature sandalwood and sea salt. "Did you shower?"

Ivy nodded. "Yeah, wanted to get the oil off. Go ahead."

I rushed through a shower and slipped on my sexiest underwear before joining Ivy on the bed. "May I have this dance?" I teased, holding out my hand.

He took my hand and pulled me to stand. "I think we're supposed to be naked. You know, for the challenge."

"Right, for the challenge," I teased, biting my lip in anticipation of our nude dancing as we stripped from our underwear. "Naked challenges are weird. Nothing like the most unspontaneous situation possible," I said, shivering in the cool room. "What song did you pick?"

"'You and Me' by Lifehouse," Ivy said.

I cocked my head. "Random or specific?"

He smiled. "I remember that song playing around the time my dad left. I think I liked it before he dropped his bomb and then, after, it was like salt in a wound. But something about the song—some of the lyrics—remind me of you." He shrugged. "Figured I might as well make it a better memory."

"I don't think I know it," I said, cocking my head to listen as he pressed play and placed the phone on the dresser

Ivy chuckled. "You would have been like five when it came out."

As the first strains of the song played, I realized I did recognize it. Stepping into Ivy's arms, I tucked myself into his warmth as the music and lyrics washed over me. It was a pretty song and I let myself savor the gentle sway of our bodies, the protective strength of Ivy wrapped around me.

The song ended, Ivy and I lost in our own little bubble.

Set to repeat, the music started again and I made myself listen to the lyrics closer the second time. By the third time the song played, our dicks had definitely gotten impatient with the dancing, but my head and heart kept getting stuck on a few specific lines in the song.

The song hit me right in the gut. Ivy hummed along, singing bits and pieces about words tripping him up, his head spinning, and not knowing where to go.

The lines of the song reflected perfectly how mixed up I was over Ivy.

Can't keep my eyes off of him?
Check.
Something about him?
Definitely.
Beautiful? Right?
Yes and yes.

As the lyrics played, describing how I felt about the man holding me, I squeezed my eyes shut and sank back into the blissful warmth of Ivy's arms. "I like this song." Running my hands up and down Ivy's back, I smiled into his chest as he gently rocked his hips into me. *I like you. I like this. I want it to be real. I'm not asking for forever, but can't we give it a go?*

As the song looped, Ivy pulled back just enough to take my face in his hands and press a kiss to my lips. "Your glasses need cleaned," he whispered. "Later." He slipped the frames off and placed them next to his phone. And then he was on me, the kiss starting slowly, but growing hot and desperate. "Fuck, you do things to me," Ivy murmured against my lips.

"And oh, the things I want to do to you." I pulled his bottom lip between my teeth, loving the way Ivy growled.

He gripped my hips, pulling me flush against him, pressing our hard cocks together.

"Show me," Ivy demanded.

I glanced toward the cameras.

Ivy grumbled, let go of me long enough to toss underwear over one blinking red light and a t-shirt over the other. He made short work of locking the door and put both of our phones on mute. In record time, he was back, taking me in his arms and kissing me. "Show me what you want to do."

Like a kid being given permission to do something he never thought he'd be allowed to do, I spun Ivy around, pushed him to the mattress, and crawled between his legs.

"Fuck." Ivy's chest heaved and his cock smeared pre-cum against the dark line of hair on his lower abdomen.

Taking his cock in my hand, I flicked my tongue over his leaking slit. "Is this okay?"

"Fuck."

Cocking a brow, I said. "Not sure if that's a yes or no."

"Yes," he panted. "Fuck, yes."

Gripping his dick, I lowered my mouth over him and took him deep. Well, as deep as one could when one had very little experience with giving head. Baby steps were appreciated by my gag reflex. An expert deep-throater I was not, but I damn sure was going to give it my all.

Especially if it made Ivy moan and buck his hips the way he was each and every time I stroked up and down, my tongue caressing the underside of his dick.

"Fuck, Em," Ivy growled. "You look so damn good." Propped on an elbow, watching me suck him off, he ran a hand through my hair. Blown pupils, lips puffy from our kisses, chest heaving, Ivy was a man on the edge of bliss. "Fuck."

"What?" I popped off, his pre-cum and my spit glistening on my fist.

"Can we...I want..." Ivy took a breath and glanced toward the ceiling. "I wanna taste you."

Trying not to make a big deal of the fact my fake boyfriend—who I'd fallen head-over-heels with and assumed was straight my whole life—wanted my dick in his mouth, I quickly picked my jaw up from the mattress and swallowed thickly. "Yeah, sure. Sixty-nine?"

"It's a number I'm familiar with," he said with a grin, "just more tabs than slots this time around." Ivy sat up and bent to kiss me. "I apologize now if I blow down your throat in thirty seconds."

"Same."

Our struggles to get into a doable position was absolute proof-positive that porn was a production and not the same as what us normal people dealt with. But the rush of desire that washed through me when we opted for stretching out on our sides and Ivy's arm came around my waist to pull me close was possibly as close to perfection as I'd ever get.

I took his cock between my lips, savoring his salty bitterness and praying I didn't explode before he even got his mouth on me.

A whoosh of breath escaped me when Ivy ran his tongue over my slit. I pulled off his cock to watch when he swirled his tongue around my cock head. But when he sucked me between his stretched lips, I knew I was dreaming.

There was no way the guy I'd crushed on for *years*, my

big brother's best friend, had his mouth on my dick. No way his cock leaked and bobbed enticingly right in front of my face. On the off chance I wasn't dreaming, I tongued his shaft and took him as deep as I could without gagging.

Holy shit.

Talk about a fucked mash-up of my poor synapses.

My mouth and tongue fought to savor the moment while begging to tease and taste, to take his hot load and swallow it down.

My hips wanted to thrust, to fuck into his mouth until I fell over the edge of that cliff.

My dick and balls pleaded for release, begged to unload and make Ivy's mouth mine.

And all of this happened at once, my brain and body a jumbled mess of sensation and want.

When Ivy's hand caressed my ass, his fingers skimming between my cheeks and pressing against my hole, I lost it. My orgasm came quickly, rocking me from head to toe as my cock pumped my load between Ivy's lips. I wanted to apologize, wanted to tell him I was sorry for coming in his mouth if he didn't want it, but his dick between my lips kept me quiet—or as quiet as one can be when sucking off his crush and jizzing his brains out.

The frantic thrusting of his hips and pulsing of his cock were the only warning I got before Ivy exploded. Hot, thick spurts coated my tongue and I swallowed to keep it from leaking out of my mouth.

When the extreme explosions of pleasure waned, we each let the other's spent dick slip from our mouths. Ivy nuzzled his nose against the sensitive skin of my groin, his hand caressing my ass.

"Letty's gonna kill us," I murmured.

Ivy chuckled. "Yeah, but what a damn fine way to go." He shifted and moved so we were both lying with our heads by the headboard.

I automatically cuddled under his arm and we spent the next several moments riding out the last wisps of bliss.

"I think I liked that challenge," I said, softly rubbing my fingers through the smattering of hair on Ivy's chest.

Ivy snorted.

"Was it okay?" I asked, hating the doubt in my voice.

He jerked his gaze to mine and gripped my chin. "Are you fucking kidding me right now? That was fucking amazing. All of it. Maybe I'm a selfish prick, but I like that I'm one of the few you've ever done that with."

"Had you done it before?" I thought I knew the answer, but I had this deep need to know Ivy had enjoyed every second of what we'd done.

Ivy ran fingers up and down my arm for a few moments before answering. "No. Never really thought too much about it."

"So, why me?"

Quiet again for several heartbeats, Ivy sighed. "Why you. That seems to be the question." He pressed a kiss against my head. "I don't know. You make me want things I didn't know I wanted. You make me crazy, craving you in a way I never thought I'd *need* a person."

Tell him.

Tell him right now.

Ask him if things between you could maybe be more than just a fake set up to win a game.

But the moment passed when Ivy's stomach growled.

"Hungry? I brought up snacks."

Ivy got a wet cloth and cleaned us up while I spread out the food and found a movie. We spent the rest of the evening in bed, laughing over a Christmas comedy Ivy liked, and cuddling.

When we settled under the covers to sleep, wrapped in each other's arms, my heart ached.

Ached with how much I loved this man.

And with how damn much I was going to miss this when it all came to an end.

⛄

"Thanks for taxiing me around," Trevor said from his place in the back seat of my car a few days later. His leg still needed to be stretched out and neither my Mazda or Ivy's vintage muscle car had much room, but my brother was making do with what he could just to get out of the house. He'd talked Ivy and me into taking him to the mall and grabbing dinner.

The December day was unseasonably warm—not *warm*, but definitely not as cold as winter days could get in Peppermint Hollow—and we enjoyed the drive.

"Park farther out so I can walk more," Trevor demanded as I circled the parking lot near the food court.

"Is that a good idea?" Ivy asked.

"I need the exercise and I'm supposed to be challenging myself to do a little more each day. Hurts like a bitch sometimes, but it's worth it if I can eventually get back to my norm."

Once we reached the food court, we ended up at a lone table as far away from the kids' play place as possible, sharing loads of food between the three of us—a tradition

Trevor and Ivy had kept up forever. We each ordered too much of our own food and then spread it out on the table like a buffet.

As we ate and laughed and talked, I wondered if we'd be able to keep this up when Ivy and I were no longer living together. Trevor and Ivy would still be friends, but would I still be a part of their little group? Would Trevor be upset with Ivy—or me—for possibly messing up their friendship and making him choose between his brother and his best friend. Would it even be a choice?

"What challenge are you on?" Trevor asked, glancing between Ivy and me. He must have seen something on our faces because he held up his hands. "You know what, never mind. Nope. Not only are you not supposed to talk about the show—and the camera crew isn't doing a very good job of being discreet—" He nodded to where one of our poor crew looked bored out of his mind as he sat a distance away and recorded our dinner—it helped they didn't record our private conversations and we always knew which parts of recorded footage was being mic'd up; the crew was really good at using footage, recorded conversations, and interviews to portray our daily comings and goings. "But I also don't want to know *shit* about whatever you're doing. Bad enough to have to see it on the footage"—he jabbed a fork at Ivy—"you better be treating my baby brother right."

Thoughts of our nude dance and mutual blow jobs filled my head. Oh, Ivy was treating me just fine.

My stomach quivered at the thought of what we had planned for that evening. Was it presumptuous of me to have all the supplies for a thorough prep tucked away in a bag at home? Maybe. But better prepared than caught off guard.

Right?

"Oh god," Trevor groaned and ran a hand over his face. "Could you at least *try* to hide shit on your faces? You two both look like the damned cats who ate the canary and that has my mind going places it definitely doesn't want to venture when my brother and best friend are involved."

"Then stop thinking about it," Ivy muttered, tossing a fry at Trevor's head.

"Stop blushing and looking like you want to eat my brother alive," Trevor shot back, launching a wadded-up napkin at Ivy.

"I'm not blushing," Ivy said.

"Mmhm, I see you're still not being honest with yourself," Trevor said, more to Ivy than both of us, but I still caught his words.

"I know my truth," Ivy said. He wiped his mouth on a napkin and pushed back from the table. "Gotta piss."

My eyes glued themselves to his ass clad in signature black jeans as he walked away and I couldn't help but grin, but I quickly bit back the smile when Trevor cleared his throat.

"Let me guess, you haven't told him you're in love with him," Trevor said with an eye roll and frustrated huff.

"You heard him, he knows his truth. Even if he were interested in me like that, he's never even hinted that he wants a relationship of any type."

"You're kidding me, right? *Even if he were interested in you like that?* Have you *seen* the way he looks at you? It's like a kid gazing at the toy he's lusted over all year just waiting for Christmas morning. Or a hungry man at the holiday buffet. He wants you. He's got it bad for you." My brother waved off my protests. "And you're just as bad. You've always been gaga over him, but now it's not just a crush. *Tell. Him.* He deserves to know and you deserve to be true to yourself. Ivy's not going to get hung up on the same-sex thing—he's not like that."

"No, he's just going to get hung up on the *I don't do relationships* and *I don't know how to love* thing," I grumbled. "You know he will. His dad fucked him up bad."

Trevor was quiet for a bit. "Yeah, he did. And Ivy might get hung up on that—but I don't think it will last. He's clinging to the past—and he has every right to feel whatever he feels about his shithead father—but if he knew the truth about how you feel, I think he'd think again."

"You really think so?" I asked, begging my heart not to get my hopes up too much.

"I do. I may be wrong. And I apologize now if it doesn't go the way I think it will—hell, maybe I'm just wishful thinking. But I really think he's not letting himself consider anything with you because—well, for one, because he's convinced himself he can't love or do a real relationship—but also because he thinks you're still just doing this whole fake thing as a favor. He thinks you deserve better; he doesn't want to tie you down to something that may end up hurting you."

My brother's words played through my head as I watched Ivy make his way back to the table.

I wanted to grab his face, kiss him breathless, and tell him I was done with faking things, done with holding back my truth.

I wanted something real with him.

But did he want the same?

And even if he did, would he allow himself the chance for something amazing?

Or was he so convinced he didn't deserve love, couldn't *do* love, that he'd let the spark of something between us fade like one last dying ember?

Ivy glanced between Trevor and me. Him and Trevor had a tiff with their intense eyes and clenched jaws before his gaze landed on me and he smiled. Ruffling my hair, he slipped my glasses from my face and cleaned them on his t-shirt before placing them back where they belonged.

Trevor watched this with his jaw in his lap. When Ivy and I started to clear the table, my brother snorted and shook his head. I wasn't exactly sure of his words as he used his crutch to get himself into a standing position, but it sounded something along the lines of *bunch of damn idiots*.

Maybe he was right.

Maybe I was being stupid.

But if Trevor was right, why hadn't Ivy made a move? Why hadn't *he* said something?

Yeah, the guy whose father left a loveless marriage for another family on Christmas morning—the guy who is one thousand percent sure he has no capacity to love or treat someone the way they'd deserve in a real relationship—is totally the guy who is going to take back the whole fake-boyfriends-to-win-a-game ploy and admit he might have feelings for his best friend's little brother.

Now it was my turn to snort.

Okay, okay, so Ivy wasn't going to make the first move.

I could appreciate his position.

But it wasn't like I had the best history with relationships either. Could I be the one to speak up? Or were both of our hearts safer if we just let the game play out and went on our separate ways?

My brain said one thing, but my heart screamed otherwise.

The three of us wandered the mall for a bit until Trevor declared he'd pushed it a bit too far and he needed to get home.

By the time we dropped him at my parents' place, he was definitely in pain and dragging. He thanked us, wished us well on the game, and mumbled something about getting our heads out of our asses.

Soon, we were walking up the pathway from where we parked our cars to The Christmas House. "It's kinda surreal, huh?" I asked, taking Ivy's hand.

"What?"

The way we used to touch and play it up for the cameras and now it just comes naturally and I'd love for the damn cameras to disappear. I shook away the thought, my hand cozy in Ivy's.

"Just that this place used to be such a mystery, such a fantasy, so...out of reach and beautiful and part of our dreams...and here we are walking right on in like we own the place."

Ivy chuckled and squeezed my hand. "Well, technically…"

"Yeah, yeah, but you know what I mean. It's this childhood dream come true and it's just kinda crazy to me."

"Yeah, I get it. Believe me, every damn day I walk in that door, I remember how seeing this house used to make me feel when I was a kid."

"Does it still make you feel that way?" I asked as I tossed my keys on the counter and stood close to Ivy.

He cocked his head, absently wrapping his arm around my waist. "In a way, yes. As much as I still hate the holidays, this place has brought me a calm I never expected. Maybe spending Christmas in this house, seeing it through your eyes, has helped me find some peace."

I hummed, cuddling into Ivy's chest. "I like that. For you, I mean. I want you to have peace, all year long." My phone buzzed with a text and I pulled it from my pocket. "Letty wants to know the timeline for meeting our next two challenges."

My heart immediately picked up the pace and my dick perked up at just the mention of porn and *something sexual out of our norm*.

"Tell her we plan to have both completed by the time we meet her for our interview tomorrow," Ivy said, his words gruff in a way I hoped meant he was anticipating the challenges as much as I was.

I shot a text back to Letty and then muted my phone. "Showers?"

Ivy nodded. "I've got a couple things to work on in the shop—shouldn't take me long—and then I'll shower out there. You can have the bedroom shower."

I wasn't sure if Ivy was giving me the extra privacy and time because he needed it, or if his mind had gone to preparations as well, but I appreciated it. "Sounds good. I'll see you upstairs in a couple hours."

First things first, I hit the shower and took care of all things preparation-related. After a thorough cleansing of myself and the tub, I poured in bubble bath and let the hot water run. By the time my fingers were pruny and I was the poster child for *loose-limbed*, I pulled the plug and toweled off.

With a towel wrapped around my waist, I made sure the tablet was charged, lube was within reach, and the only light spilling into the room came from the cracked bathroom door. The scent of citrus mint filled the room as I contemplated the cameras.

Yes, they were filtered and only showed shadows and silhouettes.

But I selfishly didn't want to share anything Ivy and I might get up to when spurred on by the *watch porn together* challenge. I hoped the producers would reconsider some of the camera details if they did a second season of the show—some things could definitely be improved on.

Knowing Letty's head would explode if we covered the cameras again, I set to work *organizing* and *tidying up* the room with my wait time. Once finished, both cameras mysteriously—and completely accidentally—had something in front of them just enough that they'd only be recording the very edge of the frame.

What? I was just cleaning, it wasn't on purpose.

Smiling to myself, my heart lurched when the door opened downstairs. A few moments later, Ivy's footsteps sounded on the stairs.

And then he was in the room, fiery eyes traveling up and down my body. Pushing freshly-washed, damp hair from his eyes, Ivy yanked off his t-shirt and tossed his shorts to the side. This night was possibly going to kill me.

"You okay with this?" Ivy asked, wrapping me in a warm hug. "Challenge or not, we don't have to do anything you're not comfortable with."

Sighing into his chest, I nodded my head. "I'm good. Anxious, but not uncomfortable."

He kissed the top of my head. "You smell good." Leading me to the bed, he got us situated under the blankets before taking my hand and turning to face me. "I think it's best if we talk about a plan up front. Porn is a given. What are you thinking as far as *something sexual out of our norm?*"

With my cock straining against the towel, I bit my lip. "Maybe we get each other off? I've never jerked anyone else off while watching porn. You?"

"Same. Anything else?"

Maybe I couldn't find the courage to be honest about my *feelings* just yet, but I could at least be honest with Ivy about what I wanted to do with him. Truly, if what we had was going to have to come to an end, I couldn't stand the thought of saying goodbye without knowing what it felt like to have him inside me.

I cleared my throat.

"That good, huh?" Ivy teased. "That's an awfully pretty pink on your cheeks, little Bell. What are you thinking about?"

Squirming, more from desire than embarrassment, I huffed out a laugh. "Just thinking that we could watch and get off. Then maybe watch some more and go further with round two?"

Ivy's eyes burned into me and he caressed my cheek with the back of his fingers. "Just so we're on the same page, can we define *further?*"

"I want to feel you inside me," I whispered. "Want you to fuck me."

"Shit, Em," Ivy growled. "You're going to fucking kill me."

"We don't have to, if you're not comfortable with it," I started, but Ivy shut me up with a kiss.

"There has *never* been something I've wanted to do as badly as taking things further with you. Not to be the one to break us from the moment," Ivy said, "but condoms? No condoms?"

"We know all the results were negative," I said, referring to the mandated medical testing the show had required before filming. "Without, if I have a choice."

"You always have a choice," Ivy said, brushing a kiss against my lips. He grabbed the tablet. "Now, let's get this party started."

My heart ached, torn between being giddy Ivy wanted *more* physically with me and being devastated that seemed to be *all* he wanted. Nothing *more* as far as emotions or romance, just sex.

But I couldn't bring myself to turn that down, finally understanding the whole beggars can't be choosers phrase.

"What videos do you like to watch?" Ivy asked.

"Gay," I answered. "But we can do bi if that helps you."

Ivy snorted. "I don't know if labels are my thing—and if they are, I'm not sure which would fit—but I *do* know I'm into *you*. Pick something that would turn you on. If it gets you going, I'm sure I'll be right there with you."

I signed into my Twitter—not the Emory Shae one, the secret screen name one I used just for following porn accounts. What? Don't act like you don't have something similar.

Scrolling through my feed, I saw some of my favorites and clicked on the clip.

Ivy and I watched three or four clips in silence, my dick screaming to escape the confines of the towel.

Then Ivy cleared his throat. "So, you, uh, seem to have a type."

"Huh?" I turned to look at his gorgeous face.

"Tattooed tops and kinda geeky bottoms."

Shit.

"You caught that, huh?" My cheeks burned, but there was no denying it.

Ivy gave me a wicked grin and put the tablet on the bed between our knees. Shifting the blankets down, he shimmied out of his underwear. I licked my lips when his cock smacked against his stomach. Swallowing thickly, I watched in heated anticipation as Ivy reached for the towel and loosened it. His eyes caught mine and he cocked a brow.

I nodded.

With both of our cocks leaking against our stomachs, Ivy lifted his chin toward the tablet. "Pick one."

Going straight to my *liked* videos, I clicked on the first one I knew always got me off. Within seconds, Ivy and I had each other's cocks in our hands, thumbing through pre-cum, and stroking as we watched the dark-haired, tattooed guy on the screen destroy the bespectacled twink spread open on the mattress.

When I could no longer keep my eyes on the screen because I wanted to watch Ivy's throbbing dick thrust into my fist, I shifted, blocking the tablet with the blankets to face Ivy.

In one swoop, he wrapped his arm around my waist and pulled me to straddle his hips. My tight balls pressed against him. Our slick cocks rubbed together. "Hi," I panted, my hands going to his shoulders before trailing down to explore his tattooed chest.

He slipped my glasses from my face and placed them gently on the nightstand. Ivy's hands traveled from my bent knees up my thighs. Thumbs circling over my hip bones, big hands palming my ass and squeezing. His gaze roamed in tandem with his hands, watching my reactions, the dark brown of his eyes catching mine, locking us together, bringing his lips to mine and devouring my mouth with a fiery, wet kiss.

When one hand played with my nipple and the other caressed up the middle of my back, I arched, a whimper escaping as I rocked our hips together.

"Love when you arch that pretty back for me," Ivy said, pulling me close and tonguing a nipple as I writhed on his lap. His words flamed the heated desire inside me.

I wanted more.

As if reading my mind, Ivy teased his fingers between my ass cheeks and brushed over my tight hole. "You think you could come twice?" His words a gruff challenge at my ear. "Get off with my fingers inside you and then when my cock fills you with my cum?"

Anticipation shivered through me and I moaned, fisting my cock in hopes of staving off my orgasm before Ivy had done more than whisper a few dirty words.

He brought his fingers to my mouth. "Suck'em, get'em wet."

My eyes never leaving his, I sucked his fingers like I'd sucked his dick. My ass clenched when he took his wet fingers into his own mouth and tongued them. Pre-cum leaked over my fist when Ivy pressed his spit-slick fingers to my hole. He tapped and teased, pressing in and retreating. He fucked his tongue into my mouth in time to his fingers breaching my hole and my body slipped into overload.

"You gonna take my cock in this pretty hole?" Ivy asked and I suddenly didn't care if he'd fucked a thousand other people—his touch, his words, *this* was just for me.

For us.

I sobbed into his neck, my tight ring of muscle gripping his invading finger.

"Talk to me," Ivy crooned. "Tell me what you want."

"Have you done this with girls?" I asked, not sure *why* the answer mattered.

"Yeah," Ivy said, pressing a kiss against my temple as he worked his finger in and out of my pucker.

"How do you get them ready?" I knew Ivy wouldn't hurt me, but I wasn't naïve enough to think it wouldn't be without some discomfort.

Ivy smeared more spit between my ass cheeks, chuckling when I gasped as he slid his finger in again and added a second. "Done toys before, but usually just eat their ass, rim them until they're wet and open." His big hand closed around mine, jacking me as his words hit home.

The orgasm rolled through me, my release spurting over our knuckles, my ass clamping down on Ivy's fingers as his kiss absorbed my cries. When I caught my breath, I sucked Ivy's earlobe between my teeth. "Then eat my ass and rim me until I'm wet and open."

I found myself rolled to my back, the earlier-discarded towel under me, the tablet thunking to the floor. Between my knees, Ivy stroked himself, his eyes aflame as he looked down on me. Shoving a pillow under my ass, Ivy shifted to his stomach and pressed kisses to the sensitive area where the back of my thighs met my ass. Having no idea if I'd really be able to come again, I ignored my spent dick and just enjoyed the high. When Ivy's big hands spread my ass cheeks and his tongue teased over my hole, I bucked and cried out.

In that moment, I knew.

Knew why nothing had worked out with any other man.

I was made for Ivy.

For his touch.

Made to be his.

"Fuck, look at that pretty hole," Ivy muttered against my pucker. "Wanna watch it open for me, spread around my cock."

Fists clutching the sheets, breaths coming too fast, and incoherent begging filling the air, I rocked into the rimming, giving myself over to Ivy. To the experience. The pleasure.

Just when I'd determined my dick wasn't going to get on board for round two, Ivy's long finger brushed over my prostate and my world went white.

Ivy chuckled, his nose nuzzling against my balls. "How about that for some holiday *magic*?" he teased.

"Fuck, Ivy, please," I babbled. "Please. I need you."

He adjusted the pillow under my ass as he took his dick in hand. Without my glasses, he was just fuzzy enough in the dim room to look like a black and white painting of a dream.

I watched in silent awe and anticipation as Ivy lubed his cock and my hole. I was there, experiencing every heartbeat of ecstasy, but it had to be a dream.

Right?

When Ivy bent to press kisses to my spread thighs, my heart melted. I was ruined. No man would ever mean to me what he did.

And he was convinced he couldn't have happiness, couldn't find love.

Love was a cruel bitch.

With the leaking head of his cock pressed against my pulsing hole, Ivy ran a hand down my sticky stomach and took my fingers in his. "This okay? You want this?"

On a sob, I whispered, "Yes."

And then I shattered to pieces as his flesh became part of me.

The sting made me gasp and the fullness took my breath away.

But the knowledge Ivy and I were one, joined in the most intimate of ways, overshadowed any discomfort.

"Fuck," Ivy grunted, one hand squeezing my fingers and one hand gripping my knee as his eyes flickered back and forth between my face and our connected bodies. "Fuck, Em, I wish you could see this. Wish you could see how beautiful you look on my cock. Open for me, taking me so good."

His words, like his touch and his heart, took me apart once again.

My dick twitched back to life with each deep brush of Ivy's cock against my prostate. "Ivy," I whispered. No other words came, just his name, like a prayer.

And then he moved my legs to wrap around his waist and dropped to his elbows. With his face buried in my neck, Ivy thrust into me, over and over. Our grunts and groans mixing on the air, the slap of our skin pairing with the scent of sweat and sex.

"Come for me, Em," Ivy pleaded. "Wanna feel it."

The orgasm came in a slow, gentle wave. Small dribbles of cum spattered between us and my ass clenched around Ivy's pulsing cock. Two final thrusts and Ivy grunted, his hot release filling me as his teeth bit into my collarbone.

I fought the urge to tell him I loved him.

Battled to keep anything serious from my lips.

But damn, I did.

Love him.

I was so in love with Ivy Lane Gregory I didn't think my heart could survive it.

Somehow, I'd found myself in an impossible relationship. I didn't know how to approach it. Didn't know how to make it better. Didn't even know if there was a chance of fixing things. Or if there was anything to *fix*.

Relationships took two people—or however many were agreed upon—working together. If one or both weren't willing—convinced they weren't *able*—there was really nothing to be done.

Right?

Tears stung my eyes as Ivy's spent dick slipped from my body. We lay together quietly for several moments, savoring the high and keeping the connection between us.

When we finally caught our breath and cleaned up— nothing more than a few words between us—both of us crashed. I didn't go to sleep worried that Ivy was freaking out, but I definitely got a bit of a *maybe we need a bit of distance after what we just shared* vibe.

Morning brought our usual cuddling, but Ivy determined we needed to get our day started early because of the elimination that evening. I didn't take it personally —and truly, I was too sore to do much of anything besides snuggles before the blankets were removed and reality set in—but Ivy was for sure in his head a bit.

I should have straight up asked him what was bothering him.

Maybe he *was* freaking out over having sex with a man.

Or maybe he felt the same connection you did and it's throwing him for a loop.

Not letting my wishful thinking distract me, I did what any gay boy who's madly in love with his big brother's emotionally unavailable best friend would do after the hottest sex of his life—yeah, I know, we don't need to examine that—I ignored Ivy's vibe, pretended my gut wasn't trying to warn me, and headed toward the shower.

By the time we'd each worked an entire day—me at the diner and the shop helping Ivy get things set up more and more each day—grabbed dinner, showered, and done our interviews with Letty, I was exhausted.

But we had a show to do.

Based on the interview questions and clips, I knew *Once Upon a Christmas House* was really playing up the new physical between Ivy and me—okay, the viewers didn't know it was *new*, just that we'd been accepting challenges to make things different. The *After Dark* episode would cap off with the Spicy challenge, assuming we made it through the vote. But the clips and questions had me pretty confident we'd survive the current round.

Later, on the couch, Letty and the crew off to the side, Ivy holding my hand, we watched the elimination.

The bottom two turned out to be Sarah and Dean, the goat farmers, and Rae and Mallory, the two women from Texas.

Jackson and Andy were safe.

Cody and Jackie were safe.

And, obviously, Ivy and Bell.

I was shocked to see both couples in the bottom two and had no idea how the votes were going to play out.

When Rae and Mallory were eliminated—the audience comments indicating the women were spread too thin and not committed enough to the game—my brain went into overdrive.

The viewers also made some of the same comments about Sarah and Dean. How they thought brand new parents trying to run a goat farm weren't going to be spread pretty thin, I had no clue.

But it made me stop and think.

Ivy and Bell needed to be one thousand percent in the game. Convincing. Competitive. Together and ready to win.

No distractions.

Nothing to throw us off our game.

Five hundred thousand dollars was on the line and I wasn't ready to say goodbye.

CHAPTER 13

IVY

WE'D MADE IT THROUGH ANOTHER ELIMINATION.

If we got through this week's vote, we'd be in the final two.

But all I could think about was how Emory Shae Bell had completely obliterated my world. Every damn day, he broke my heart. And every damn day, every single smile, touch, gentle word from his lips pieced me back together.

He owned me.

But our time together was slipping away.

Just give it a try. You don't know you can't make something work. You've never *felt this way about anyone else. Maybe it would be different with Emory.*

No. I wouldn't do that to him. He deserved better than being a trial-and-error experiment on my part to see if I could overcome the shit my dad put me through.

In the early morning darkness, I stared at the ceiling as Emory's soft breaths puffed across my skin. My chest ached to think of mornings coming soon when Emory wouldn't wake up beside me. When I wouldn't thrill at the caress of my fingers down his perfect torso or the plump of my dick when I palmed his ass. Mornings when we wouldn't share chicory coffee from those stupid Christmas mugs and Emory wouldn't giggle every time he pulled me under the damn mistletoe.

The day before, we'd completed the week's challenge of adopting a child from the town's Christmas Angel Tree and shopping for their gifts. How something so simple could embed Emory Shae deeper in my heart was beyond me, but somehow, he'd done it.

I'd known he wasn't just giving good soundbites when he jabbered on and on about how many kids he'd adopt from the tree next year if we won the game. Emory had the biggest heart and I was a lucky bastard to get to experience it firsthand.

We'd agreed to *each* adopt a kid from the tree—Emory insisting we get older kids because they were usually the ones to go last. "People like buying gifts for the cute and cuddly babies and little kids. Teens get looked over."

The day of shopping had been fun. Exhausting and long, but fun. I'd been gifted with an insight into Emory I hadn't seen before. Yeah, I'd already known he was generous and sweet and smart—and a ton of other great things—but he had a heart for the underdog, the overlooked, the ones who might get glossed over. He fiercely stood his ground when looking for a teen who maybe was hoping for gifts others might have seen as weird or different—off the beaten path—and then poured his entire being into finding the requested gifts to make that teen's holiday happy.

I maybe hadn't given myself over to the whole Christmas magic thing, but completing that challenge proved to me that folks like Emory brought magic to people's holidays—to their *lives*.

As I lay in bed, I wondered about Emory's determination to pick the kids who maybe would otherwise be overlooked. He'd had a great childhood. I knew he did because I was there for most of it. So where had the protectiveness of forgotten children come from?

If you'd grown up in the shadow of Trevor, how do you think you would feel?

The thought hit me like a ton of bricks, but I couldn't say it was shocking.

Trevor was the golden boy. Outgoing, charismatic, perfect at everything he did. He loved Emory with every ounce of his being, but Trevor could be a lot to take—a lot to live up to—even when he was your biggest fan. Todd and Lisa Bell had never once—at least in my large amounts of time spent with them—expected Emory to be like Trevor, but the shopping trip had shown me Emory had a few demons when it came to making his way out of the shadows.

If I was being honest with myself, I had to hope that our time together—the show, the challenges, all of it—had maybe helped Emory step into the light in his own way, even just a little.

With the main challenge out of the way—we'd spent the night wrapping the gifts...okay, Emory had spent the night laughing at me and re-wrapping the messes I made when I got within two feet of the paper, tape, and scissors —all we needed to do before the next vote was the audience challenge.

The audience challenge we'd be given when Letty arrived after breakfast.

For some reason, the unknown of what the viewers would challenge us to do this time had me on edge. Maybe it was because we were so very close to the win. Or maybe it was because my heart wasn't sure just how much more it could take without splintering into a million shards when I had to let Emory walk away.

But I had a cement block in the pit of my stomach and a bad feeling the audience challenge was going to change things. For worse? Better? That remained to be seen. I just knew something was brewing.

"Good morning," Emory whispered against my cheek, his hands roaming over my chest. When he rocked his morning wood into my thigh, I snorted. The guy was insatiable—not that I minded.

Running my hand down his back and cupping his ass, I stroked fingers over his tight little hole. We'd ended the night with my cock buried inside him—something I'd quickly decided was heaven on earth and my heart wept with the thought of giving him up. Pressing a finger into him, I groaned when I found him slick with lube and cum from the night before. "You too sore?"

Emory shook his head and moved to straddle me. He'd gained more and more confidence in the bedroom with each passing day and I loved watching him bloom before me. Reaching behind himself, he took my hard dick in hand. Pressing my cockhead to his tight ring, Emory lowered himself onto my dick, whimpering with each inch he took deep.

Leaning forward, he braced his hands on my chest and rode my dick. When my hands trailed up his back, to his shoulders, and down to his wrists, Emory took my hands in his and pressed my arms up by my head. With our fingers entwined, Emory ground his hips, taking me deeper.

"Ivy," he begged.

I sat up, holding him around the waist, bringing our mouths together in a slow, sensual kiss. "What do you want?" I nipped at his lips.

Emory's preferences in bed ranged from slow, gentle, sweet lovemaking to wild, hard, dirty fucking. And I loved each and every moment of it.

He bit my lip, grinning when I gasped. "On my knees."

Smacking his ass, I let go of him so he could move to the middle of the bed. Knees spread, leaning on his elbows, perfect back arched, Emory was a work of art presenting himself just for me.

Moving between his legs, I slid my cock back inside his ass, loving the way he took me so easily. Hands on his hips, fingers digging into his smooth flesh, I fucked him. Each thrust a reminder of what I'd soon lose. Every whimper escaping Emory's pretty lips tormenting me while driving me toward bliss.

He shifted, pressing up onto his hands. "Touch me," he begged.

Pulling him up, one arm wrapped around his chest, a hand fisting his dick, I pumped in and out of his ass while stroking his cock. Emory stretched, his arms moving over his head to grasp for me, urging my mouth toward his, accepting my seeking tongue as eagerly as his tight little hole took my dick.

"Wanna make you come, then I'm pounding you into the mattress," I growled in his ear.

Emory whined, shuddering in my arms as his orgasm shot onto the pillows—we'd had a ten-fold increase in laundry since things had gotten physical between us—his ass clenching around me, his balls emptying.

Before he'd even stopped pulsing in my fist, I pressed him to the bed, my arms wrapped tight around his chest, and railed him in long, smooth, pounding strokes. Sex with Emory was different, better, so much *more* than anything I'd ever experienced before. I wasn't in the headspace to puzzle through the *why* of that—and I wasn't sure it mattered—but I knew no one after him, if I could even bring myself to take another person to bed, would ever live up to what Emory and I shared.

My release thundered through me, my load shooting deep in Emory's well-used ass while his whimpers and my sex-crazed grunts filled the air. Then we were spent, floating in an orgasm-induced haze, just enjoying the connection as we savored the bliss.

"How much time do we have before Letty gets here?" Emory asked, his words sounding like he could sleep for a week.

"About two hours."

"Set an alarm? We can sleep for another hour or so before showers. Save water, shower together," he mumbled.

"Definitely won't save time," I teased. Slipping from his body, I reached for my phone and made sure an alarm was set so we wouldn't oversleep. Gathering him close, I kissed the top of Emory's head as he tucked himself under my chin, and we slept.

Two hours later, after much-appreciated sleep and a

shared, sensual shower, Emory and I found ourselves on the couch with a way-too-chipper Letty across from us.

"We're so close to the end, gentlemen," she chirped with a wink. How did she already have lipstick smeared on her teeth? "*So* close. Are you ready for the audience challenge?"

Emory and I breathed in deeply as if we shared lungs. "Not like we can avoid it," he said and I realized he was feeling the same unsettled vibes as me.

"Well, we spun things a bit this week and challenged the audience to go deeper with their submissions. Since we're so close to the end, we wanted to get more emotional, more real. We're easing away from the spicy after dark type stuff and looking to give the viewers something to really chew on as they decide who they want to give their votes to." She waved an envelope. "Are we ready? Brace yourselves. Let's do this, okay? Okay."

She slid a perfectly manicured fingernail under the flap of the envelope as Emory squeezed my hand.

"This week's challenge is..." she paused dramatically, annoyingly, and for just long enough for me to know I wasn't going to like what she said next, "to tell each other a truth."

I was sure the editing crew would have a field day splicing together clips of the footage because I knew my face showed terror. Not only were Emory and I on the show based on an untruth, any truths I had for Emory weren't things I wanted to share.

Letty gestured at the cameras to cut.

"Okay, boys, we're going to have to make this one work." She cocked her head and studied us. "While I'm one thousand percent sure you both have some very real truths that very much need shared between you, the biggest truths are likely ones we can't air because they'd uncover facts I'm not sure the viewers would be very happy learning this late in the game."

"So, what do we do?" Emory asked, an edge of panic in his voice.

"We can go the easy route and have you tell some very superficial truths on camera," Letty suggested.

"But it sounds like the show wanted the viewers to get deep, do you think the audience is going to like it if we gloss over the challenge and take the easy way out?"

Emory's words echoed my thoughts.

"No, I don't. The other option is for you both to tell a deeper truth, but not *the* truth you've been keeping hidden." Letty tapped a finger against her chin. "But either way, I'd like to encourage you to hole yourselves away and have some real-talk. Just the two of you." She gave us a look. "Don't tell me you don't need that."

Yeah, well, maybe we needed it, but that didn't mean we wanted it.

Or, at least, I didn't want it. If I could avoid my truth about Emory for a little bit longer, maybe it wouldn't hurt so bad when he left.

Or maybe it will hurt even worse.

"If you're both on board, I say you take a bit of time and decide what you're going to tell each other—on camera, for sure, but maybe think about what you might want to say off camera as well—then we'll get the footage and be out of your hair."

Letty gave us twenty minutes and told us we couldn't speak to each other as we came up with what would work for our on-camera truths.

By the time we returned to the couch, I was going to puke.

Emory grabbed my hand, stopping my keychain which had been flipping back and forth like a jackrabbit on a pogo stick. "We've got this," he whispered in my ear. "For five hundred thousand, we can give each other a truth."

He was right. I took a deep, calming breath and nodded.

Letty signaled the cameras to start rolling. "Let's do this, gentlemen, okay? Okay. The audience has challenged you to tell each other a truth. The floor is yours."

Emory shifted on the couch, bringing one knee up under him and facing me. I turned toward him, taking comfort in the warmth of his hand on my knee. When he nodded at me to begin, I swallowed thickly.

"You know why I don't love the holidays. What happened back then is why, before you, I'd never even attempted more than serial hookups. My truth is that, because of what he did, I've been terrified I can't love a person the way they deserve to be loved."

There.

It was the truth.

It was pretty deep.

And it didn't spoil the fact Emory and I had been faking it since the very beginning.

Emory's glossy eyes caught mine and held for a moment. "Thank you for sharing your truth." He cleared his throat. "My truth is, until you, I felt like I'd never be seen for who I truly am. It's scary to think you might not ever be enough to find love."

Fuck.

How the hell were we supposed to work through that?

Me knowing I didn't have the capacity to love, knowing I couldn't trap Emory in a relationship that would only fall apart because it was all I knew, and him thinking he wasn't enough to earn love I didn't know how to give; love he should never have to *earn*.

What kind of fucked up situation had we gotten ourselves into?

"Thank you for your truth." My words were gravel on sandpaper.

Letty cut the cameras and stood. "That was good. It was real and it was honest without screwing up your storyline." She snorted. "Truths and lies, oh what a tangled web we weave." She shook her head and jabbed a finger toward us. "Now I suggest you tell each other your actual truths—the ones you're still hiding from each other. Before it's too late."

And then we were alone. My keychain began its clicking again and I stood, desperate to escape the tension. Fleeing to the kitchen, ignoring the damn little snow globe house, the creepy nutcracker, and the mistletoe, I wanted to forget everything about truths and lies. Forget about faking it, saying goodbye, and life without Emory in it.

But I had to be fair to him.

"My truth," Emory said, talking to my back as I stared out the kitchen window above the sink. "My truth is I want you as more than my fake boyfriend."

"Em," I started.

"No, just let me get this out."

I closed my eyes and waited for him to gut me.

"I agreed to do this game because you're a friend and I wanted to help. It didn't hurt that I'd had a crush on you for years and getting to play house didn't seem like a bad gig at all." Emory came to stand next to me, our arms pressed together. "I thought I could keep everything easy. Sure, we'd need to kiss and touch and play it up as a couple—and I'd enjoy the hell out of it—but it was to win the game and help you out, so I had no problem with it." He paused and huffed out a breath. "But along the way, the lines blurred. I'm sorry for changing up what we'd agreed to. I know we said it was fake from the very beginning. But I think my heart must have missed out on that part." He bumped his shoulder into me. "I'm not trying to change the rules, I just need you to know my truth. I want this to be real—if I had my choice, I'd make it real."

We were silent for a long moments.

"Can you say something?" Emory asked and I hated the unsureness in his voice.

"I can't lie and say I don't feel something for you. I do. It shocked the hell out of me, but there's no denying it."

"Then—"

"But I can't start something with you that could end up hurting you. My truth remains the same. I don't know how to love, don't know what a healthy relationship looks like. I'm not going to experiment with you and run the risk of hurting you in the process."

"But—"

"Em," I whispered, turning to face him and cupping his cheek. "You deserve so much more than me. You deserve someone who gets just as excited as you do about decorations and lights. Someone who knows what it means to fall in love and build a future on that foundation. You deserve to know that person is your forever. I can't promise a forever—I wouldn't even know where to start."

Tears glistened in his eyes. "I hate that you think you could ever hurt me. Yeah, I get it, love can hurt. But you're one of the best people I know and you'd never purposely put someone through the pain you went through—I feel that in my heart." Emory took a shaky breath. "I won't beg for more. I don't like it, but I knew from the beginning this was all fake for you and I'll respect that. Whether it's because our feelings aren't the same or because you truly believe you can't do love, I'll respect your stance." He reached up and brushed a chunk of hair from my eyes. "Because I'd never try to change who you are in here," he said, moving his hand to press against my chest. "Yeah, I tease about turning you into a Christmas-lover and believer in holiday magic, but I'd never try to change who you truly are. You're Ivyrson Lane Gregory and you deserve to be loved just the way you are."

"What does this mean?" I asked, my heart aching in my chest.

Emory gave a weak smile. "I think it means it's time to start preparing for our goodbye. We're so damn close to winning, but things are starting to hurt a bit too much. We've done a great job faking it and we keep it up, but maybe we take a few steps backward as far as the intimacy?" He huffed a shaky breath. "I'm going to need to learn to sleep by myself and not have my fake boyfriend around for kisses." Big tears threatened to spill behind his glasses, but he put on a brave face. "I will *never* regret playing this game with you. And I hope we can keep the friendship intact. I might just need a while to lick my wounds after it's all over."

Shit.

Just tell him. Admit you're scared shitless and you have no clue what you're doing, but you want to try something real with him.

But that wouldn't be fair to Emory. He didn't deserve to be someone's experiment. Not that I was unsure of my attraction to him or my ability to be in a same-sex relationship. No, it was just my ability to be in *a relationship* period. And Emory deserved someone who knew what a healthy relationship looked like.

When he walked out of the kitchen that day, it was like watching my heart slip away from me, separated by a damn gulf between us.

The rest of the week was hell.

Emory took to working in the shop when I was asleep. He signed up for more shifts at the café. We became total clichés, ships passing in the night, as he fell into bed just as I was getting up or vice versa.

I missed him.

Missed his touch, his kisses, his body. But more than anything, I missed *him*. Talking with him, laughing with him, just being with him.

Emory had become my world and I was getting a glimpse of what it was going to be like to lose that world.

I didn't like it.

But there was nothing I could do about it.

I wouldn't put Emory through the time and effort of building a relationship—with someone who had no clue even *how* to do it—and the potential heartache when it became evident I just couldn't do it. Couldn't love the way he deserved to be loved. Couldn't give him what he needed.

We ended up in the bottom two in that week's vote.

Jackson and Andy were safe.

Sarah and Dean were safe.

Cody and Jackie shared the bottom spot with Ivy and Bell.

Comments poured in about the rift between Emory and me. Viewers didn't like it, but could I expect Emory to put himself through pain just to get a few more votes? It was probably best he took a few steps back to ease the pain of saying goodbye.

I breathed a sigh of relief when Cody and Jackie were sent home. I thanked whoever was watching over Bell and Ivy for the stroke of luck I wasn't sure we'd deserved.

The viewers suggested they loved Cody and Jackie, but they'd lost a connection with them over the last couple weeks. The hipsters from San Francisco were given tons of well wishes with a lot of comments saying if they'd been in the bottom two with anyone but Bell and Ivy, they likely would have been safe.

Which left Jackson and Andy, Sarah and Dean, and Ivy and Bell in the final vote.

Popular friends with benefits from South Carolina.

Beloved new parents from North Dakota.

And fake boyfriends from Peppermint Hollow who were already sending up red flags because their fake relationship had gone through a very real heartbreak.

Could we patch things up just long enough to ensure our win? Or was that too much to ask? Would going back to faking it for the game just make it that much harder when everything ended for real?

Or would a split five hundred thousand dollars help ease the pain?

We wouldn't know unless we won.

And I wasn't going to make Emory do something that would hurt him more than I'd already done.

CHAPTER 14

EMORY

Telling Ivy my truth had been the best and the worst.

I felt better at least knowing I'd been honest with him and let him know what I wanted. While I hadn't spilled my guts about how head-over-heels-in-love I'd fallen, I told him I wanted something real.

It sucked because I had to respect that he didn't want the same thing.

Don't twist his words. He never said he didn't want something real with you. He said he didn't know how to do something real and he wouldn't put you at risk of getting hurt.

Yeah, well, either way, the outcome was the same.

The final week's challenge was simple.

Play your best game and give the audience what they want.

After barely squeaking by during the last vote, I was determined to do everything in my power to make sure we won. We'd worked so hard and come so far, I wasn't going to let a little heartache knock us out when we were so close to winning.

Give the audience what they wanted?

Easy.

It was the exact same thing as what I wanted.

Bell and Ivy, together.

In love.

Playing our best game.

After a few hours of working in the shop, I'd come to a decision.

"Can we talk?" I asked as Ivy looked over an online parts catalog in his office.

He clicked the site closed and gave me his full attention.

Clearing my throat, knowing taking a step backward would be enjoyable and probably worth it in the long run if we won, but would also hurt like a bitch when everything came crashing down, I perched on the edge of his desk.

"I know I said we needed to pull back, but I think I was wrong. Maybe it will hurt worse, but I want this time together with you. It's what the audience wants and I don't want to give it up." I brushed a chunk of Ivy's dark hair from his brow. "I wish things were different. Wish the Christmas magic would fix everything. But I've always known where you stood on this, so it would be unfair of me to expect anything different."

"What are you saying?" Ivy asked, his dark eyes locked on mine as he stared up at me from his seat.

"I want to go back to the way things were. We can deal with the fallout when the show is over." I ran my thumb over his lips. "I'm greedy, but I want this last little bit of time."

Ivy stood, his chair rolling backward and slamming into the wall. He wrapped his arms around me and brought our mouths together for a kiss. Like coming home, like heaven, our lips met and heat sparked. God, how I'd missed the taste of him on my tongue, the grip of his hands against my skin, the press of his body on mine.

"Ivy," I begged.

The days we'd been apart had been a million years and the air between us hung heavy with need.

Ivy's hands slid under the waistband of my basketball shorts. He groaned at the discovery of my bare ass. "Get these off," he demanded.

When I went to toe off his borrowed work boots, he grunted and gripped my chin. "Just the shorts, leave the boots on."

My shorts hit the floor and I yanked my shirt over my head. Standing naked before him in just the unlaced work boots, I watched in awed anticipation as he stripped his shirt off and unbuttoned his black jeans. Pushing them down just far enough to release his rock-hard cock, Ivy crowded me into the wall.

"Fuck," he growled. "No lube."

I glanced around wildly, trying to think of a suitable replacement. "Vaseline." He kept it for scrubbing off the worst of the dirt and stains before his showers.

After a beeline toward the tiny little bathroom, Ivy was back.

Within seconds, I was slicked and worked open.

"Put your arms around my neck and hold on."

With my legs tight around his waist, I gasped when his

lubed cockhead pressed against my hole. Whimpering as Ivy pushed into me, inching his length deeper and deeper as he held me against the wall, I rejoiced in our reunion. "Ivy," I panted against his neck, nipping at the sensitive skin, sucking away the sting.

"Fuck, Em," Ivy grunted, slamming into me.

An ocean of wishes, shoulds, and uncertainties spread out between us, but in that moment, none of it mattered. It maybe wasn't healthy, it would maybe lead to regrets, and my heart already ached with what was to come, but I couldn't help myself. Like a kid absorbing the last few days of summer before school started, I knew what lay ahead was going to suck, but if I could just slow down these last moments and engrave each and every second with Ivy into my soul, I'd have something to get me through when he was no longer mine.

We showered off the slick, sticky mess we made once we'd fucked ourselves into oblivion. With Ivy's too-big work boots flopping on my feet and his hoodie keeping me warm, we rushed from the shop to the house where I made a big bowl of peppermint stick and dark chocolate ice cream while Ivy started a pot of coffee.

"Did you read any of the viewer comments?" Ivy asked as we settled in on the couch.

"A few, why?"

He shrugged.

"What?"

"Just a couple of them bothering me."

I pulled out my phone and scrolled through the comments after the most recent vote. "Which ones?"

"I don't know, I guess it's just the ones saying shit about my past."

I took a moment to read through the comments more carefully.

Ivy is way too hung up on whatever happened in his past. Let me guess, daddy issues. The d*ck cheated? Left? Whatever. Does Ivy not realize he's losing out on happiness by letting that a**hole win? ~tellitlikeitis

If Ivy was being honest with himself, his whole "truth" is a crock. Maybe he thinks it's his truth, but he needs to dig deeper. That whole thing about being scared he didn't know how to love? Bullsh*t. He's scared of loving and someone leaving. ~psychmajorhereforluv

"These two?" I asked, pointing to my phone screen.

"Yeah, I guess. Like, who are those dicks to act like they know anything about my past? It happened. My dad fucked me up. End of story. They don't know shit."

I took his hand and waited to see if he wanted to say more, but we sat in silence from one commercial break to another before he finally cleared his throat to speak.

But the topic had changed.

"Remember you said you know where I stand as far as a relationship between us?" he asked, my heart clawing its way to my throat.

"I do."

"Well, I don't know if you *really* know where I stand." Ivy squeezed my hand. "I need you to know, if I could do a relationship I'd want it to be with you—total no-brainer." He leaned in and brushed his lips over mine. "If things had happened differently for me, we'd be having a totally different conversation."

I kissed him back and shook my head. "If things had happened differently for you, neither of us would be the people we are today. Don't get me wrong, I'd never wish the pain of your past on you, but what happened back then made you who you are today. Our experiences growing up together helped to shape me into who I am."

Ivy's forehead rested against mine. "If ever there was a person I could love it would be you."

Huffing out a frustrated breath, I closed my eyes, breathing in his sandalwood and sea salt scent. "You just don't get it do you? You've been *doing* a real relationship this whole time. Maybe we've been faking it, but we've been in a relationship." I forced a sad smile. "And you'd be the person I could love too. Always."

We fell asleep on the couch, wrapped together in our impossible situation as much a soupy, sticky mess as our leftover ice cream melting in the bowl.

CHAPTER 15

IVY

I COULDN'T GET THOSE DAMN COMMENTS OUT OF my mind.

Of course, I was fucked up thanks to my dad.

He left us for a whole new family. Didn't love us enough to stay. It made perfect sense I'd live my life worried I'd turn out just like him.

Or maybe you should give some space to the flip-side of that. Maybe you are scared to love someone and have them leave you. Maybe you're not so scared you can't love, maybe you're just more worried about turning out like your mom than your dad. Or maybe it's a combination of both.

Growling out a frustrated breath as I stirred the fire before heading out to the shop the day before the final vote, I glanced at the nutcracker on the hearth. "Creepy fucker," I muttered.

An air of unsettledness washed over me as I thrust the fire poker back into its slot. My eyes roamed the room and landed on the snow globe.

Moving closer, I studied the little house. A perfect

replica of the one I now called my own. Inexplicably, the wall of ivy had grown thicker—on both the tiny house and the real one—the wreath Emory insisted on putting on the front door showed up in miniature on the snow globe house, and a wisp of smoke still curled from the chimney as the fire burned down.

"I don't understand any of this," I mumbled. "Makes no damn sense." When a twinkle of light, almost like a star inside the snow globe flashed—so quickly, I almost thought I'd imagined it—I finally gave in. What did I have to lose? "Okay, I'm not saying I believe it completely, but I can admit there seems to be very little other explanation." I cleared my throat. "So, if this whole holiday magic, Christmas spirit thing is real, show me what to do." Running a hand over my face, I thought about the next night being my last with Emory. "Am I scared of being my dad? Afraid I'll end up alone like my mom? Or just hiding behind excuses?" I picked up the snow globe and swirled it in my hand, an icy draft washing over me as the snow whirled inside the fragile glass ball. "Can Emory and I make it work? Or should I let him go before one or both of us end up hurt because I'm too fucked up?"

The tiny star-light twinkled again, but nothing else happened.

"Christmas magic, my ass," I mumbled, feeling like a fool to have fallen for it.

Whether I didn't know how to love thanks to my dad or I was scared to be left alone like my mom, Emory deserved better than me.

What about what you deserve? And did you ever think that maybe Emory is a grown-up who can decide what he deserves for himself?

Pushing aside the thought and giving a big *fuck you* to...well, I wasn't exactly sure what I was giving the middle finger to, maybe my past? My inability to move on from the fear? Fuckin' whatever...I cursed under my breath and headed out to the shop.

My phone dinged while I was elbow deep in an engine. Knowing Emory was expecting me for lunch at the café, I wiped my hands quickly and checked the text just in case plans had changed.

It wasn't Emory.

It was Iris.

My sister.

> Iris: Hey there, just wanted to say you're on my mind with Christmas being so close. I know how much you hate it, but I also wish you could move on from that. The past is in the past and it's okay to be happy. I've found replacing the old bad with the new good is helpful to ease the pain and makes for happier times. Anyway, love you and hope to see you soon. You have a niece I'd love for you to get to know.

My heart clenched. I hadn't heard much from Iris since she moved away. A few texts dropped here and there to let me know she was settled in, how she was doing, and a picture of the baby now and then.

Why in the world would she have texted me out of the blue today?

I called Emory to check if he still wanted me to stop in for lunch.

"Yeah, we're swamped right now, but should be able to take a break in about an hour," he answered sweetly, although I could hear the frazzle in his words.

I returned to the engine and lost myself in the work for a while.

Then my phone rang.

Trevor.

I loved the guy like a brother, but I wasn't in the mood to defend myself against his well-intentioned advice. And I needed to finish up so I could head to the café.

As I washed my hands a bit later, I pressed play on his message.

Hey, man, it's me. Just wanted to let you know I'm rooting for you and Em to win. I think you have a real chance. Whatever happens, don't forget that you both deserve to be happy. Basically, what I'm saying is you both seem to be struggling because you're idiots and need to take your heads out of your asses. We can't change the past and we can't control the future, but we can choose to be happy in the here and now. Love you, man.

When I got to the café, I spotted Emory finishing up with a customer.

A very attractive customer who was very clearly interested in getting more than the check from Emory. The man flirted and Emory blushed, but when he spotted me his eyes lit up and he waved. He handed the check to the guy and moved toward the kitchen.

A few moments later, he was back and took my hand, leading me to a table. "Oh my god, I've never needed a lunch break so bad in my entire life. Sit here. I'm going to go wash my hands and pee. Order me a water and a Coke if Shelly comes over—she had to cover for one of the servers whose two kids are sick with a stomach bug."

While I waited, surreptitiously watching the man who had definitely been interested in Emory, I thumbed open my text app to look at the text from my sister. Her words spoke to me. *Replacing the old bad with the new good.* I liked that. Was it something I could do?

I pressed the play button on Trevor's message and listened to it twice.

We can't change the past and we can't control the future, but we can choose to be happy in the here and now.

I thought of the damn comments from viewers.

Does Ivy not realize he's losing out on happiness by letting that a**hole win?

He's scared of loving and someone leaving.

Emory returned to the table with drinks and I forced the thoughts away. "I said I'd help Shelly since she let me take my break. What do you want to eat? I'll go put it in."

We spent an enjoyable hour in the tiny corner booth, eating, laughing, and talking about how we thought the last episode was going to go down. I didn't miss the camera guy over in the corner getting footage, but I'd grown pretty used to them being around over the last eight weeks. It was funny how I'd gotten to the point I didn't worry much about what they captured or the soundtrack—it was weird, but I trusted them to make sure we looked and sounded our best so we could get votes. I guess the crew wanted to be on the winning team as well.

"I can't believe it's almost Christmas," Emory said as he munched on a fry. "This eight weeks has absolutely flown by."

It really had. Part of me wanted to stop time and never have to let Emory go, but I also wanted to win the damn game.

We chatted a bit more about the show and the bits and pieces Letty had given us clues about. We knew one couple would be voted off early in the show and the other two would face the final vote to end the show.

Beyond that, we didn't have a lot of information.

"Hey, I'm going to work an extra shift to help out. I've got those schedules and orders to work on in the shop, but I can get them done easily tomorrow before we need to be ready for the recording," Emory said.

"No problem, I appreciate your help." And I did. He'd done an amazing job in the shop.

Outside the café, I gave him a quick kiss and told him I'd try to wait up.

"Don't even worry about it. I'll be late and you need to sleep. You were up early this morning." Emory brushed a kiss over my cheeks. "See you at home."

Home.

For one more day.

Once Emory was gone, it wouldn't feel like home ever again.

I was asleep before Emory got home from his late-night shift at the café, but it was a restless slumber. I dreamed of the man in Emory's section flirting with him and asking for his number. The rest of the dream was flashes of Emory out on the town with this guy—laughing, dancing, having the time of his life. I woke in a cold sweat, terrified of losing him. True, I'd convinced myself I didn't know how to love him, but I couldn't stand the thought of someone else getting to share his life with him.

Fuck.

"You okay?" Emory asked, his hand on my chest as he snuggled closer.

"Yeah, just a weird dream," I muttered. I took a trip to the bathroom and crawled back into bed, pulling Emory close and refusing to believe it was our last night together.

What are you going to do when he takes the confidence he's learned from faking it with you and applies it to something with a guy who wants nothing more than to build a future with him?

Or worse, a guy who doesn't treat him right. Hurts him. Doesn't appreciate his heart and everything that makes Emory Emory?

"You sure you're okay?" he asked.

"Yeah, all good," I lied, kissing the top of his head.

Emory's soft snores told me he was asleep within a few minutes.

My night consisted of winks of sleep and a snowstorm of worries.

When I finally dragged myself from bed the next morning, I knew immediately something had changed—my head? My heart? Something was different.

The smell of breakfast and coffee wafted up the stairs with the sound of Emory singing Christmas songs. After a shower, I made my way down the stairs, that weird feeling not changing at all. Nothing seemed out of place, but the entire house, my entire *soul* felt different. The damn mistletoe still hung from every doorway, the creepy nutcracker still watched me from the hearth. Hell, I could even smell the chicory coffee and knew Emory had filled the Christmas mugs—the *magic* Christmas mugs.

I couldn't explain it, but *something* was in the air.

Glancing at the snow globe, the windows reflecting sunlight—an exact replica of what the real house would have looked like in the winter morning sunlight—smoke from the chimney thanks to the fire Emory had started, and even a snow angel in the side yard.

Ha! There. Proof it wasn't magic, just some sort of fuckery. There was no snow angel in our side yard.

"Did you see it snowed last night?" Emory called from the kitchen.

What.

The.

Fuck.

I walked to the window and looked out.

"I made a snow angel," Emory said from the doorway as I stared at the imprint in the dusting of snow. "It wasn't wet enough for a snowman, but an angel worked."

Glancing over my shoulder at his cute ass as he walked back to the kitchen, I rushed to the snow globe again.

What in the hell was going on?

The text from my sister, the call from Trevor, the dream.

I didn't know how to explain any of it, but I could no longer deny there was something there. In the air, in the house, in my heart.

Magic?

Spirit?

Love?

Whatever the fuck it was, it had me all bamboozled, but I didn't hate it.

My mind went a million miles a minute for the rest of the day as we worked and prepped for the show.

And then it was time.

"Okay, we'd like to give a big final episode welcome to all of our *Once Upon a Christmas House* viewers. On behalf of Season's Streaming, we'd like to thank you for tuning in, commenting, submitting challenges, and voting over these last eight weeks," Silas said, his smile a mix of smarmy and calculating from where I sat at the dining room table watching the tablet with Emory. "We're going to get right down to it with our first vote. This vote was determined earlier in the week and we're sad to see anyone go, but we can only have one winning couple." He flashed an envelope. "When I announce the couple voted off, your name will disappear from the screen and you'll lose connection to the feed. We invite you to tune in with the rest of the viewers to see how the show plays out. Here we go," Silas said, flashing a mega-watt smile. "Saying goodbye right now is...Jackson and Andy."

The little rectangle with the live feed of the friends-with-benefits went black and my heart jumped into my throat.

"Hate the see them go," Silas said and sounded genuine. "They've been a favorite from the beginning. We gathered audience comments and it seems our viewers found Jackson and Andy highly entertaining, but they wanted a romance. Wanted to see our friends-with-benefits fall in love and that just never happened. We're going to take a commercial break and we'll be back with our final two couples and their last speeches to the viewers—last appeals for votes."

Shit.

I'd guessed we'd likely be asked to say something to the viewers, but I hadn't really planned a speech.

"Just speak from your heart," Letty said. "Really never thought we'd make it to the final two, but you've got as good a chance as any. Speak the truth. Give the audience what they want. In any other case, those two things might not coincide, but in this situation, I really feel you can do both."

"Welcome back," Silas announced. "We are down to our *final two*. We're going to give Sarah and Dean, our new parents and goat farmers from North Dakota a chance to appeal to the viewers for your votes first."

To be honest, I was so lost in my head, my hand gripping Emory's as Sarah and Dean spoke, I didn't have the slightest idea what they said. I was sure it was good, they were a cute couple and the audience clearly liked them. The baby was a definite plus.

And then it was our turn.

"Bell and Ivy, it's your turn to convince our viewers why *you* need to be our winning couple. The stage is yours," Silas said with a flourish of his hand.

Emory squeezed my hand and went first. "I've had so much fun playing this game and it's been even better because of getting to play it with Ivy. We came into this game as a new couple and getting to know Ivy while having so much fun has been a blast. We'd really love your votes."

With absolutely no plan of what I was going to say, my mind short-circuited as words started pouring from my mouth. "I've loved this game and I love you. I wouldn't have wanted to play this game with anyone else by my side." I turned to the screen. "We appreciate any votes you're willing to give us."

Emory's eyes glistened and he gave my hand a

squeeze. "Hopefully, these two months have helped make Christmas happy for you again."

"*You* made the holidays something special again. You're my Christmas magic."

I had a vague impression of Silas cutting to commercial.

And then everything was silent.

"That was really good," Emory said, his words raw.

I shifted in my chair, moving us both so my legs could encase Emory's. "That wasn't for the show," I said, pressing our foreheads together. "I meant every word." My words whooshed out in a soft rush of air. "I'm in love with you and I'm done with the fake boyfriend thing and being an idiot who thinks I can't love you."

"What do you mean?"

"I want you to be my real boyfriend. Live with me. Work with me." I closed my eyes and made a wish. "Love me?"

"Yes," Emory choked out. "Yes, of course." A tear spilled down his cheek. "What changed?"

I cleaned his glasses and slipped them back on his face, although the tears splattered right back on the lenses. "Revelations, thanks to…Christmas spirits? Hell, just call me Scrooge, I guess. Anyway, I realized I'm done letting my past hold me back and control me. I deserve to be happy—*you* deserve to be happy—and I'm not going to let my father continue to bring me down." The guy from the café and the dream about Emory dating flashed through my mind. "And I can't lose you. The thought of you sharing your life with someone else takes my breath away. If you'll have me, I want to be the one holding your hand, putting a smile on your face, even celebrating Christmas together."

Emory smiled and kissed me through his tears. "Even if we don't win?"

"This," I touched my chest and then his, "what we have, is worth more than any game show prize. Win or lose, I want this."

I knew the money would be a huge help. I knew we both wanted to win. But I also knew, money or no money, I wanted to move forward and replace the bad memories with good ones. With Emory by my side, I planned to take back Christmas.

As Silas welcomed the audience back from the commercial break, I saw Letty smiling and trying to inconspicuously wipe away a tear. I'd forgotten she was in the room, but I had a feeling they'd definitely captured a good bit of that on film and the editing crew was likely in a frenzy getting it ready to roll. No doubt in my mind the show had specifically gone to commercial after the speeches to gather a bit of extra footage before the final vote.

Emory gave my hand a squeeze just as the door opened and the rest of the Bells walked in. Trevor smirked at me like the knowing asshole he was. Todd and Lisa each gave a smile and a wave as the trio sat off to the side. It meant the world to me they were there to support us.

Win or lose, with Emory by my side and the Bells as my family, I could face whatever came my way. No matter what happened with the show, *Once Upon a Christmas House* had changed my life and I would forever be grateful.

The screen flickered to a video of Sarah and Dean with

the baby during the commercial break. Just regular parent things, cuddling, being cute.

Then the screen showed Emory and me. We looked... very much in love. The editing team had done a fabulous job of laying only certain sections of our words over the video so as not to give away our secret.

"I know, I know, you all want to know the winners right now, but we need *you* to cast your votes. If you've been on the fence about who you want to win, now is the time to make a decision." Silas winked. "One last commercial break—come on, we've got to pay the bills— and we'll see you on the flip side."

Amazing how one minute could seem like a lifetime.

"And, we're back." Silas beamed into the camera and waved the envelope. "Let's get right down to it. We want to thank the viewers who made Season's Streaming and *Once Upon a Christmas House* a smashing success this year. We'll be taking audience feedback and suggestions for the next week. If you'd like to submit your application to be considered for next year's show, be sure to subscribe to our social media so you're up-to-date the moment we start taking entries. But until then, let's find out who's getting this five hundred thousand dollars and a house remodel." Silas slipped a well-manicured finger under the flap to break the seal and took a big, dramatic breath.

I was going to lose my mind if they went to another damn commercial.

But Silas just winked, opened the envelope, and announced, "The winner of this year's *Once Upon a Christmas House*—brought to you by Season's Streaming —is..."

EPILOGUE

EMORY

"Please, Ivy," I begged. Bent over the bed in the downstairs den where we'd moved our room while the upstairs was being remodeled, I gripped the sheets and cried out with each and every thrust. "I'm so close."

"Come for me," Ivy demanded, his fingers gripping my hips as he plowed into me.

We'd missed spontaneous daytime sex over the last year because there wasn't a day that had gone by that we didn't have a crew of some sort working on repairs, remodels, and updates in the house.

Now, just a few days before Christmas, the crews were gone for the next two weeks and we could have all the sex we wanted.

Except, Iris and her husband and their little girl were coming for Christmas this year. Robby and his boyfriend were coming for dinner. And Trevor was bringing someone special he'd met in therapy last year.

We really couldn't complain, though.

Ever since winning *Once Upon a Christmas House*, life had

gone from good to better to best—and it wasn't just the money or the house remodel. Ivy and I were madly in love and spent every single day laughing and falling harder for each other than the day before. That love—what started growing between us when we first started the game—was what won the show for us.

The viewers stated in their votes they absolutely loved Sarah and Dean just as much as Bell and Ivy, but watching us fall in love more and more as the show went on was what made us special. The married couple with the baby were sweet and in love, but the audience fed off of watching love grow between Ivy and me right before their very eyes.

"Fuck, Em," Ivy grunted. "Shit, I'm close. Turn over."

He pulled out gently and rolled me to my back. Spreading my knees, he stroked my cock and slid back into my ass with a groan.

Wrapping my legs around his waist, I pulled him down, bringing our chests together. Kissing him slow and sweet while he fucked me hard and fast was one of my very favorite things to do. And Ivy was so very good at mixing dirty and sweet.

Moments later, with my ass clenching around his pulsing cock, greedily taking his load as my own release splattered between our stomachs, I panted, "Fucking love you so much," against his lips.

"Love you too," Ivy grunted out, burying his face in my neck as we caught our breaths.

"As much as I hate to break up this sticky little love fest, we need to get ready," I said.

Ivy groaned but pulled from my body slowly, making me shudder when he pressed his thumb into my slick hole. "If we have to, we'll hit the shop while everyone else sleeps."

"We can go three days," I teased, but the thought of sneaking off to have sex in the shop while his sister was here wasn't the worst.

After showers, I caught Ivy in the living room. The keys clinking in his hand were something I hadn't seen in a while. They only came out when he was feeling super anxious these days. Placing a hand on his in hopes of calming his nerves, I said, "Your sister is going to love the house. Iyrie is going to love the five million presents you got her. You and Brett will have plenty to talk about."

"I just want it to be perfect," Ivy said. He'd hired a crew to decorate the outside of the house—focusing on an amazing design on the ivy wall side. "Do you think the presents are too much? Take some of them back?"

"No, it's fine." I led him to the couch. "We've got some time to kill. Iris said they'd text when they were an hour out. Lunch is in the oven. Robby will be here a little later—I swear, he and his boyfriend are fucking adorable." Robby had been working for us in the shop when he met Bruce—one of the mechanics I'd helped Ivy hire to take on some of the extra appointments we were able to take at Ivy's Autos ever since expanding the shop layout.

"They are," Ivy mused, his voice sounding somewhat less anxious. "I hope his parents take it okay when he decides to tell them."

"We'll be here for him either way," I said.

"Maybe we should put the creeps away," Ivy said.

I chuckled. *The Creeps* were what he'd started referring to the nutcracker and the even creepier vintage Santa—yes, I insisted on him making his way out of the attic this year—we'd decorated the living room with. "Nope. They stay."

"But Iyrie might be scared."

"She's seen them on video calls, she'll be fine. She's kinda a firecracker, if you haven't noticed. I bet she'll be so busy playing with her favorite uncle, she won't even notice."

Ivy put his arm around me and pulled me in for a kiss. "Favorite *uncles*," he corrected and my heart soared. How was this my life?

"What time is dinner at your parents?" Ivy asked, sipping coffee from our magic mugs.

I snuggled deeper into his hoodie which had slowly just become mine over the last year and said, "After six, I think."

We sat quietly for a moment.

"This year is a lot different," I said, "but still kinda the same. If that makes sense."

"Yeah, it does. It's the same, but better. Especially without the cameras."

I nudged him. "I don't know, the video we made the other night was pretty hot."

Ivy groaned. "Fuck, yeah. That was good."

We both chuckled remembering our little foray into making our own sex tape. It wasn't going anywhere but for our eyes, but we'd had fun with it for sure.

"How are we doing on replacing the bad with good?" I asked.

We talked a lot about bad memories that could be replaced with good ones in our monthly therapy sessions. Ivy went to a solo appointment once a month as well.

He turned to me and kissed me gently. "Pretty soon,

we're going to run out of bad to replace and just be overflowing with the good."

"Is the tatted, dark, and broody Ivy Lane getting all gushy with holiday goodness?" I teased.

Ivy took my hands. "Real talk? Ever since the day you agreed to fake it and play that game, everything's been moving perfectly into place. I still hate what my dad did. Hate the way things played out for Iris and me because he and my mom couldn't get their shit together. But I don't hate Christmas—thanks to you. You helped me remember the good times—helped me create new positive memories. I don't want to pass along a negative experience to my niece, or our kids if we decide to have them. From now on, this family celebrates Christmas the way it was meant to be celebrated—with joy, love, and all the damn holiday spirit we can dig up."

We lost several hot and heavy moments to kissing and touching, but the text from Iris saying they were about an hour away brought us back to ourselves.

"Do you want your gift?" Ivy asked. "I think you and Iyrie will have fun with it."

I'd already surprised Ivy with an amazing lighted sign for the outside of the shop. It was a custom design with lush green ivy leaves and fluorescent tube lighting that spelled out *Ivy's Auto*. I'd also sprung for uniform shirts for the entire shop crew and I couldn't wait to see how professional they all looked once we returned to business after the new year.

"Do I want a gift? Um, yeah," I said.

Ivy sprinted out the door and I watched as he made his way to the Sheffield's. He spoke to Mrs. Sheffield for a bit and she handed him a box. Ivy was beaming when he walked back into the house. "Sit on the couch."

I sat, wondering what in the world he could have gotten me that he needed to hide at the neighbor's house.

The box wiggled and whined when it was placed on my lap.

"Ivy, what did you do?" I asked.

"Figure we have to make sure we can survive this before we talk marriage or kids," he said, yanking the lid off the box to reveal the cutest Black Lab puppy I'd ever seen.

"Oh my god, he's adorable," I cooed, picking up the puppy and cuddling him close. "Did you name him?"

"Not yet."

"It has to be perfect, I'll need to think about it."

We snuggled with the puppy, laughing when he just conked right out to sleep in the middle of playing.

"Would you really want kids?" I asked.

"I don't know. It's something I'm willing to talk about. What about you?"

"Never really given it much thought. Maybe ask me after Iyrie leaves," I teased. "You think Trevor has actually found someone to meet his standards and pull him away from work long enough to date?" The thought of Trevor meeting someone and falling in love was one that made me happy, but it was still a bit foreign to me.

"Stranger things have happened," Ivy said.

"Yeah, like what?"

"Like me believing in Christmas magic," he said, cupping my cheek and kissing me.

With my eyes locked on his, hardly able to believe Ivy Lane loved me back, I whispered, "Like falling in love with the most amazing man I never saw coming and getting to spend the rest of my life building a future with him in The Christmas House?"

"Yeah, just like that," Ivy murmured against my lips.

We took advantage of our time together to make out like horny teens.

Until the puppy peed on Ivy's jeans.

He cursed as he stood with the little fur ball in his arms and pulled me up next to him. "Probably need to take him outside. Gonna have to get him potty trained."

As we made our way toward the door, Ivy came to a dead stop by the fireplace. "Em, look." He smoothed a hand over the snow globe. "Well, I'll be damned. Guess we know what his name is."

The tiny little replica house, decorated exactly like we'd paid to have it done this year, had its usual wreath, ivy wall, and chimney smoke. But in the yard, chewing on a stick, was a Black Lab puppy.

"Christmas Magic," we whispered together as the wiggly puppy let out a tiny little bark.

~THE END~

ALSO BY A.D. ELLIS

Holly Hills Christmas- **Holly Hills Christmas** is a steamy, feel-good, M/M age-gap holiday romance.

Listen to Your Heart- **Listen to Your Heart** is a steamy, second chance, M/M romance with just enough holiday magic to make you believe. It shares the same world with **Follow Your Heart** by Declan Rhodes.

The Heart of St. Nick- *The Heart of St. Nick is a steamy, forced proximity, small-town M/M holiday romance with a slight age gap between a bowtie and suspender-wearing good guy and an emotionally-stunted man with a cold heart just waiting to be melted.*

Two Weeks in Paradise- an opposites-attract, forced proximity M/M romance between two widowers nearing fifty. This low-angst love story is perfect for fans of kinky steam mixed with sweet fluff.

Jett & Leighton: On Cravenwood Block- a steamy, opposites-attract, bisexual-awakening, roommates-to-lovers M/M romance featuring a sexy-as-sin tattoo artist and a fresh, flashy barista with a smile that lights up the room.

The Perfect Blend- A steamy, M/M age-gap, marriage of convenience, coffee shop romance

Perfect Timing is a steamy, M/M romance with an introverted, demisexual writer and a big, soft teddy bear of a nurse trying to navigate a love they've always dreamed of but most definitely weren't expecting.

Adore (Remington Place 1) is a steamy, age-gap, bi-awakening, dad's best friend M/M romance with a sassy smartass and a sexy silver fox. It's the first book in the Remington Place series and can be read as a stand-alone.

Crave (Remington Place 2) is a steamy, friends-to-lovers, fake relationship M/M romance with a virgin nursing student and a gruff, grumbly construction worker.

Desire (Remington Place 3) is a steamy, age-gap, hurt/comfort M/M romance featuring a heart-of-gold mechanic and a twink who's a lot stronger than he realizes. *Please note: This story has mention of sex trafficking and sexual abuse.*

Yearn (Remington Place 4)- a steamy, enemies-to-lovers, forced proximity M/M romance between two EMS workers who have hated each other for a decade.

Power Struggle is a steamy M/M, age-gap, forced proximity romance set in a small town. A twenty-year history, rival schools and jobs, and a hotel with only one bed make for a hot and heavy, sweet and sexy, HEA-guaranteed love story.

Take Me Home M/M age-gap, opposites-attract romance with plenty of steam and a scene that will make you appreciate camouflage and work boots

Let Love In M/M age-gap, forced proximity, dad's best friend, bisexual-awakening romance. Available on AUDIO!

Let Love Win M/M brother's best friend romance. Available on AUDIO!

Buried Secrets Romantic suspense stand-alone title. Available on AUDIO!

Silver in the City (3 books- meet the Silver crew you read about in Forged in the City) Available on AUDIO!

Forged in the City (3 books- a spin-off series from Silver in the City) Available on AUDIO

The BJ Boys Series (3 books, small town, big love) Available on AUDIO

Forever Better Together (friends to lovers) Available on AUDIO!

His Reluctant Cowboy (age gap, opposites attract, cowboy romance) Available on AUDIO!

What Blooms Beneath (LGBT Fantasy romance) Available on AUDIO!

Sawyer

(this was the first M/M I wrote and you may remember Sawyer and Luke being mentioned in Barrett & Ivan as well as in Ryker & Gavin)

The Something About Him series has been revamped with revised stories, updated blurbs, and spiffy new covers.

The series is available on ALL of your favorite book platforms!

Bryan & Jase

Brody & Nick

Barrett & Ivan

Braeton & Drew

Ryker & Gavin

Kade & Cameron

A.D.'s first stories (all male/female except Sawyer which is male/male) are in the Torey Hope and Torey Hope: The Later Years series. Find the 8 book box set HERE or you can find each individual title on Amazon.

For Nicky

Because of Beckett

Christmas in Torey Hope

Loving Josie

Decker

Sawyer

Zach

Kendrick

ABOUT THE AUTHOR

A.D. Ellis is an Indiana girl, born and raised. She spends much of her time in central Indiana as an instructional coach/teacher in the inner city of Indianapolis, being a mom to two amazing teenagers, and wondering how she and her husband of over two decades haven't driven each other insane yet. A lot of her time is also devoted to phone call avoidance and her hatred of cooking.

She loves chocolate, wine, pizza, and naps along with reading and writing romance. These loves don't leave much time for housework, much to the chagrin of her husband. Who would pick cleaning the house over a nap or a good book? She uses any extra time to increase her fluency in sarcasm.

A.D. uses she/they pronouns.

Sign up at http://www.subscribepage.com/ADEllisNewsMMRomance for a FREE books!

Website http://adellisauthor.com/

Find me EVERYWHERE at https://www.adellisauthor.com/mylinks/

CONNECT WITH A.D. ELLIS

Follow my website http://www.adellisauthor.com or find me on Facebook

http://www.facebook.com/adellisauthor

If you want to get updates about releases, interviews, sales, giveaways, and more please sign up for my newsletter http://www.subscribepage.com/ADEllisNewsMMRomance

Check out my TikTok- https://www.tiktok.com/@adellisauthor

You can also find me on Twitter http://www.twitter.com/ADEllisAuthor

Find me on Spotify if you'd like to listen to the playlist for this book (mainly just the songs I listened to while writing). Just search for A.D. Ellis.

To make it easy, find me EVERYWHERE here- https://www.adellisauthor.com/mylinks/

ACKNOWLEDGMENTS

It's always so hard to write this part because I'm worried I'll forget someone without meaning to.

Readers- you are the reason I write. As long as you continue reading my stories, I'll continue writing them. Thank you for your support.

Bloggers- your support, reviews, and promotion are very much appreciated. Thank you!

My author buddies- I don't know that I could keep doing this without our brainstorm sessions, laughter, road trips, meals, wine, and friendship as my support.

Thank you to my alpha readers, betas, editors, proofreaders, and ARC readers! Your eyes and input are beyond important to me.

Brett and Gage- as usual, I doubt you even grasp how much your support, input, and friendship mean to me. This author journey has brought many wonderful things into my life, and you both are two of the BEST! I'm blessed to call you friends.

My family and friends- thank you for your love and support, always.